THE MAPMAKER'S SECRET

A THOMAS THE FALCONER MYSTERY

JOHN PILKINGTON

Boldwood

First published in 2004 as *The Mapmaker's Daughter*. This edition published in Great Britain in 2026 by Boldwood Books Ltd.

Copyright © John Pilkington, 2004

Cover Design by JD Smith Design Ltd.

Cover Images: Shutterstock

A CIP catalogue record for this book is available from the British Library.

Paperback ISBN 978-1-80600-914-5

Large Print ISBN 978-1-80600-913-8

Hardback ISBN 978-1-80600-912-1

Trade Paperback ISBN 978-1-80656-166-7

Ebook ISBN 978-1-80600-915-2

Kindle ISBN 978-1-80600-916-9

Audio CD ISBN 978-1-80600-907-7

MP3 CD ISBN 978-1-80600-908-4

Digital audio download ISBN 978-1-80600-909-1

This book is printed on certified sustainable paper. Boldwood Books is dedicated to putting sustainability at the heart of our business. For more information please visit https://www.boldwoodbooks.com/about-us/sustainability/

Boldwood Books Ltd, 23 Bowerdean Street, London, SW6 3TN

www.boldwoodbooks.com

1

The fire started in the hour before sunrise, when the unsuspecting folk of Boxwell Farm were yet to stir from their beds. The first intimation of disaster came when Beatrice Ames, wife to the farmer John Ames, having risen for some reason she could not fathom, threw wide the farmhouse door and saw smoke swirling above the big aisled barn. Even as she opened her mouth to cry out, she saw the small flames, lurid orange, licking at the edge of the thatch. Shouting at the top of her voice, she ran to the well and heaved the bucket over the side. The spindle sang out, its whine audible above the crackle of the burning pales that infilled the frame walls of the heavy-timbered barn. It had taken John Ames's grandfather many months to build the great structure, with its stone threshing floor in the middle and generous space for corn sheaves on one side, hay and beaten straw on the other. Now, the whole thing could become ashes in a matter of hours.

Ames, followed by his two sons, stumbled half-dressed into the yard. While the boys filled pails and ran to dash them where the fire seemed fiercest, John Ames, balanced precariously on a pile of hurdles, tore at the thatch with a billhook, seeking to cut a firebreak before the whole roof was ablaze. Calling to his wife to aid him, he wrenched the charred and smoking pales from the oak frame with his bare hands, heedless of the pain, coughing as smoke billowed about his head and shoulders. Beatrice seized a mattock and began demolishing the wall, both of them becoming aware that the fire had got a firm hold. Fortunately there were no livestock within, and most of the hay had been used for winter fodder...

Then it was that Matty, the older son, ran up and shouted to his father. 'Haylock – where is he?'

Ames ceased ripping away the thatch and looked down. 'Is he not with you?'

The boy shook his head, then threw an anxious look at the barn doors, which were firmly shut. 'We must look within!'

'No!' his father shouted. 'You open the doors, the draught will fan the flames and the whole barn will go up!'

The boy looked desperately to his mother, whose hand went to her mouth. 'We cannot leave him!' she cried. 'He's likely been overcome by the smoke. He'll burn to death!'

With a curse, Ames leaped from the hurdles and thrust the billhook into her hands. 'You pull the thatch down,' he said. 'I will go.'

'For the Lord's sake, be quick!' his wife called, before clambering onto the hurdles and attacking the roof. If anything, the smoke had increased, though there were no flames now in the thatch. As her husband and older son hurried round to the doors, she called to the younger boy, Gilly, to run with the pail and douse the wall, higher up.

Ames and his son heaved open the heavy doors. At once a

thick cloud of acrid smoke engulfed them, making both cough and retch, driving them back. As it cleared, they ventured forward, peering into the gloomy interior. Flames were visible about the base of the right-hand wall. Shouting hoarsely, Ames stepped onto the threshing floor.

'Simon! Simon!'

There was no reply. Their day labourer, Simon Haylock, had slept in the barn, as he did some nights, especially around lambing time. What dreadful turn of fate had made this night one of them?

'Father!'

Matty darted towards a heap of straw on the opposite side from the fire. Heart in mouth, Ames hurried forward. The next moment both of them had seized the motionless form of Haylock and were dragging him across the threshing floor. In seconds they were out in the open air, coughing hoarsely, eyes streaming from the smoke. Ames dragged Haylock by the shoulders towards the well, while his son seized the barn doors and slammed them shut again.

For a moment there was something like silence. Round the end of the barn, Beatrice still hacked at the thatch. Slumped against the stonework of the well, Ames took the dipper his younger son handed him and dashed water over his face. Then, still coughing, he struggled to his knees and gazed upon the face of Simon Haylock, who lay prone beside him.

'Lord God... Father, look at the state of 'im...'

Blinking, Ames tried to focus. The older boy had come over and stood beside his brother, both of them staring downwards at the terrible sight.

For poor Simon Haylock had succumbed neither to smoke nor flames. Instead, his rigid body, and the face set in a grim rictus of a smile, told a different tale. The front of his shirt was covered in dried vomit, which was also about his half-open mouth.

Whatever the cause of it, he was already dead before the fire started.

2

Thomas awoke with a start, breaking an uneasy dream. He sat up, breathing quickly, and tried to collect himself. In recent years, he had been relieved to find that the old nightmares about his short but harrowing experience of soldiering were starting to decrease. He had even begun to hope that one day they might disappear altogether. This one, he sensed, was all too familiar: someone nearby had screamed.

Nell stirred beside him and mumbled softly in her sleep. He looked down at her thick hair, its deep red colour indiscernible in the early dawn, hiding her face. How long was it since she had begun sharing his bed? Three years? He realised at that moment that it was a long time since he had dreamed of Mary. But then, he had been a widower now for nine years – too long, the Petbury folk said – and what in heaven's name was stopping him marrying Nell? Were they not already husband and wife in everything but name?

Then came the distant cry: piercing but, he knew at once, quite harmless. It was dawn, a May morning, and already the avian choir had begun. Along with other summer visitors, the swifts had arrived. Devil-screamers, the Downland people called them. He almost smiled at the notion.

He realised Nell was awake, watching him with her emerald-green eyes.

'Fretting about the chicks again?'

He shook his head. 'Ned has taken to the work – I've no fears on that score.'

Thomas's new helper, young Ned Hawes, was shaping up well as assistant falconer. Thomas had given him charge of raising the eyasses, newly taken from the nest of a wild falcon near Whitehorse Hill. The boy seemed to relish the task.

Nell sat up, yawning. 'I must to my work. The kitchens will not wait.'

He nodded and got up. Outside, a cockerel crowed in the pens. Nell stood and pulled her working kirtle on over her shift. Meeting her eyes, he saw something unspoken, an old battle as yet unresolved between them.

'My mother always warned me not to let the sun set on an argument,' Nell said.

He sighed. 'We can speak of it later.'

'Always later!'

Thomas eyed her warily. Used to her humours now, he sensed a storm brewing.

They did not speak again until they stood at the cottage door, where she turned abruptly to face him.

'Do you know what tomorrow is?'

He shook his head.

'It is my birthday. I have reached my thirtieth year.' When he merely nodded, she added, 'While you turned forty in March. I saw a glint of silver in your hair last night. Soon you'll become a grey-bearded sage among the falconers of West Berkshire.'

She was not smiling. 'Tell me, Master Thomas – how long do you expect me to keep on warming your bed?'

He sighed. 'I have said, we will marry...'

'Yes, you have said. Yet the moment I make so bold to ask when, you must needs hurry off to tend your hawks.'

'Falcons,' he muttered absently. 'My master has no hawks at present...'

That was careless, and Nell's eyes blazed. 'Mayhap you think to keep me on a leash too!' she snapped. 'Until I am too old for childbearing!' She had said more than she intended, though he knew well enough how she felt.

'We will marry, and...' He broke off.

'And?' She looked fiercely at him, then gave a little snort and stepped out of the door. The first fingers of dawn poked above the beech trees east of the cottage. Dew glistened on the sloping sward, with the grey bulk of Petbury manor lying below them. She half-turned, gathering her skirts to keep them off the wet grass.

'I've been a widow five years, Thomas,' she said in a different tone. 'You a widower for twice as long. Do you mean to wait until we are both grey-headed?'

He shook his head and took a step towards her, but her expression stayed him. 'Sir Robert and Lady Margaret are expecting company,' she said. 'We will be late in the kitchens. I sleep in the house tonight.'

He watched as she turned and walked downhill, towards the arched doorway which led to the kitchen garden. On the Downs, larks and pipits greeted the sunrise. With a sigh, he pulled the door to behind him and went to his work.

* * *

The nursery mews, a near-circular structure of plain timber, stood in a remote spot away from tracks and footpaths, where the young falcons could be raised in quiet fashion. As Thomas trudged up the gently sloping hill, his boots swishing through the still-wet grass, Ned Hawes appeared at the entrance, looking forlorn. At once, Thomas knew what had happened.

'Have we lost one?'

Ned nodded. 'I know not why. They all appeared in good sort yesternight...'

He held out the pitiful body of the dead chick, wisps of fluffy grey down visible among its adult plumage. Thomas examined it. 'Sometimes a weakling dies, for reasons none can fathom,' he said finally. 'I know there was no lack of care on your part.'

The young man looked relieved. One could read Ned like a child's horn-book, Petbury folk said. He was utterly devoid of guile, despite his fine light-brown hair and boyish looks which turned the heads of many girls in Chaddleworth village.

'They ate all the ground-up dove's flesh,' Ned told him. 'I thought to try milk-and-egg for the runt.'

Thomas shook his head. 'Feed them all the same,' he said. 'They'll learn to take wild birds soon enough.'

It was Ned's job to make up the chicks' special diet, to resemble as closely as possible the food regurgitated by their mother in the nest. Having earned Thomas's trust in the few months since he had come to work under him, the boy was still at times somewhat too eager to please.

'Shall we fly Tamora and Caesar later?'

Thomas signalled his assent before moving inside the semi-dark mews to look at the eyasses. They sensed his presence, squawking and fluttering their stubby wings. Soon it would be time to give them their first taste of the outdoors.

He came outside again to find Ned digging a small hole with a trowel.

'Nay,' Thomas said. 'Don't bury it. Cast it upon the hill for carrion.'

Ned straightened up and stared at him. 'Is that your usual custom?'

But Thomas was preoccupied this morning. He gazed up at the cloudless sky, then downhill in the direction of Petbury.

'The new tercel has worms,' he said, turning at last. 'I have a mind to make a trip into Wantage to see the apothecary. Mayhap it's time I took you along with me.'

Ned broke into a smile. Such a visit meant a rare opportunity to take in the pleasures of Wantage, the nearest thing to a bustling market town within ten miles, unless you counted Lambourn.

'When do we go?' he asked eagerly.

'I will ask Sir Robert,' Thomas told him, then frowned at the look on Ned's face. 'We'll have little time to tarry in the Blue Boar inn, if that's what's firing you up,' he added, but Ned shook his head.

'Nay – I have a mind to buy a gift for someone, is all,' he said. 'I have some money put aside.'

It was common knowledge that Ned had designs on Thomas's daughter Eleanor, who would turn seventeen later in the month. These days, as favoured maid to Lady Margaret, she lived in the big house, and carried herself as if she were a gentle-woman. Of late she and her father had seen little of each other, which was no accident since the business of the missing letter.

Thomas shrugged. 'Well, it's your affair how you spend your money,' he said.

Ned's face fell. 'You think whatever kickshaw I can afford would seem but a trifle to her,' he began.

'Nay, I thought no such thing. Though it's true she is become a little high and mighty of late.'

Ned lowered his eyes. 'I wish you and she would make peace,' he said.

Thomas looked away. The recent bone of contention had unsettled Ned as well as he and Eleanor. A week ago there had been an unprecedented occurrence at Petbury: a letter had come, brought by a carrier, addressed to Master Finbow, falconer to Sir Robert Vicary. The event was the talk of the stable yard as well as the kitchens. Yet no sooner had an astonished Thomas taken delivery of the precious missive – from the hands of the steward, Martin, who clearly disapproved of the matter – than it had gone astray. It had lain the morning in his hut, unread, while he fed and exercised the falcons; by dinner time it had vanished. A theft at Petbury was unheard of, and to Thomas's mind the culprit was plain: Eleanor, who came and went at her pleasure these days, forgetful of her duty to her father as she was of many other things. Though for her part, the girl hotly denied having touched the offending letter. There had been rash words between the two of them, and the mystery as yet remained unsolved. It had given Thomas several restless nights as he turned over the baffling question: who on earth would wish to write to the Petbury falconer?

He managed a smile, and clapped Ned on the shoulder. 'If Sir Robert is willing, we'll go tomorrow,' he said. 'I have a mind to make a purchase or two myself.'

Ned's grin grew so wide, his teeth flashed like beacons.

* * *

Later that morning, to her chagrin, Eleanor found herself being reminded of the matter as she and the other lady's maid began the elaborate business of dressing Lady Margaret.

Now in her forty-fourth year, the Lady of Petbury was still a beautiful woman, quiet-spoken and dignified, if somewhat distant. Each morning and at other times throughout the day, though her servants performed the most intimate of tasks for their mistress, they were never in any doubt that though she spoke with them readily enough, there was always a screen of some kind between her and them. Indeed, they knew such a barrier existed between her and Sir Robert too, even though she still shared his bed. Though being a dozen years her senior, the knight seemed to care less than he once did about such matters, and if the noise of his snoring were aught to go by, slept as soundly as his hunting dogs in their kennels.

Eleanor finished placing the linen smock with the square-cut neck about Lady Margaret's shoulders, while the other servant, nimble Alice Latter, laid several pairs of stockings on the bed for her to choose from. After pointing to those of finest silk yarn, Lady Margaret threw a glance at Eleanor.

'This quarrel with your father. It must be settled.'

Eleanor bobbed, then found a thin ribbon of garter to tie the silk hose. 'I'm certain it will, my lady.'

Lady Margaret sat while Alice knelt before her. 'I have a high regard for the both of you,' she added. 'It pains me to see you at loggerheads.'

Alice stood up, and it was Eleanor's turn to kneel and tie the garters. When she got to her feet, Alice had already brought the corset of reed and whalebone. Today guests were arriving, and their mistress would, as always, dress to the occasion.

'Do you wish for the horn busk, my lady?' Eleanor asked. Below her shoulder she heard the diminutive Alice, who was less than five feet tall, stifle a giggle.

'Do not attempt to change the subject so boldly,' Lady Margaret told her. 'The matter I speak of has gone on long enough.'

'My lady, we have searched high and low for that—for the letter,' Eleanor answered, unable to keep exasperation from her voice. 'It is lost, and that is all—'

'Not the Spanish farthingale,' Lady Margaret said abruptly, admonishing Alice for not paying attention; the item was now out of fashion. The girl bobbed obediently and took a larger frame, tautened with willow wands.

'I will hear no more about the letter,' Lady Margaret said to Eleanor. 'Whatever the cause of the coil, your duty is to your father.'

'Yes, my lady.' To her dismay, Eleanor found tears starting to her eyes. She drew a breath and turned to pick up the sky-blue kirtle her ladyship would wear over the farthingale. Alice pointedly looked away.

Lady Margaret sighed and glanced through the tall window of her chamber, which looked southwards towards the Lambourn Valley. Then she lowered her gaze to the courtyard below.

'Isn't that Ames, from Boxwell Farm?'

The two maids followed her gaze, seeing a figure in a battered hat and nut-brown jerkin striding towards the house. As they watched, he skirted the courtyard and turned to his left, heading for the stable yard.

'John Ames it is, my lady,' Eleanor confirmed, relieved at the diversion.

Lady Margaret turned to Alice. 'Go and find Master Martin,' she instructed. 'Tell him one of the tenant farmers is come. There must be a reason.'

Alice curtseyed, put aside the farthingale and went out. For a moment there was silence, before Lady Margaret turned a deliberate gaze upon Eleanor. And though the girl flushed she stood her ground, trying not to bite her lip.

'You are so like Thomas,' Lady Margaret said finally. She hesitated before adding in a kindlier tone, 'Whoever is at fault, please me and make your peace with him.'

Eleanor lowered her eyes, and nodded obediently.

Yet within a matter of minutes, even the tale of the missing letter would be eclipsed by the commotion that followed the arrival of a tired John Ames, his face still blackened from the struggle with the fire in his barn that morning. And when the general dismay turned to alarm at news of the discovery of Simon Haylock's body, it was all but forgotten.

3

Thomas and Ned had spent an easy enough morning exercising Sir Robert's favourite falcon, the mighty Tamora, and her lifelong companion Caesar, who was beginning to show his age. In unhurried fashion they had followed the birds west along the Ridgeway, as far as the path that led from Lambourn to Wantage, bagging up the larks and plovers they killed, before calling them down. It was almost midday. The sun was warm, and both were glad to take a drink from the costrel of weak beer Thomas had brought. By this time Ned's stomach was rumbling, Thomas told him, like approaching thunder. Each with a hooded falcon on the wrist, they began the long walk back to Petbury. But they had barely covered half a mile before Ned stopped and pointed. Following his arm, Thomas saw two figures standing in the long grass some distance away, watching them. After a moment the taller figure raised a hand in greeting. For no other reason than curiosity, the falconers changed course and walked towards them.

As they drew close, their curiosity increased. A dun-coloured horse – not of the best quality – was grazing some way off. Scattered about was a jumble of objects, among them a saddle and packs, a leather carrying-case, and a strange-looking wooden device on legs, the like of which neither Thomas nor Ned had ever seen. But neither of them gave it more than a glance, for their attention was taken by the two people who stood before them, quietly composed as if awaiting the arrival of guests.

The man was of middle years, tall and sunburned, his sleeves rolled back to the elbows. He smiled, lifting his wide-brimmed hat in greeting. After a glance at Ned he addressed Thomas, as the senior of the two.

'I give you good-day, falconer. A warm one for May, is it not?'

'It is,' Thomas answered. The accent aroused his curiosity further. It was the voice of an educated man, yet the travel-stained breeches and well-worn boots pointed to one of humble means. His glance shifted to the man's companion: a young woman, simply dressed, with silky, crow-black hair poking out of a hood. There was an intake of breath from Ned Hawes, standing rigid at his side.

She was of perhaps twenty years, clear-eyed, her face sunburned though not so brown as the man's. She favoured both falconers with a warm smile, then lowered her eyes. Words like *pretty* and *well-favoured* were inadequate; her beauty was imbued with a depth of natural charm that was rarely seen on the Downs – if, indeed, anywhere else.

Thomas sought for some words of greeting, when the tall man stepped forward. 'Christopher Mead,' he said. 'I am the Queen's mapmaker. Permit me to present my daughter Grace.'

Thomas inclined his head. 'Thomas Finbow, falconer to Sir Robert Vicary of Petbury Manor. Here is my helper, Ned Hawes.'

Christopher Mead smiled at them both – somewhat slyly,

Thomas thought, or was it his fancy? – then turned to his daughter. 'Have we refreshment enough to share with these men?' he asked. 'They look as though they've walked far.'

Thomas was about to decline the offer politely, then he glanced at Ned and was nettled by the boy's demeanour. The fool had not taken his eyes off Grace Mead since their arrival. He was struck dumb.

'I thank you for your kindness, sir,' Thomas said, 'but we have a long walk to the manor. Dinner awaits us there, along with our work.'

He looked pointedly at Ned, whose attention had been diverted from Caesar; the bird shifted on his gauntlet and looked as if he were about to bate. Coming to his senses, Ned drew his arm closer to his body and began stroking the falcon to quiet him. Yet again, his gaze strayed towards the mapmaker's beautiful daughter.

The girl spoke suddenly. 'The bird is thirsty,' she murmured. 'Indeed, they both are.' She looked at Thomas. 'We can spare a little brook-water, can we not?'

The question was addressed to her father, who nodded. 'Of course. Would that please you, Master Finbow?'

'Again, I thank you,' Thomas said. 'They could use a drink, it's true.'

Grace went to the packs and found a small wooden bowl. Unstopping a leather bottle, she poured water, then brought the bowl to Thomas and held it out.

Thomas took it in his right hand, watching her. 'You knew not to place it on the ground,' he said. 'Are you used to the ways of falconers?'

The girl said nothing, only smiled and turned away. Going to the saddle, she sat down upon it, took some needlework from her dress and busied herself with it – a little too deliberately, Thomas thought.

He and Ned walked some distance away, unhooded both falcons and let them drink. When it was done, Thomas walked back towards Christopher Mead, allowing his glance to stray towards the object on legs. Closer, he saw it consisted of a small, upright wooden board, well-shaped and mounted by means of a brass swivel on a circular base with markings upon it.

'I have heard naught of a mapmaker coming to the Downlands,' he remarked. There was a wooden case near the foot of the machine, in which lay what he assumed were drawing instruments. Rolls of paper poked out of one of the packs.

Mead raised his eyebrows. 'My commission is no secret,' he said, 'even if few are aware of it. I have mapped the counties of Surrey, Middlesex and Hampshire. This year I find myself in Berkshire. I am surveying the Lambourn Valley, from its source down to the Kennet.'

Thomas glanced at Ned, who was trying to look as if he were listening to the mapmaker, though it was plain his attention was fixed upon his daughter.

'Do you survey with that device?' Thomas asked, indicating the machine. He struggled to see how it worked.

'My dioptra,' Mead smiled. 'Men seldom wait long before enquiring as to its purpose.' The smile faded. 'Some in their ignorance have accused me of sorcery, for using what appears to them a devilish instrument. Yet its operation is straightforward – a matter of observation, and simple mathematics.'

Standing before the dioptra, he rotated it on its stand, pointing out what Thomas now saw were graduated numbers.

'The flat base is the alidade,' he said. 'By means of this I can take sighting of any distant object, be it castle, hill or steeple. By triangulation I can calculate how far away it is, and hence mark it on my chart.' Turning to Thomas, he added, 'There are many great mapmakers now at work on the continent, like the learned Gerardus Mercator. To such men England is but a backwater – most of her inhabitants scarcely know what county lies beyond their own!'

'If I might speak for myself, I have been in many counties on my master's business,' Thomas said mildly. 'Surrey... Salisbury Plain in Wiltshire, to name but two.'

'Indeed,' Mead nodded, and Thomas caught a tiny gleam of contempt in his eyes. 'And what lies beyond Wiltshire, can you tell me that?'

Thomas eyed him. 'Somerset.'

'And beyond that?'

'I believe it is the Bristol Channel, and thence the open sea.'

Mead gave a little sniff. 'You are well-informed.'

'For a falconer?' Thomas asked. Mead did not reply. Tamora lifted her wings slightly, as if impatient to be on the move.

'I will tell my master Sir Robert you are here, sir,' Thomas said, at which Mead stiffened suddenly.

'I need no landowner's permission,' he said sharply. 'The Queen's commission is enough.'

Thomas paused, then when no further words were uttered, he added, 'He is known on the Downs for his hospitality. If you require aught while you are hereabouts, I'm sure he will extend you every courtesy.'

Mead took a breath, then spoke in a different tone.

'Master Finbow, your fair words do you credit.' He glanced at Grace who sat with head bowed, giving no indication that she had heard the conversation.

'I fear I have little time to pay my respects to your master,'

Mead said. 'We shall be moving on in a week or two. We have adequate lodgings in Great Shefford.'

Thomas gave a slight bow, then turned to Ned, who had managed to tear his eyes away from Grace. Raising hand in farewell, both falconers took their leave of Mead and his daughter, trudging off across the empty Downs. Glancing back after a few minutes, Thomas saw the mapmaker's tall form above the grass, bent over his dioptra. Of Grace there was no sign.

Neither of them spoke for some time. Finally, when they struck the downhill path towards Petbury, Thomas felt Ned's eyes upon him and turned deliberately, at which the boy dropped his gaze. He sighed, thinking about their trip on the morrow. Who would his assistant be thinking of, when he made his small purchase in Wantage – Eleanor, or Grace Mead?

* * *

An hour later, with his stomach threatening to announce its emptiness at any moment, Thomas stood in Sir Robert's small morning chamber. He had been summoned the moment he appeared at the kitchen door, and while Ned took his dinner, he had been obliged to attend upon his master. With him were Martin the steward, who these days used his staff of office to lean on rather than to display his rank. With them, to Thomas's surprise, was John Ames from Boxwell Farm, a man he had not set eyes on for months. He listened as Martin recounted the news, frowning at the untimely death of Simon Haylock, then divined what was coming next.

Sir Robert sat at his writing table, scattered with papers, quills, ink and sandbox. 'I have arranged for aid to be sent to Boxwell,' he was saying, with a nod towards Ames, who stood clutching his worn-out hat, ill at ease in the great house. 'Skilled men will be engaged to repair the barn and replace the thatch.' He glanced at Thomas. 'Ames thinks the fire was no accident.'

Thomas looked towards the farmer.

'There was no reason for it, falconer,' Ames said in a voice hoarse with fatigue. 'No means by which a flame could have been set to one end of the barn, save by design. I would swear to it.'

'Yet you can think of none who would wish you such misfortune.' Martin peered at the farmer from beneath his white eyebrows.

'None, master steward,' Ames replied. 'I'm not a man who makes enemies.'

Sir Robert exchanged a glance with Thomas, who said, 'The misfortune fell hardest upon Simon Haylock, surely?'

Ames sighed. 'I've thought upon it, yet my sons and I are certain he was already a corpse before the fire began. If you'd looked upon his face...' He winced at the memory. ''Twas pale and of a terrible aspect, like a man dead of plague, only there's no marks upon him. And he'd retched up all that his stomach could hold.'

Thomas's own stomach threatened rebellion at any moment. He opened his mouth, but Sir Robert forestalled him.

'Will you go back to Boxwell with Ames and take a look around?' he asked. 'I have sent word to the high sheriff. There will have to be an inquest, I suppose.'

Thomas nodded. 'Might I take a little dinner before I leave, sir?' he ventured.

Sir Robert gestured his assent. Martin cleared his throat, signalling that the discourse was over. Ames bowed and murmured his thanks to Sir Robert before heading for the door. From the kitchens came the sound of ladles clattering, and Nell shouting at one of the wenches.

'Sir Robert, may I beg leave to go to the apothecary at Wantage tomorrow?' Thomas asked, remembering. 'I need physic for one of the birds.'

Sir Robert frowned. 'Not sick, is it?'

'Naught but worms, sir.'

'Then go, so long as you won't tarry long.' The knight looked up suddenly. 'How's the boy shaping up?'

'I think he'll make a falconer,' Thomas replied. Seizing the moment he asked, 'Might he accompany me tomorrow? It will be a lesson for him.'

'Very well...' Sir Robert was already turning back to his papers. Ignoring Martin's disapproving stare, which was part of a frequent, unspoken ritual between the falconer and the steward, Thomas made his bow and got himself outside. To his relief he managed to reach the passage before his stomach growled its displeasure. Only then did he realise that he had forgotten to mention the mapmaker. He thought of turning back, then dismissed the notion; the matter could wait.

* * *

By mid-afternoon he stood in the yard at Boxwell Farm, two miles south of Petbury, surveying the devastation.

It was worse than he had expected. One end of the barn was a blackened ruin, the wall and part of the roof gone, leaving the interior open to the elements. Ames's younger son was still clearing up. A heap of charred and broken reeds spoke of the family's alacrity in cutting a firebreak before they lost the entire thatch. Thomas commiserated with the farmer, before voicing the question. 'Where have you placed him?'

Silently, Ames led the way round the side of the farmhouse.

In a small tool-shed, Haylock's body lay on the beaten earth floor, covered with an old cloth.

Thomas drew the cloth back and looked. He had known Haylock slightly, a Chaddleworth man who worked his own humble acres as well as helping out on neighbouring farms. He was a widower who lived alone, his daughters married and long gone. As far as Thomas recalled the man had never been in any trouble, unless taking too much drink now and again were counted a crime.

He noted the dried excrescence on Haylock's clothing and sniffed it. He pulled the jerkin aside and saw it was as Ames had said: there were no marks of any kind. He began to form the opinion that Haylock had merely drunk to excess, and choked on his own vomit. The odd twist of the mouth bothered him, however – it was as if the man had died in pain. He replaced the covering, thinking the matter were best left to the surgeon and the coroner's jury. What could he add?

He left the lean-to and walked outside into the afternoon air, where Ames was waiting. When Thomas gave his opinion, the man nodded his agreement.

'I thought something of the same myself. Mayhap you should take this, and pass it to Simon's folk.'

He held out a worn leather costrel. Thomas took it, drew out the stopper and sniffed at the contents, then met Ames's eyes. The man nodded grimly.

'Strong sack. I found it inside, after we finished dousing the fire. He was drinking more than was good for him of late, though it never hindered his work.'

'Odd though, is it not?' Thomas mused. 'To die of drink on the night of the fire?'

Ames shook his head, no doubt weary of the whole matter. Seeing how tired he looked, Thomas put a hand on his shoulder.

'You should rest, John,' he said. 'Thank God none of your family was harmed, nor your stock.'

The man nodded dumbly. Together they walked slowly back to the yard, and the big aisled barn with one side burned away.

Yet some undefined notion tugged away at the back of Thomas's mind, and he knew it would stay there until he could give it form. He sighed. Another night of broken sleep loomed, and there would be no Nell to divert him.

4

Thomas took a late supper in a corner of the kitchen, while the Petbury servants scurried about him. Sir Robert and Lady Margaret did indeed have guests in the Great Hall, among them no less a personage than Richard Ward, the high sheriff of Berkshire, who had ridden the twenty miles from Hurst Manor beyond Reading soon after receiving word of the events at Boxwell Farm. Some recalled that he was not always so conscientious; could the visit have aught to do with his passion for hawking, and the chance to indulge himself in the company of a like-minded nobleman like Sir Robert?

Nell had been too busy to speak with Thomas all evening, and no one else had time to notice any rift between them. One or two turned their heads when Eleanor came hurriedly into the kitchens on some errand for her mistress. Seeing Thomas seated alone she hesitated, then walked over to him.

'I heard about what happened, down at Boxwell.'

He pushed away his empty trencher and eyed her. As usual she wore one of Lady Margaret's cast-offs: a partlet of dusty-pink taffeta, altered to fit her own slighter frame. Her hair, dressed by the clever-handed Alice, went as far as any lady's maid would dare go towards imitation of her mistress's grand style. His daughter, Thomas was only too aware, was growing into a very attractive young woman.

'You look tired,' she added, seeing a line or two of strain about his eyes. Or had they been there for some time, and she too preoccupied to notice?

'So do you,' Thomas answered. 'My lady keeps you busy.'

She nodded. 'She orders me to look to my duty, and ask pardon for offending you.'

He gazed at her, then gave a smile. In spite of herself, a smile flickered briefly about Eleanor's lips in return. They knew each other too well. There was no remorse being shown; she was merely doing her mistress's bidding. From the corner of his eye, Thomas saw Nell busy herself mixing something in a bowl.

'You may tell her I have forgiven you. Though not for losing —' He broke off, berating himself; but it was too late.

'I have told you a hundred times, I did not lose it! I never even touched it!' Eleanor's storm-grey eyes flashed at him, as her shoulders rose in anger. 'How can you even think I would lie to you? Have I ever done so?'

'Nay, I know you would not,' Thomas answered quickly, keeping his own voice low. One of the serving-men glanced at them as he passed by with a loaded platter. Further off, Nell kept her gaze averted.

'Then why...' Eleanor began, but Thomas had taken hold of her arm. 'I have accused you of naught but forgetfulness,' he told her wearily. 'Yet, if you still swear you know not what happened—'

'I have sworn it, and do again!' she retorted. 'Mayhap you should look to your own carelessness. The cottage minds me of a pie's nest these days, the way you cast things about.'

But it was her turn to look as if she regretted her words. Despite the arrival of Ned Hawes as second falconer, it was well known that Thomas often did the work of two men. Small wonder that he had little time for housekeeping.

He was frowning. Nell had stopped pretending, and was watching them both. With a quick, almost furtive gesture, Eleanor touched his arm.

'I ask pardon, Father. Truly I do,' she murmured, and turned away. The matter remained, as ever, unsettled.

He watched her walk over to Nell to exchange a few words. She and Eleanor liked each other well enough. Indeed, it was not his daughter who stood in the way of Thomas making a wife of Nell – that much was plain to all at Petbury. Some had grown impatient with him, and accused him of becoming a ditherer in his middle years. But then, others said, they knew not his mind, and he usually had a reason for what he did. He watched Eleanor go out the passage door without glancing back, then got to his feet and went out to feed the falcons before night fell.

* * *

Dawn found him already at the mews when Ned arrived, wide awake after walking the mile from Chaddleworth. His cheerfulness was so great when he learned that the journey into Wantage would go ahead, Thomas had to smile.

'I've put fresh water out,' he said. 'If you'll feed the others, I'll take a look at our invalid.'

Ned nodded and busied himself putting broken meat down. There was much calling and beating of wings from the hungry falcons, of which there were half a dozen in the mews at present, not counting Lady Margaret's merlin. Tamora, no longer young now but every inch a princess, was the undisputed ruler. Her consort, Caesar, a third smaller in height, was losing a little plumage from his chest, but still ranked as a prime hunting bird. Then there were the three sisters, named in jest by Sir Robert after the daughters of Zeus: Euphrosyne, Aglaia and Thalia. Ned had long since given up trying to pronounce their names.

Isolated in the darkest corner was a high perch, with a sheet of sacking hanging from it in case its occupant fell and had to claw his way back up. Each falcon had its own perch, at a safe enough distance from its neighbour to prevent fighting. No bird was ever placed on the ground; its wing and tail feathers would soon become damp, which could lead to infection. Brutus, the ailing tercel, had been prone to ill health from the day he arrived, a gift to Sir Robert from the well-meaning widow of an old friend, who knew not how to care for her late husband's falcon. Thomas had already spent more time in the bird's care than he could spare. Fillanders, tiny thread-like worms and the bane of falconers, were a common enough problem among all birds of prey, even those as well cared for as the ones at Petbury. But of course it was Brutus who now had them, and none else.

Thomas approached him slowly, keeping his body half-turned away, all the while murmuring soft words. The falcon blinked at him. Reaching into his pouch, Thomas drew out a piece of well-cooked pheasant, which had somehow slipped from a platter in the kitchen last night. He held it out. Brutus hesitated, then pecked at it. After placing it at the bird's feet he watched for a minute, then walked outside and took a lungful of sweet morning air. White clouds drifted in from the west, yet there was no threat of rain; nothing to spoil the trip to Wantage. He was looking forward to the diversion more than he had expected.

Ned was in talkative mood as the two set out, walking north-eastwards up the hill above Petbury until they struck the

Hungerford to Wantage road below Woolley Down. He had promised his young sister a ribbon for her hair, he said, and his mother a packet of sewing needles, for she had not set foot in Wantage for a year. Then, how many did? Chaddleworth folk worked mainly on the farms, and were busy now with the lambing. Most worked the Petbury lands or those of Poughley Manor, Sir John Mountford's smaller estate east of the village. Ned's father had once worked there, though he disliked working for a Catholic; Sir John's name featured prominently on the Berkshire recusant rolls for this year of 1592, as they had done the year before. What it cost the Poughley estate in fines, was anyone's guess.

'At least he is true to his faith,' Thomas observed as they walked. 'He has never denied what he believes.'

Ned looked shocked. 'You do not hold with papists?'

Thomas shrugged. 'A man's religion is his own affair, and our Queen thinks the same. What was it she said? She would not make windows into men's souls.'

'You think she still holds to that? After the plots laid against her life?'

'I know not,' Thomas answered. How different his days were now, he reflected, since he had had another falconer to converse with. It had been a shock to realise how lonely he must have been.

A thought struck Ned, and at once he was off on a different tack. 'Someone walked with me up the lane this morning, as far as the Petbury gates,' he told Thomas. 'Seems he's the one will likely rebuild Ames's barn.'

Thomas raised an eyebrow. 'He was quick off the mark. Who is it?'

'Name of John Flowers,' Ned told him, pleased to be the bearer of important news. 'Not from Chaddleworth – he'd come up from Great Shefford, soon as he heard there might be work going. He's not much older than me, yet he's served his prentice-ship as a carpenter and set himself up – hired two men already.' He paused, keeping the best until last. 'You'll never guess who one of them is.'

Indulging him, Thomas waited.

'Ambrose Fuller,' Ned announced.

'Indeed?'

'Aye. Proves Flowers don't know much about Chaddleworth folk. Most wouldn't have aught to do with him.'

Thomas considered. If Chaddleworth had a bad apple, then Ambrose Fuller was he. A morose, beetle-browed man given to picking fights on the slenderest pretext, he supplemented his irregular thatching work with poaching, or worse. Many branded him a thief, though those who would dare call him such to his face were few.

'Can't say I know this man Flowers,' Thomas murmured.

'I liked him,' Ned said. 'Friendly sort, and eager to work. He said if Sir Robert hired him, he'd stand me a mug in the Black Bear come the week's end.'

'It's not Sir Robert he needs worry about,' Thomas replied. 'Martin does the hiring. It'll take more than a smile to move his mind.'

'True enough...' Ned's plain features clouded. 'I won't forget the way he made me feel, standing cap in hand that day, waiting to see if I had a place or not.'

Thomas threw him a smile. 'But you did. And here you are, walking to Wantage on Petbury business.' He hesitated, then added, 'If we keep a good pace, mayhap we'll have time to step inside the Blue Boar after all, and still be back by midday.'

Ned tried to keep the smile from his face, then gave up the struggle.

* * *

It was Thursday, not a market day in Wantage, yet still the little town throbbed with life. Coming in by Newbury Street after their two-hour walk, the falconers entered the busy square, with its new cross topped with a fine sarcen stone, to be assailed by the cries of street-sellers. A cart piled with sacks rumbled by; there were corn mills on the river, beyond the square to the west. Thomas led the way along its eastern edge, then turned right into Wallingford Street. They passed an open-fronted shambles, from which came the sickly smell of raw meat and offal. Threading their way through the press of townswomen with their baskets, they entered the apothecary's, and were at once in another world, with its heady mixture of strange odours. An air of mystery, even reverence pervaded the dimly lit shop. On one wall was a chart showing the parts and humours of the human body. The small table beneath it was cluttered with basins, mortars and pestles.

'Master Halliwell.' Thomas smiled at the slight, balding man who turned at once to greet them. His breeches and doublet were dusted with some white powder. The man hailed from Oxford and had a scholar's manner, though he had never seen the inside of the university.

'Master Finbow!' He smiled in return. 'As always, you are right welcome.'

Thomas gestured to Ned. 'My new helper, Ned Hawes. Chaddleworth lad.'

Halliwell nodded a greeting. But Ned was staring about at the shelves of bottles and flasks, a rainbow of colours. To him the shop seemed a treasure-cave.

'What is it you lack, falconer?' The man asked with barely

suppressed eagerness, the reason for which Thomas would soon learn.

'Let's start with dried sea-moss,' he answered. 'Do you have it?'

'I knew it!' Halliwell almost jumped in delight. 'You are the first falconer to come in a week, and you want physic for worms – is't not so?'

'Fillanders,' Thomas nodded, but the other wasn't listening.

'*Perfectio!* For I have the very thing!'

'The very thing?' Thomas echoed.

'*Pulvis contra vermis!*' the apothecary cried. 'My own recipe, made up only this month. Swear you'll try it, and you shall have it at a bargain price!'

If Thomas looked uncertain, Dan Halliwell refused to notice. He almost ran to a table, and with a flourish produced a little bag tied at the neck.

'Open it! Sniff it for yourself,' he said, drawing the string and holding it out.

Thomas took it, trying not to appear suspicious. 'What's in it?'

'*Flos sulphuris,*' Halliwell told him. 'And *carolinum*, as you rightly requested, dried and mixed with the powdered heads of swine's fennel. Plus a little wormwood, and one or two secret additions that are mine own.' He tapped his temple. 'Do not ask, Master Finbow, only place your trust in Daniel Halliwell, who has cured as many birds as people, and more people than would fit in yonder square on the Translation of St Thomas – one of our feast days, you will recall.'

Thomas didn't recall it, nor did he share the other's enthusiasm. After sniffing the open bag, he lowered it. 'With all respect to your skills, Master, I'm loathe to use a potion which contains I know not what, on Sir Robert's falcons.'

But Halliwell's smile remained firm. 'Have I ever failed you? Do I not supply every falconer within a twenty-mile radius? Am I not renowned for the efficacy of my medicines, be they for man or beast? Am I—'

'Master Halliwell, if you will.' Thomas held out the pouch until at last, very reluctantly, Halliwell took it. 'I will do business with you and no one else – and I've never doubted you. Indulge me as one grown set in his ways, and only furnish me with what I wish for the making of pellets. It's served me well enough.'

Halliwell put on a pained look. 'You disappoint me, Master Finbow. I sought but to save you time and toil by concocting my worm remedy.' He gave a wry smile. 'Yet if truth be told, you are not alone in being set in your ways... Name me a falconer who isn't.'

'I cannot,' Thomas admitted, 'unless it be young Ned here, who is still learning his craft.' Hearing his name spoken, Ned turned from the shelves. But Halliwell merely sighed and shook his head.

'Ask what you will, Master Finbow, only indulge me in turn: say you will spread the word that Daniel Halliwell has a bespoke worm remedy especially for falconers, that begs to be tried. Once it's proven, you shall see how it sells!'

Thomas nodded. 'I will speak of it to any who will listen.'

'And you are a man of his word.' Halliwell nodded, brightening a little. 'So, tell me now, how I may serve you.'

Thomas gave a nod and named his wants.

* * *

A half hour later, having completed all their purchases, the falconers made their way back to the square. The Blue Boar lay on the south side, facing the market cross, but their attention was caught by a noisy crowd that filled another corner of the square. There was shouting and jeering, mingled with hoots of laughter. Turning to Thomas, Ned saw him frown.

'Some poor soul in the stocks,' Thomas said. 'I don't care to see who.'

Ned hesitated. 'You don't mind if I go?'

Thomas sighed. 'If you must.' He inclined his head towards the inn. 'Look for me inside.'

With barely suppressed eagerness Ned went off, pushing his way through the crowd. But Thomas had hardly found a bench in the busy front parlour of the Blue Boar and called for two mugs of beer when the boy reappeared in a state of high excitement.

'I never saw aught like it, Thomas,' he breathed. 'You should come and see.'

'Why should I?' Thomas remained seated.

'It's a foreigner, some sort of conjuror. Been whipped by the constable and put in the stocks. They're giving him a fearsome time. You should see how he's dressed. And he has an ape!'

'Have they put the ape in the stocks, too?' Thomas asked wryly, but the irony was lost on Ned.

'Nay, he's with the conjuror's man... He's not foreign like his master. Can't do naught but sit by and wait 'til he's freed...' He paused, seeing at last how distasteful the business was to his master. 'Your pardon, Thomas,' he said at last. 'I know you dislike cruelty.'

But when Thomas's gaze shifted, he looked round quickly. The noise in the parlour had dropped suddenly, and all eyes fell upon a young man with long hair, dressed in a garish suit of yellow and green, who had appeared in the doorway. But it was not the clothing which occasioned such stares: it was the brown-haired ape, perhaps half the height of a man, which crouched beside him, holding his hand like a child and looking about with frightened eyes.

The young man spoke up nervously. 'I would ask mercy of you folk, for there's none outside. Mercy for my master in his plight. He is hurt...' He looked about, seeking a sympathetic face in the room, but all he got was a wall of blank stares.

'What d'you expect from the stocks?' a fellow called out. 'He shouldn't have got himself put there.'

There were mutterings of agreement. The young man swallowed, moistening his lips. The ape drew closer to him, as if for protection. Ned felt, rather than heard, Thomas get to his feet behind him, just as the drawer appeared with two mugs of foaming ale.

'I will go with you, and take a look at your master,' Thomas said loudly. When every head in the room snapped towards him Ned turned, his heart thudding. Nothing so exciting had happened to him in years.

There was gratitude in the eyes of the young man in the garish suit. He watched, as did the entire company, as Thomas unhurriedly drained his mug, plonked it down on a table and moved towards the entrance. Ned grabbed the other mug from the startled drawer, gulped its contents and followed. None molested them, though voices rose behind them as they cleared the doorway. Thomas looked towards the crowd which still seethed about the stocks, then turned to the young man with the ape.

'How much longer must your master serve his punishment?'

'Another hour, perhaps – I know not,' the other replied. 'He grows weak... He has taken many a blow to the head.'

Some of the crowd noticed them, and the ape. There were shouts, and someone threw a stone. It missed but the ape whimpered, cowering against the boy's legs.

'Take the creature away, is my advice,' Thomas said. He looked round. 'Ned, go with him along the Hungerford Road... Wait for me outside the town.'

Ned gaped. 'You mean, we're taking them with us?'

Thomas glanced at the young man, who was doing some thinking of his own.

'Where are you bound?' he asked. When Thomas told him he nodded, hope in his eyes. 'If you'll help us to Chaddleworth, my master will reward you,' he said quickly. 'He is a good man – a genius. He's not the wizard these fools have branded him. He harms no one!'

Thomas hesitated; he had the feeling he was getting himself into more trouble than he liked. But he made the mistake of glancing down at the ape, and found its eyes fixed unwaveringly on his. 'The south road,' he told Ned, waving him away impatiently. To the other he said only, 'I will do what I can.'

The young man nodded, then followed Ned towards Newbury Street, the ape swinging along obediently by his side. Thomas watched them go, then took a breath and began forcing his way through the jeering crowd, his face taut in anticipation of what he would find.

5

Over the years Thomas had seen many individuals clapped in the stocks, that crude form of punishment meted out for everything from drunkenness and blasphemy to witchcraft. But the man who sat that day in the market square at Wantage, his feet and hands secured between the heavy slabs of unyielding oak, was unlike any he had encountered before. It was not merely the richly embroidered gown he wore, soiled though it now was, nor the curious cut of the beard, forked and trimmed to resemble the wings of some strange bird. It was the manner in which he bore his ordeal.

Ned was right: the crowd had shown him little mercy. His head and arms showed not only the results of their heaving anything within reach at him – from eggs and rotten fruit to clods of earth – they also bled from the cruel impact of stones and fragments of brick. By the time Thomas forced his way through, the man was exhausted and in some pain. Yet rather than hang his head or try to duck whatever missiles came his way, he remained defiant, trading insults hoarsely with the onlookers in a curious dialect. At times he broke into what to Thomas's untutored ear sounded like Latin.

Somewhat sick at heart, Thomas scanned the raucous crowd, his gaze falling upon a sturdy-looking man in heavy boots and fustian, dangling a bunch of keys from his belt. When he made his way towards him the fellow turned sharply, and Thomas saw the look in his eyes: discomfort. The constable, to his surprise, did not relish the grisly spectacle any more than he did.

'How much longer must he sit there?' he asked.

The man glanced at the sun. 'Not a great deal more,' he answered.

'What's he done?'

The other frowned. 'Who are you, and what's your interest?'

'Merely one who dislikes seeing any man used in such fashion,' Thomas told him.

The constable looked hard at him, then seemed to relax a little. 'He's a vagabond, a sharper and a conjuror to boot,' he said. 'Gave a tent show yesternight that scared folk witless. Some accuse him of devilry, but that's not what upset the town fathers: rather, twas the way their wives flocked to him after, to have their fortunes told.' He grimaced. 'He made the mistake of upsetting men who are in a position to give vent to their jealousy.'

Thomas glanced at the supposed conjuror, and received a jolt. The man was staring straight at him – a piercing look, the meaning of which was unclear.

'I hear he's a foreigner,' he said. 'Might he not have misjudged matters? Mayhap the laws are different where he comes from.'

'How am I to tell?' the constable demanded. 'I merely do my office.' He sniffed. 'Either way, it's a mite too late, wouldn't you say?'

The prisoner's shouts of defiance had diminished now, until

finally they ceased. Mercifully the crowd were beginning to lose interest. Some had drifted away, leaving only a hard core of scoffers and jeerers. To Thomas's relief, the constable seemed to reach a decision. 'I deem he's paid his price,' he said. 'Since you have shown a Samaritan's compassion for the fellow, mayhap you'd like to give me a hand?'

Thomas nodded and followed him to the stocks. The crowd fell back, and most began to leave now the conjuror's ordeal was over. Breathing hard, bruised and bleeding from a dozen cuts, the man turned a haggard face towards his liberator. The moment the constable unlocked the hasp and raised the top beam, he drew his arms and legs free and tried to stand. But immediately he staggered, fell backwards and sat down amid the debris.

Thomas unstoppered his costrel and held it out. With a look of surprise, which quickly turned to gratitude, the man took it and drank. Though he would clearly like to have drained it, he stopped himself and handed the vessel back to Thomas.

'*Danke*... I thank you, sir.'

Thomas nodded. 'Your prentice, the young man in the green and yellow – he awaits you outside the town, with his ape.'

At that, the man tried once again to get to his feet. This time he succeeded, though Thomas and the constable each had to put out a hand to stay him. He swayed once, then stood looking hard at Thomas.

'You are kind,' he muttered, speaking far back in his throat. He coughed, and with one of the wide sleeves of his gown, gave his face a wipe. He looked in some alarm at the blood that showed.

The constable addressed him. 'I'd advise you not to tarry here,' he said. 'Nor to return to Wantage. At least, not for a while.' He jerked a thumb over his shoulder. 'I had a man keep an eye on your cart, in case anyone had a mind to spoil your goods. It's in yon stable yard.'

The other straightened himself, looking highly relieved.

'For that, I would thank you also,' he said.

The constable turned without a word and walked off across the square. After watching him go, the conjuror faced Thomas. 'Paulo Schweiz,' he said abruptly. 'In England, some call me Paulo the Switzer.'

Thomas gave his name and station. 'We'd better go and get your cart, then find your friend,' he said. 'My helper is with him. There's a stream not far along the road, where you can clean yourself up...'

He paused, for the man was smiling mysteriously at him. He had a long, thin face, framed with dense brown hair. His facial hair was heavy and flecked with grey. 'You are in some quandary in your life,' he said. 'You see two paths, and know not which one to take.'

Thomas stared, but at once the man held up his hand. 'Your pardon,' he said. 'Such habits die hard – I did not think to ask your leave.' He stiffened suddenly, as if in pain. 'The man who put me in that box, also laid his lash across my back. Yet he was not as harsh as he might have been...' He put a hand to his head. 'I must get away from here, and restore myself.'

'Indeed.' Thomas nodded in the direction the constable had indicated. 'Shall we go and find this cart of yours?'

Schweiz nodded and stumbled out of the square, with Thomas at his side.

* * *

It was past midday before the little party halted, a mile or two south of Wantage, to allow Paulo to wash himself and recover a little. His splendid gown was taken from him by the now-silent young man in the garish suit, who seemed to fill many functions, including servant. While he attended to his master's needs, Ned and Thomas walked a few yards away to confer in private.

'His name's Kit Page,' Ned said, still excited from the morning's adventure. 'Served yon magician for years, he says. They've been all over – across the seas too, if you believe...'

But Thomas was impatient. 'I care not where they've been. We'll set them straight for Chaddleworth, then get back to Petbury. Are we not late enough?'

Ned's face fell. 'Was it wrong to wish to help?' he asked. 'Don't look like they made many friends in Wantage.'

'Small wonder, from what I heard,' Thomas told him. He glanced over to the covered cart. The single horse that drew it, a sway-backed animal of advanced years, was cropping grass at the roadside. As he and Ned watched, Paulo Schweiz emerged from the back of the vehicle, newly attired in a gown of sober black. He now looked more like a schoolmaster than a travelling mountebank – though that, Thomas knew, was what he was. The fact that the man had presumed to tell his fortune, more accurately than he liked, he chose not to dwell upon.

The mountebank climbed down stiffly from the cart and walked towards them. His face was clean, his cuts and bruises smeared with some ointment. One hand was bandaged, where it had been cut by a sharp stone. His hair, which he wore untrimmed like his assistant's, hung down past his shoulder blades.

'I wish again to extend my thanks for your kindness,' he said. 'My novitiate has told me how you alone—' he gazed at Thomas '—stood up in the inn, and said you would try to help. Paulo Schweiz would repay you, in any way he can.'

'No need for it,' Thomas answered. 'I'll point you towards

Chaddleworth. The road runs on south to Hungerford, if you like. Or you could halt at Great Shefford, then follow the valley east to Newbury.'

Paulo was nodding, his sharp eyes flicking back and forth between the two of them. Ned's glance had strayed towards the cart, where Kit Page was feeding the ape from a bag of what looked like dried fruit.

'Is it a goodly size, this Chaddleworth?' the conjuror asked.

'No, it's but a small village...' Thomas frowned suddenly. 'Not much of a crowd. You wouldn't want to go setting up this tent show of yours there.'

Paulo gave a tired smile. 'Please, you must not concern yourself further about me. I wish merely for an inn where we may rest... Is there such?'

Ned spoke up eagerly. 'The Black Bear. Master Dillamore keeps a room or two, and a goodly brew on tap.'

Thomas's heart sank. Plainly Ned already saw himself as the toast of the tap-room, after he had introduced the conjuror and his ape to the little community. He would be telling the tale of how he and Thomas rescued them for months.

'You wouldn't want to stop there long,' Thomas said to Paulo, with a glance at Ned. 'They're country folk, superstitious...' He broke off. Paulo was looking at him with some amusement.

'Please, there is naught to fear.' The conjuror levelled a frank gaze at him. 'You think I am some charlatan, like those ballad-singers who draw the crowd while their accomplice cuts purses, no?' When Thomas did not answer he added, 'I am not of that ilk, Master Finbow. My *Mundus Peregrinus* – my exotic world – is but a show, to delight folk and show them some of the wonders of foreign lands. There's no harm in it. Anyone who pays a penny may come and enjoy – as they have done in many parts of Europe.'

He paused as if waiting for a reply. When none came he looked back towards the cart. His assistant was watching them. 'Well... enough,' he said finally. 'If you will walk with us and show the way to this village, I will not take up more of your time.' He turned away, then said over his shoulder, 'A pity, for I have known falconers in other countries. We would have things to speak of.'

He walked off towards the cart. Ned looked at Thomas as if about to speak, then thought better of it.

* * *

That evening, the falconers took supper then went their own ways – Ned presumably to find Eleanor and present his gift, whatever it was, while Thomas sat doggedly in the kitchens until finally Nell realised he was not going to leave, left her duties and walked over to him.

'I brought a gift from Wantage, for your birthday,' he said.

Her face softened. 'Did you indeed?'

'If you care to come by the cottage later...' Their eyes met. 'Unless Sir Robert dines late,' he added.

'Sir Robert took the high sheriff out hunting today,' Nell told him. 'They have already supped and retired, as my lady has.'

He waited.

'I will come by in an hour,' she finished.

She found him sitting by the fireside at the little homemade table he used as a work-bench, skimming the froth from the surface of a pot which was coming to the boil. Hearing her enter he looked round, then turned his attention to the task. Wordlessly, Nell sat on the other stool beside him.

'Clarified honey,' Thomas said. 'It makes a fine base for the pellets.'

She watched as he boiled the honey until it thickened, then took a lump on a knife-point and dropped it onto a small trencher, where it began to cool. He took a pinch of wormwood and began to mix it in.

'Your gift is by the window,' he told her.

She rose and went to the falconer's pouch that lay on the window shelf, and drew out the comb. It was longer than the one she owned, its fine teeth well-carved of some substance she did not know. 'It's beautiful,' she said, and came back to sit with him. For a while neither of them spoke. Night was falling, the fire's glow the only light in the single room.

'She you never speak of,' Nell said. 'One you met in Armada year, when you went with Sir Robert to Surrey.' And when he paused at his work, she went on, 'I know you loved her. What I would know is, if you love her still.'

He faced her. 'I know not,' he answered. 'It's been four years...'

'And if you went there now and sought her out, and she was free, would you leave Petbury and stay with her?'

He hesitated. 'Again, I know not.'

She watched him finish moulding the pellet between his fingers, to the size of a small hazelnut, then drop it on a scrap of soft leather. 'You must decide,' she said.

'I know.' He took another drop of honey on the knifepoint, and turned to her. 'I wish you only happiness,' he began, but she stayed him with a glance.

'Speak no more of it,' she said, standing. Then without a backward glance she moved towards the Jacob's ladder in the corner that led to the sleeping-loft.

* * *

By the middle of the next day, Thomas had put aside his
troubles, as he and Ned occupied themselves with their work.
Brutus, the ailing tercel, swallowed his worm pellets obediently,
and while at the mews Thomas took the opportunity to give Ned
an impromptu lesson on the diseases of falcons. Though Ned
was a willing pupil, he was a lad of the Downlands, who much
preferred learning while they were exercising the birds. He was
relieved when they were about to go out, until Sir Robert came
riding up to the mews on his new hawking horse, a fine Barbary.
As usual he had taken Tamora out, and now drew rein, leaning
down so that Thomas could take her from the gauntlet.

Their master was in a somewhat sombre mood. 'I must ride
down to Boxwell Farm later,' he said. 'The inquest is being held
on Simon Haylock.' He waited as Thomas settled Tamora on his
own wrist. 'The high sheriff will act as coroner. I have offered
him the full hospitality of Petbury during his stay. You know,
Thomas, that he enjoys a day's falconing as well as I do.'

Thomas nodded. 'We have enough birds, if it please him to
ride forth at any time.'

The knight seemed not to notice Ned, who stood nervously to
one side. He became tongue-tied whenever Sir Robert was
about.

'Martin has engaged a fellow to rebuild Ames's barn,' Sir
Robert mused, seemingly in passing. 'Let's hope we can put an
end to the business soon...' He trailed off. Thomas waited;
knowing his master as he did, he guessed there was more. The
knight was not a man given to idle conversation.

'This mapmaker,' he said.

Behind him, Thomas felt Ned stir slightly.

'You encountered the man two days ago, I understand.'

'I did, sir,' Thomas confirmed. 'It slipped my mind to tell you
of it.'

'No matter.' Sir Robert gazed into the far distance, where sheep dotted the Downs, then turned back to Thomas. 'I saw him yesterday on my ride, pointing that contraption of his at Coldborough Hill. When I told him who I was, he claimed acquaintance with you.'

Thomas nodded politely.

'Odd sort,' Sir Robert mused. 'A scholar, no doubt of that – Cambridge man, though.' He wrinkled his nose. 'He claims he holds the Queen's commission to map every county in England. Yet Master Saxton carried out that same task, admirably I believe, more than a decade ago.'

Thomas was frowning. 'You think he has some other purpose in mind?'

Sir Robert shrugged, then took a firmer grip on the rein of his spirited mount which, growing bored with standing still, shook its head. 'He draws maps, anyone can see that. He showed me some of them.' He raised an eyebrow. 'What did you make of the daughter?'

'She was kind and well-disposed towards us, if a little shy,' Thomas told him.

The knight grunted, and at last seemed ready to take his leave. 'Wouldn't hurt to keep an eye on him, I'd wager,' he said. 'If you happen to notice, I mean, while you're out with the birds, or...'

'As you wish, sir.' Thomas threw a glance at Ned. Having learned in passing that Eleanor had received no gift from him last night, he had a shrewd idea which way the young man's mind now moved.

'Good...' Sir Robert shook the reins and turned his horse. Looking back over his shoulder, he seemed to notice Ned at last, and called out, 'Study hard from the book of Thomas, boy. There's no better master of your craft in all Berkshire!'

He rode off towards the stables, the Barbary breaking at once into a graceful canter. Thomas turned, and the lad dropped his gaze.

'I would guess you'd not object, should we encounter Master Mead and his daughter again,' he murmured.

Ned gulped. 'If Sir Robert wishes it,' he stammered. 'I-I'd better look in on the eyasses again,' he added.

Thomas merely nodded as Ned turned and strode away across the Downs in the direction of the nursery mews.

6

That evening, it being Friday, Thomas finished his duties and walked the mile into Chaddleworth to take a mug at the Black Bear. In reflective mood, he wished for nothing more than a quiet night by the chimney corner, but when he entered the smoky parlour he knew it was not to be.

The crowd was bigger and noisier than usual, and a mood of some excitement prevailed. Then he saw the cause of it, which made him uneasy: at the far end of the room no less a personage than Paulo Schweiz, attired once again in his splendid – and now clean – gown with the hanging sleeves, was holding court. Nearby, Kit Page and his ape performed simple tricks, to the delight of the onlookers.

Thomas had given the mountebank little thought since parting from him the previous afternoon at the Chaddleworth turning. He understood that the man intended to spend the night, then move on. Instead, having found himself made welcome, he looked as if he were here to stay. Before Paulo noticed him Thomas turned to find himself in the path of the Black Bear's landlord, Hugh Dillamore.

'Thomas!' The other grasped his shoulder. They were old friends, and had been since boyhood. Yet while Thomas had adopted the outdoor life of a falconer, the solidly built Dillamore had married the inn-keeper's daughter and taken over the business, his once muscular body quickly going to fat. Now, he seldom strayed beyond his own four walls.

'A mug of best?' The landlord led the way to the farthest barrel, cleaving the throng of drinkers before him. Thomas followed, greeting acquaintances as he went. He stood by the keg as the other worked the spigot.

'We've got entertainment.' Hugh nodded in the direction of Paulo Schweiz, in the act of raising a tankard to his lips. When he lowered it, the froth lay upon his thick moustache like snow – whereupon he blew it off, spattering the clothing of those nearest. There was a roar of laughter.

'I met him yesterday in Wantage,' Thomas said. 'Ned and I travelled back with him.' He did not feel inclined to add details.

'He's good for trade,' Hugh told him, holding out the filled mug. Thomas took it gratefully and took a long pull. 'He's going to raise his tent on the green outside, give a show tomorrow night,' the landlord went on. 'Though what sort of show it might be, I know not.'

Thomas lowered his mug abruptly, and seeing his expression, Hugh narrowed his eyes. 'Is there aught I should know?'

'The show he gave in Wantage got him put in the stocks,' Thomas said. 'From what I hear, it's not for the faint-hearted.'

The landlord frowned, then found himself distracted. There was a cheerful shout of 'Two mugs, master – and quickly!'

Turning, Thomas saw a fresh-faced young man with blond hair and a thin beard approaching them, wearing a broad grin. With him was Ned Hawes.

'Thomas.' Ned was relaxed, all smiles, the business of the day forgotten. 'Here's the man I spoke of who'll rebuild Ames's barn – John Flowers.' Turning importantly to Flowers, he presented Thomas as the chief falconer to Sir Robert Vicary, as though there were a whole company of them.

Thomas took the young man's hand, bidding him welcome.

'That he is,' Dillamore chimed in with a grin, swinging two mugs down from their pegs. Business was certainly brisk tonight.

'I hear much of you, Master Thomas, even down at Great Shefford,' Flowers told him. 'They say you're becoming the most famous falconer on the Downs.'

Thomas blinked. 'Fresh news to my ears,' he muttered, with obvious embarrassment. Both young men, already seeming firm friends, suppressed a laugh. Yet Ned was the sort who made friends so readily, it was small surprise.

'John will settle the reckoning, Master Hugh,' Ned told the landlord, taking the filled mug from him. Turning to Thomas he said, 'He's good as his word, see?'

Thomas took a pull from his own mug, while the younger men drank and toasted each other. Soon they moved away, seeking company more their own age.

'I would hear more about this show of Master Paulo's,' Dillamore was saying, but again he was called to serve more customers. Thomas went off to find a quiet spot, then saw it was impossible; there was not a seat to be had.

By the far wall, Paulo Schweiz was still the centre of attention. As Thomas watched, two village women approached him and spoke quietly in his ear. At once the mountebank drew them aside privately, smiling and nodding. Thomas felt his brow furrow; if the man were bent on telling fortunes, as no doubt he was, he could end up buying himself the sort of trouble he had got into at Wantage. But the next moment the thought was literally jolted out of his mind as a squat, round-shouldered man knocked against him, spilling what remained of his beer onto the floor.

'Here...' Thomas looked round and stiffened. The culprit was Ambrose Fuller, the thatcher, whom Ned had talked of the day before, and who generally carried trouble about him the way a pedlar does his pack.

'Mind yourself, falconer,' Fuller growled, his breath full of beer-fumes.

'It's you should mind yourself, tipping a man's mug,' Thomas retorted, though he knew to avoid provoking the man. He had no desire for a bout.

'You can afford it,' Fuller snapped. His famous eyebrows, like two black caterpillars, moved together, and those nearby eyed him uneasily. 'The way you Petbury folk live, you ought to treat every man here.'

'I hear you're in work yourself,' Thomas answered. 'Mayhap you should buy. That'd be a first time, would it not?'

There were a few chuckles. Fuller glared round, whereupon the drinkers turned away and busied themselves in conversation; the man's reputation was legendary. But at that moment his eye fell upon John Flowers, his new employer, with an arm about Ned Hawes's shoulder, the two of them in animated conversation with a couple of village girls.

'You'll wait, falconer,' Fuller muttered. 'I got business...' He moved off.

Thomas glanced wryly down at the pool of spilled ale, and began to make his way back to the barrels for a refill. Kit Page, now seated beside his master, was doing tricks with coins. The ape sat docilely on his lap.

Dillamore, as skilled a drawer as any in West Berkshire, was filling mugs as fast as he could in between hurrying to the tables and back. Waiting his turn, Thomas gazed about. Most of the population of Chaddleworth and its surrounds seemed to be in the Black Bear. The tiny village on the hill, clustered about St Andrew's Church, boasted little more than a hundred souls.

There was a cry, from somewhere outside. A few heads turned towards the door. There was another shout, more akin to a scream: a woman's cry. Voices rose in consternation, and those nearest the door began to move outside. Others further off, and those clustered about Paulo Schweiz, had heard nothing. Thomas joined the group that spilled from the inn onto the green outside, where dogs began barking. It was almost dark, and lights showed at nearby cottages. Beside the open door of one stood a small, stout woman, crying out to anyone who would hear.

'He's dead! God's mercy on us, for he's dead!'

'It's Jane Kirke,' someone muttered. Village folk were appearing at cottage doors, as more emerged from the inn to see what the fuss was about. They milled around the distraught figure of Jane Kirke, wife to William Kirke the joiner.

'Who's dead, Jane?' someone asked, rather foolishly, for the answer was becoming plain. The dumpy little woman burst into tears, pointing wildly towards her open door. Women gathered to comfort her. Several men, Thomas among them, moved past her into the tiny cottage, only to stop dead in their tracks.

The single downstairs room was illuminated by the light of the dying fire. At the table, in one of the oaken chairs he had fashioned with his own hands, William Kirke was slumped, his dead eyes staring glassily upwards. One hand was clamped rigidly to his own throat, as if he had suffered pain or even choked. On the board before him was a bowl of porridge, half-eaten, and a cup lying on its side. He had vomited the entire contents of his stomach down his shirt front, spattering the table in the process. More alarming, however, was the look on Kirke's face: one of desperation, as of a man who knows he is dying and can do nothing.

But something shook Thomas, more than the discovery of the dead man, and at once he knew what it was. Perhaps because of the way Kirke was soiled, or the mouth which hung open... He thought of Simon Haylock, back in the burned barn, and knew in his heart that both men had died in the same manner.

* * *

The next hour was one of alarm and confusion, until cooler heads began to prevail. One was that of Giles Frogg the constable, fetched from the Black Bear where he had been enjoying the traveller's tales of the visiting showman, Paulo Schweiz. In fact, Paulo had asked the constable's permission to accompany him and view the body, citing a professional interest in sudden deaths. And now, piecemeal, the story began to take shape.

Jane Kirke worked some days as a laundress at Poughley Manor, and had been out all day. Her husband had come home in the evening as usual, being engaged on a job at Brickleton, a few miles north, and taken his supper alone. A bit of bread and a dish of porridge was all he ate at such times. On this occasion, though, having sat down at the table, he had never risen from it. That was how his wife found him when she came home at dusk. Now she sat in a neighbour's cottage, pale and shaking, swearing she would never set foot inside her house again. She would always see him, she maintained, sitting in his chair, dead as a stockfish.

Frogg, a mild-mannered man who kept bees, was at something of a loss. Was the death truly suspicious? Kirke was not a young man. Could he have died of some sickness or heart failure? It was then that Thomas drew him aside and voiced his private fears. He had barely finished speaking when he caught sight of Paulo Schweiz, standing some distance away, gazing at him intently.

'By God, Thomas,' Frogg said, with a shake of his head. 'If it be as you say, it's beyond my powers. I'd best send word to the sheriff.'

'As it happens, he's a guest of my master at Petbury,' Thomas told him.

Frogg brightened a little. 'Then will you...?'

Thomas nodded. 'I'll go now. Sir Robert will not be abed yet...' He stopped. Schweiz had come forward, and was hovering behind Frogg's shoulder.

'My friend.' He smiled at Thomas. 'Once again you seem to be close at hand, when there is trouble.' Thomas blinked at this; there was more truth in that than he liked.

'*Herr* constable...' Paulo laid a hand on Frogg's arm. 'Might I be permitted to look at the body?'

Frogg looked doubtful. 'Nay, it's a matter for the coroner, and such folk.'

Paulo threw a knowing glance at Thomas, who was reminded uncomfortably of the way the conjuror had told his fortune so promptly, back in Wantage. Somewhat to his own surprise, he spoke up.

'This man's got a keen eye, Giles,' he said to the constable. 'Mayhap we can discern something together?'

Frogg hesitated, glancing over his shoulder. A small crowd still clustered anxiously about the doorway. Already there was talk of some sickness in the village. Seeing that it was his part to offer what reassurance he could, the constable made up his mind quickly. 'Look him over then,' he told Thomas. 'But if you find aught, you'll tell me of it.'

Thomas signalled his agreement and, knowing him as one

to be trusted, the constable went out, leaving the other two men alone. Taken aback, Thomas saw that the mountebank, barely awaiting permission, had moved swiftly to the body. At first he bent down and sniffed. Then he looked into William Kirke's mouth and, pulling the eyelids back, peered into his eyes.

'Here, have a little respect,' Thomas began, but the other straightened and looked round with an odd half-smile.

'The porridge,' he said.

Thomas glanced at the bowl. 'What of it?'

'Poisoned, my friend. I would stake crowns on it.'

Thomas stared. 'How can you know?'

But Paulo had caught up the bowl, to sniff fiercely at it. Carelessly he threw it down, then took up the overturned cup, thrust his long nose inside it and sniffed that as well. 'I cannot know for certain, Master Thomas,' he said finally. 'Yet I may make an opinion, may I not?'

'Mayhap you have an opinion as to what form of poison it was, then,' Thomas answered, still sceptical.

Paulo sighed. 'You have not heard of how the porridge was poisoned in the kitchens of the Bishop of Rochester?' he asked. 'Back in the time of your King Henry the Eighth, that was. The culprit, a man named Rose, was discovered, and boiled alive. 'Twas the penalty for such a crime then – as it still is, in some places.'

Thomas shook his head. 'You have more knowledge than I of such, that's plain. But this is no bishop – just a plain Chaddleworth man who made tables and chairs for a living...' He stopped, for Paulo was nodding vigorously.

'Indeed, a puzzle! And yet, like me, you suspect this man did not die of natural cause. For he is not the first, *nein*?' And when Thomas merely gazed at him, he smiled. 'I know what you told our friend the constable, about a man named Haylott – is it not so?'

'Haylock.' Thomas stared. 'Yet, how could you hear?'

With a sigh, Paulo laid a hand on his arm. 'I'm no sorcerer, Master Thomas. There is a skill I learned many years ago, known to a very few men. You watch the lips, and the way the mouth moves, and you can tell the words.'

'You're a dangerous man, Master Paulo,' Thomas said at last.

Paulo gave a yelp of laughter. 'So I am told!'

'And if it were poison, could you tell which one?'

Paulo shrugged. 'Wolfsbane, would be my guess. The choice of murderers through the centuries... Indeed, they say it was the choice of Catherine de' Medici herself.'

'Here...' Thomas felt matters spiralling alarmingly. 'We can't speak of murder...' And then, he remembered the costrel. 'Yet, there is one thing,' he murmured, bringing a gleam of satisfaction to Paulo's eyes. 'If you know a way to divine whether a man was poisoned, I have a drinking vessel that was beside the other one when he died.'

Paulo spoke quietly to him. 'Let me have it, and I will do a simple test. I cannot swear as to which poison was used, but if poison was in the vessel, I should be able to tell.' He turned quickly. 'And I will take a little scoop of this poor soul's porridge, and do the same test.'

Thomas hesitated. If there were any bad intent on Paulo's part, he could not see it, but the man was tricky as a weasel – of that he had small doubt. Yet what harm could it do?

'I'll give you the costrel,' he said. 'Though I ask you to tell no one of this, until I have spoken with my master.'

'You have my word,' Paulo said.

They walked out of the cottage together. Thomas would head back to Petbury at once, while the other returned to the Black

Bear. But as they parted on the Chaddleworth green, the mountebank gave Thomas a curious look, before saying, 'It is not the means that should concern you, my friend, but the cause of it,' he said gravely. 'And that is something I care not to delve into.'

But the next moment he was smiling again. 'Come to my *Mundus Peregrinus* tomorrow night, and you shall enter free of charge,' he called as he walked away. 'I swear there is naught like it in the whole of England!'

Thomas watched him go, then turned to take the road back to Petbury. Suddenly, a thought flew up from his memory that stopped him in his tracks.

William Kirke, it was once rumoured in the village, had a sum of money salted away somewhere. Kirke had always denied it, and it was true none had seen evidence of it and the matter was all but forgotten. Now, Thomas recalled that Simon Haylock had once let slip, while in his cups, that he would want for naught when he was too old to work. At the time most folk had dismissed this as merely the drink talking... But then, if the two men had truly been murdered, as Paulo was so quick to suggest, might these matters put together, constitute a cause?

Thomas walked home slowly, so deep in thought that he barely saw the gates of Petbury when they loomed out of the gathering dark. Curiously, what now came to his mind was that he had forgotten to pay Dillamore for his drink.

7

By the time he returned, Thomas was disappointed to learn that his master had already retired to his chamber. Hence he was obliged to wait until the morning, after he had finished his tasks at the mews. Ned arrived late, having imbibed too freely last night at the Black Bear, to Thomas's mind. But the lad was filled with excitement at the events, and spoke in animated fashion as they worked.

'There's talk of some malady that's come here,' he said. 'What with Haylock, and now Will Kirke – two dead in three days, and in such terrible manner. Folk are afraid.'

Thomas thrust a besom into his hands. 'Sweep up,' he said shortly. 'Only save the sick tercel's muting, so I can look at it.'

Ned glanced at him, knowing better than to argue. But at that moment a stable boy came hurrying up the slope, and called to them to be ready. Sir Robert and the high sheriff would ride out shortly, with a bird each.

Relieved, Thomas slipped on a gauntlet and untied Tamora from her perch. But as Ned followed suit with Caesar, for some reason the tercel bated on his fist. Despite Ned's efforts to calm him, the bird was clearly agitated.

'You were too quick with him,' Thomas chided. 'I warned you about sharp movements.' While Ned struggled to quiet the falcon, Thomas caught up a small bowl, filled it with water from the pail and took a mouthful. Then he moved close to Caesar and, to Ned's surprise, sprayed water from his mouth onto the bird's chest. The startled tercel shook himself, then quieted at once.

'You'll remember that trick, I hope,' Thomas murmured.

As they emerged from the mews two horsemen appeared, riding at a leisurely pace towards them. The high sheriff, Richard Ward, was a man in his middle years, alert and well-attired. He came from a grand Berkshire family, being the son of the Queen's late cofferer, and was said to be destined for a knighthood. When he and Sir Robert reined in to receive their birds from the falconers, and Thomas begged leave to speak to his master on a matter of importance, the man would have drawn away for courtesy's sake. But a frowning Sir Robert gestured him forward.

'There has been another death, like the one at Boxwell Farm,' he told Ward. Turning to Thomas, he bade him tell all that had transpired, which he did. The two men listened in silence.

'Here's a turnabout, Sir Robert,' Ward said finally. 'Fate must have lent a hand.'

Sir Robert nodded. 'Perhaps you should hold an inquest on both men at once, Master Sheriff.' Seeing Thomas's puzzled expression, he offered an explanation. 'The inquest on Haylock is postponed. We are at some pains to find enough able men to make up the jury.'

Thomas was surprised. 'Surely there's no shortage of folk in Great Shefford, sir? Or close by – at East Garston, or Weston.'

'Indeed, falconer, I'm in agreement with you,' Ward said. 'And seldom have I heard such an array of excuses. They plead everything from lambing time to wives about to go into labour. It must be a boom year for Downland births.'

He glanced at the hooded Caesar, sitting docilely on his gauntlet, then peered closer. 'Was this bird distressed?' he enquired. 'I see you have doused him.'

Thomas smiled. 'You have a keen eye, sir. But he is content now, and will serve you well.'

Ward nodded briefly, then turned to Sir Robert. 'Will you make arrangements concerning the body of the village man?' he asked. 'And the widow – she will need to be provided for.'

Sir Robert was thoughtful. 'She must look to her master, Sir John Mountford, at Poughley.' Ward glanced at him, and something unspoken passed between the two men. Sir Robert then looked pointedly at Ned Hawes, standing stiffly behind Thomas.

Thomas turned to him. 'You'd best get on, Ned,' he said, not unkindly. Ned bowed clumsily to Sir Robert and the sheriff and disappeared inside the mews.

Beginning to divine the trust that existed between Thomas and his master, Ward was moved to speak freely. 'This matter needs looking into, somewhat more closely,' he murmured.

Naturally enough, Thomas thought, he knew of the circumstances of Simon Haylock's death. Sir Robert was nodding, and Thomas seized the moment. Without going into details, he mentioned Paulo Schweiz and his theory, as yet untested, that William Kirke, at least, had been poisoned. But both men reacted sharply to the notion.

'That's idle talk, Thomas,' Sir Robert snapped. 'More likely they fell victim to the same bad ale, or contaminated food.'

Thomas inclined his head politely. 'Yet, as they were both Chaddleworth men, sir, surely more would have fallen ill?'

Ward eyed him. 'Who is this foreigner, who claims to know so much?' he demanded.

Thomas told him a little about Paulo, omitting to mention the Wantage stocks.

'And which way, pray, does your mind move?' Ward asked him.

'I cannot be sure, sir,' Thomas admitted. 'Yet there was something unnatural about Haylock's death, as there is about Kirke's. The man never had a day's sickness in his life. And if you'd seen his face...'

Ward hesitated, then said in a different tone, 'I have heard something of your reputation hereabouts, falconer. They say you're an accomplished rummager.'

Sir Robert was beginning to exhibit the same restlessness as his horse. 'We will talk further as we ride, master sheriff,' he said, watching the hooded Tamora, who had sat patiently on his wrist. To Thomas he said, 'Will you take time to go down again to Boxwell and talk to Ames? You can exercise the birds as you go.'

Thomas hid his displeasure. 'I fear there is little more I can discover, sir,' he began, but Sir Robert was already making ready to ride.

'The body of Haylock is being taken to Chaddleworth for burial,' he called out. 'This would be your last opportunity to look it over.'

Thomas sighed inwardly and bowed, as Ward too shook his reins and urged his horse forward. As he went, he said, 'Keep me well versed if you find anything, falconer. I would be interested to see whether your reputation has any true base.'

He waited until both men had ridden away, whereupon Ned appeared from inside the mews. He opened his mouth, then saw the look on Thomas's face.

'Jesu – you're looking a mite sick yourself.'

Thomas threw him a pained look. 'What's this reputation I seem to have brought upon myself?' he asked, recalling John Flowers's words of the night before. 'Have you been wagging your tongue about me?'

Ned shrugged. 'Nay, but others have... Ever since I was a little tapper, I've heard such.' He looked away. 'I was proud as a peacock to come and work under you.'

Thomas stared down at his boots, then moved off towards the mews. 'After you've seen to the eyasses, meet me back here. We've got to go down to Boxwell.'

Ned nodded, berating himself for his clumsiness. Only now did he realise the extent of Thomas's embarrassment.

* * *

Towards the latter part of the morning both falconers walked into Ames's farm with their birds, to find the place filled with activity. The farmer and his sons were at work in the fields, but the yard was cluttered with tools, stacks of thatching reeds and assorted builders' jumble. A ladder stood against the barn wall, with the bull-headed figure of Ambrose Fuller at the top of it. Thomas looked in surprise at the amount of thatch that had been torn down, exposing the beams to the sky. Then he realised what the man was doing, and frowned. True to form, Fuller had seized the chance of making more of the job than it required, and was bent on replacing the entire roof.

From the open doors of the barn, John Flowers appeared. Seeing the newcomers, he broke into a grin. 'Ned, and Master Thomas – welcome! Are you come to chew the fat with us? It's near dinner time.'

Ned indicated the bird on his wrist, one of the sisters with the unpronounceable names. 'We've had a long walk,' he grinned. 'A bite and a drink wouldn't go amiss...' He glanced at Thomas and his face fell.

'Master Flowers.' Thomas's tone was friendly enough, but his face was taut. 'I see you've let yon thatcher have his way, and make a whole new roof.' He indicated Fuller, who had stopped work and was glaring down. Keeping his gaze on Flowers, Thomas went on, 'John Ames and his family worked hard to save what they could – they are not wealthy folk.'

But it was Fuller who answered. 'Sticking your nose in, hawksman?' he called down angrily. 'Well, save your breath, for I'm only doing as I'm bid. 'Twas Flowers's notion to tear down the old thatch.'

Thomas looked at Flowers in surprise, but the man was nodding. ''Tis the truth, Thomas,' he said mildly. 'I told master Ames I would save his thatch if I could, but it wasn't worth the candle. Mildew, and old bees' nests and lord knows what else have rendered it poor. It will save him money in the long run, to have us make it anew while we're here.'

Seeing the sense of the young man's reasoning, Thomas began to relax. 'Your pardon then, John,' he murmured. 'I spoke in haste.' But he was unable to resist adding, ''Tis but that, not being a Chaddleworth man, you may not know the reputation of Master Fuller here.'

There was a silence, soon broken by the sound of Fuller deliberately descending the ladder. 'You take those words back, Finbow!' he shouted. 'Or I'll make 'ee...'

'Ambrose!' Flowers held up a hand, showing more authority than Thomas expected in one so young. 'You see to your work. I'll speak with Master Thomas.'

The thatcher stopped on the bottom rung, gripping the sides of the ladder. 'You're the master, John,' he muttered finally, and began to ascend again. To Thomas he added, 'I told you yestern-ight, falconer – you'll wait!'

Thomas ignored him and favoured Flowers with a smile. 'I meant not to disturb your work. My master ordered me to come here...' He trailed off. A lad in work-stained shirt and breeches, with long, dark hair tucked behind his ears, had emerged from the barn to stand behind Flowers.

'What's the coil, John?' he asked.

'There's no coil, Tom,' Flowers replied. Gesturing to Ned and Thomas, he presented his labourer, Tom Brazier. The young fellow nodded, though his manner was none too friendly. To his master he said, 'I've cleared the base of yon wall, ready for the sill.'

'Good, then we'll stop for a minute or two,' Flowers said, and turned to Thomas. 'Will you take a drink with us? It's a warm day.'

Ned looked hopeful, but Thomas was hesitant. 'A mouthful would be welcome, but we can't tarry long,' he said. 'My errand isn't a pleasant one.' He began to explain about Simon Haylock, but seeing the other's expression, stopped himself.

'I fear you've had a wasted journey, Thomas,' Flowers told him. 'A man came yesterday afternoon with a cart and took the body away.'

Thomas frowned. 'Do you know by whose orders?'

'I do,' Flowers nodded. 'Sir John Mountford's.'

Thomas considered briefly. This was a matter for Sir Robert. He glanced up, to see the sun was reaching its zenith. And it was indeed a warm day...

'Then we'll accept your hospitality,' he said to Flowers. 'And next time you take a mug at the Black Bear, the reckoning shall be mine.'

Everyone relaxed then, save Ambrose Fuller who remained

defiantly atop his ladder, showing his refusal to drink with the interlopers. Having taken the falcons some distance away and tethered them, Thomas and Ned were glad to sit with the other two and share a costrel of tepid ale. And before long, the talk turned abruptly to Christopher Mead, the mapmaker.

'We saw him yesterday, on the road to Eastbury,' Flowers said. 'He was leading the horse, with that daughter of his in the saddle.'

'Do you not see him more often?' Thomas enquired. 'He told us he was lodging in Great Shefford.'

Flowers looked surprised. 'Nay, they don't dwell in the village. I've only ever seen them in the lanes, or out on the Downs.'

Thomas glanced at Ned, who was all ears, the reason for which he knew well enough.

Having taken a generous pull from his costrel, Tom Brazier wiped his mouth with the back of his hand and spoke up. 'That Grace Mead.' He smiled, with a knowing look. 'What I wouldn't give for a night with her.'

Flowers threw him a scornful look. 'You wouldn't stand a chance, boy.'

'Wouldn't need much of a chance,' Brazier replied. 'And wouldn't it be worth it? Prettiest little callet I've seen in a long while.' He leered at the other two. 'Any man who says he wouldn't tumble her in the nearest ditch, is a liar.'

Thomas tensed, realising Ned was angry. He also realised that he had never once seen him lose his temper.

'She's a princess, is Mistress Mead,' Ned said, fixing Brazier with a hard look. 'Well-named, for grace is what she has, aplenty. John speaks aright – she wouldn't look twice at the likes of you... or me.' The last words were added as an afterthought.

Brazier stared at him, then put on a wide grin. 'Look here,

John,' he said to his master. 'I believe young Ned pines with love for the mapmaker's girl.'

With a barely concealed sneer, he added, 'You don't truly believe she's his daughter, do 'ee?' He grinned at Ned, who had gone white. 'Name me a craftsman, be he mapmaker or what, that ever had a woman for his prentice. She'm his doxy, boy. I'll wager you a shilling she cleaves to him every night. Maybe out there in the long grass, too... Jesu, I'm in a sweat just picturing it!'

Ned was on his feet in an instant. 'You're lying,' he said hotly. 'She's a fine lady, any man can see that – even a dirty-mouthed cove like you!'

Brazier laughed, but his teeth showed. 'By the Christ, you're blinded with love,' he cried. 'That, or a plain fool. They say Chaddleworth folk are short on wits.'

Then deliberately he stood up and faced Ned, the two of them locking horns like young bullocks. Thomas and Flowers exchanged a look, and rose as one.

'Ned.' In spite of his anger the boy turned at once, and caught the look in his master's eye. 'Go and loose Aglaia from her perch. Time we were on our way.'

Ned hesitated, threw a dark look at Brazier, and went. Meanwhile Flowers had moved to stand in front of his labourer. 'Fetch those timbers off the cart,' he ordered in a harsh tone. 'And hurry it up.'

The young man spat deliberately on the ground, then went off in his turn.

Flowers turned to Thomas, who said, 'Once again, I should ask your pardon.'

The other shook his head. 'Nay, I've begun to see how Tom enjoys baiting folk,' he muttered. 'He'll get himself a broken head one of these days. And you know Ned is my friend.'

Thomas nodded. 'As he is mine. And I'd not stand by and brook injury to one I hold dear.'

But there was no resentment in the other's face. 'Mayhap it's my part to ask pardon,' he said. 'For the behaviour of both my men.' There was a rueful look on his face. 'I've been away from my village too long... I took no advice as to the calibre of the fellows I hired. I wonder now whether I have acted in haste.'

Thomas was relieved to find that this young man impressed him more, the longer his acquaintance with him. 'Your senses do you credit, John,' he said. 'And you'll see I keep my word, when you next come to the inn at Chaddleworth. We're not all short on wits.'

Flowers smiled, then walked with Thomas to the fence where he had settled the hooded falcons. Ned was waiting for him, eyes fixed firmly on the ground.

But his anger was not spent.

8

They were silent throughout the walk back to Petbury. Only when they were at the mews once again, settling the birds, did Ned at last venture to speak.

'I ask your pardon, Thomas.'

'For what?' Thomas was busy unhooding Tamora.

'For my angry words towards Brazier?'

'Is that all?' Thomas faced him. 'I thought you touched on another matter.'

Ned said nothing.

'I've wondered of late, how matters stand between you and Eleanor.'

Ned looked up. 'As they always have since I first saw her,' he began, trying to ignore Thomas's gaze and failing. He made a show of pulling off his gauntlet and stowing it in his belt.

'It gladdens me to hear it,' Thomas answered. 'You know how protective I can be towards my daughter.' But when the boy refused to meet his eye, he sighed and let the matter drop. Was it so long since he had been Ned's age, and prey to the same stew of emotions?

'Let's take a bit of dinner,' he said at last. 'Then we'll walk out with the other birds and bring down some game for the supper-table.'

But that afternoon, having walked far out on the Downs north of Lambourn, they were surprised by a figure who appeared suddenly out of the grass, leading his horse uphill towards them. While their charges hovered in the sky above, Thomas and Ned stood waiting for the mapmaker to ascend the slope. He was alone.

'I saw the birds,' Mead called out as he drew close, indicating the soaring falcons, one of which dropped suddenly, having fixed upon her prey. 'Though I knew not twas you, Master Finbow.' He halted, slightly out of breath, wearing the same slightly ironic smile that Thomas remembered. It would be difficult, he thought, to tell when this man spoke the truth and when he lied. And in spite of himself, he recalled Tom Brazier's bawdy accusation of that morning. Suddenly, for some reason it did not seem so unlikely.

'Is your daughter not helping you today, sir?' Thomas asked.

Mead's smile faded. 'Poor Grace pleads *mal à la tête*,' he replied. 'One of those several ailments that troubles women more than men. I've left her at our lodging.'

'That would be at Great Shefford,' Thomas observed in a casual tone.

'Close to Great Shefford,' Mead agreed after a moment. 'Yet not within the village.'

Ned watched them. But there followed a whirr of wings and Thalia appeared, the limp body of a partridge hanging from her talons. At once the lad busied himself taking the prey and settling the bird on his wrist.

Thomas's gaze had strayed towards the horse, which bore only a saddle and a small pack. Of the mapmaker's tripod and other equipment, there was no sign. 'You travel light today, sir,' he smiled. 'Is your survey of the Lambourn valley then complete?'

Mead raised an eyebrow. 'If you refer to my dioptra, I do not employ it on every excursion,' he answered, then changed his tone. 'How fares your master, Sir Robert? I will endeavour to take up his kind invitation to sup with him and Lady Margaret.'

Thomas accepted the assertion of status with a smile. 'He's well, sir, and asked me to look out for you. You have become the talk of the Downlands.'

Mead appeared not to like that notion. 'I'd not marked you as a flatterer, Master Finbow,' he replied with some sarcasm. 'I but do my work, as you must do yours.'

Thomas gazed upwards, shielding his eyes from the afternoon sun. The other falcon was still soaring, a distant speck. And suddenly, Mead seemed eager to take his leave. 'Commend me to your master,' he said, catching up the reins of his horse with an abrupt movement.

Thomas inclined his head and looked to Ned, who followed suit. But without a glance Mead yanked the reins, turned his horse and led him back the way he had come. A dozen yards away he changed direction and turned off at an angle, northwards towards Greenhill Down.

'What's he doing heading for the Ridgeway?' Ned asked, walking over to Thomas. Thalia sat hooded on his wrist.

'I know not,' Thomas replied. 'But it's an odd place from which to map the Lambourn Valley.'

Together, they watched the mapmaker disappear from sight.

* * *

They parted company that evening, tomorrow being Sunday when Ned would stay home in Chaddleworth, helping his father with their own little plot of land. But before he went Thomas brought a bag, tied at the neck, out of the mews and handed it to him.

'Will you do me a service?' he asked. 'Drop by the Black Bear on your way, and give this to our friend the conjuror.'

Ned was about to ask what was in it, but held his tongue.

'And tell no one,' Thomas added.

Ned nodded, about to take his leave, then stopped. 'The show!' he exclaimed. 'His *mundus* what-do-ee-call-it, on the green. Are you not coming to watch?'

'If there's naught else to do,' Thomas said, and after making his farewell went back into the mews. He knew that once out of sight, Ned would look inside the bag. But all he would find was a costrel, which would soon pale to insignificance beside the impending excitement of the tent show.

Whereupon he realised how intrigued he was to see it for himself.

When he dropped by the kitchens an hour later with the day's bag of game birds, the heat from the great chimney hit him at once. The place buzzed like a hive, and Nell signalled to him that she was fully occupied for the night. Sir Robert and Lady Margaret, it seemed, had not only the high sheriff but other company at their table. Though Thomas expected it, he was disappointed; it would have pleased him to take Nell to the tent show. Taking what supper was on offer – half a roast capon with some greens – he retired to his usual corner, then was obliged to get to his feet as Martin appeared from the passage doorway.

The steward rarely came into the kitchens, and every servant strived at once to look busy. Stooping over his staff, Martin made his way towards Thomas. 'I've spoken with the grooms and the head gardener,' he said. 'Now I ask you too to be alert, for I fear there is a thief on Sir Robert's land. Not one of our known poachers,' he added. 'I speak of someone bolder, and more cunning.'

Thomas frowned. 'What's gone missing?'

'Some loaves from the bakehouse…' The steward shook his head. 'Worse, a silver dish is lost, and a pair of embroidered sheets. The women swear that someone has been inside the wash-house.'

'That's bold indeed, when we have the high sheriff as our guest,' Thomas observed. 'Yet I will keep an eye out.'

'I expect no less,' Martin replied drily. 'More, I have a mind to set a watch each night, for the coming week at least.' He waited a moment before adding, 'I may call upon you in a day or two, to serve your turn.'

Thomas nodded as the old steward turned about and made his way towards the door. There was some relief when he had gone.

'What've you done now, Thomas?' the kitchen boy asked cheekily. 'Lost another letter?' Then seeing the expression on the falconer's face, he darted away and made himself scarce.

* * *

The green at Chaddleworth had been transformed.

Lanterns hung from the beech trees to its east side, illuminating a large tent, much mended and travel-stained but brightly painted, which stood but twenty yards from the doors of the Black Bear. Pennants fluttered from the tops of its two main poles. Adjoining one of its sides was a much smaller tent, its entrance flap tied shut. Village children ran excitedly about, a few bolder ones peeping under the walls of the main tent. But clearly there was little to see, for they soon lost interest and came out again.

It was sunset, and Thomas made his way into the Bear to find it full to the corners again, and not only of Chaddleworth folk. Clearly word had spread, and many from neighbouring villages had arrived to see the *Mundus Peregrinus*. Of its proprietor, however, there was no sign. This night, Dillamore's wife Ann was helping to serve tables. Seeing Thomas, she smiled and gestured him towards the barrels.

'I never paid Hugh for last night's mug,' he murmured as he drew near, prompting a snort from the big, raw-boned Ann.

'Only you would have thought to say such,' she laughed, wiping her hands on her apron. 'You think he'd remember, after all that's been happening hereabouts?'

Thomas felt a smile spreading; Ann's company always cheered him. 'It's my habit to forget much, when I'm away on the Downs,' he began, then broke off. Giles Frogg was moving purposefully through the noisy throng towards him.

'Aye, you always were one to forget what suits him,' Ann threw back, and bent to fill a mug from the spigot. 'Like the way you and me once was, before you went and married Mary Blount.'

Thomas coughed and turned to greet Frogg, with more warmth than the constable expected. 'Giles, you're welcome.'

Frogg blinked. At the same moment Ann stood and handed Thomas his full mug. 'You better pay me now,' she said flatly, 'lest you forget again.'

Thomas found a coin, took his mug and turned back to the constable, who was eying him. 'I would speak privately,' he muttered.

'Yon conjuror,' Frogg said when they had moved stood some way off, towards the door. 'He spoke with me a while ago. Said you'd given him something, would tell him how Simon Haylock died.' And when Thomas nodded, the constable looked crestfallen. 'Is there aught I should know?'

At once Thomas told him about the poison theory, whereupon the man's jaw sagged. 'Nay, here in Chaddleworth?' He frowned. 'And what in heaven's name is wolfsbane?'

Thomas shrugged. 'I've yet to see Master Paulo. If he confirms it is such – or some other poison, as he claims he is able – I will tell you at once.' He looked frankly at the honest fellow, a plain man he had known all his life. 'I ask pardon for not telling you sooner. It was late, and I wished to find my master.'

Frogg was nodding. 'Did you tell the sheriff, as I asked?' Thomas told him what had passed between himself, his master and Richard Ward that morning. Frogg seemed relieved.

'Then I'll take my leave, for the present,' he said, and jerked his head towards the door. 'Like Lambourn Fair out there tonight.'

As the constable moved off, Thomas was startled to feel a tug on his sleeve, even more so when looked down to find a long, hairy hand grasping his shirt. He whirled around, almost dropping his mug, before the truth dawned. Men nearby roared with laughter, and Thomas was obliged to join in. Still holding on to his sleeve, Kit Page's ape was standing beside him, looking up at him with its huge deep-brown eyes. Kit himself stood close by, wrapped in in a plain cloak.

'We meant not to fright thee.' As ever, the young man wore a sombre look. Thomas had yet to see him smile. He took a pull from his mug and waited.

'Master Paulo sends a message,' the young man went on. 'He's preparing for the show now, yet he bids you wait on him afterwards. He says to tell you he has done the task you wanted, and found what he sought.'

Thomas gave a quick nod, whereupon Kit and the ape moved off abruptly. And a moment later, it was time.

The audience were summoned by a sudden, loud blast on a trumpet. In the Black Bear, drinkers downed their beer in haste and joined the crush to get outside, mingling with the throng surging about the tent. Now its entrance flap was flung wide, and lights showed from within. As Thomas drew near, he saw rows of benches arranged inside. And there was Kit on the door, bowing and taking the money, while the ape swung from a guy rope nearby. None could fail to note the remarkable change in Paulo's young assistant: he had cast off the cloak and was clad in the bright yellow-and-green suit in which Thomas had first seen him, and now radiated excitement.

'Come, sirs, and ladies – ye are honoured this night!' he called. 'The *Mundus Peregrinus* of Master Paulo Schweiz the traveller has delighted folk in every country in Europe – nobles, gentles and common people all! See the true images of far-off lands, from the forests of Afric to the Sultan's Seraglio! From ancient Athens to the Court of the Grand Mogul! Marvel at sights never yet shown to mortals this side of the English Channel! And more – with each likeness, ye will hear sounds, made by scientific process, its secrets known only to the most learned men, like Master Paulo! Here now, for but a short time – hurry, and pay your penny!'

The crowd needed little encouragement. They huddled round the entrance, pressing against the tent. Guy ropes creaked, and the ape leaped in alarm onto Kit's shoulders.

'Steady, sirs!' Kit Page cried, though there was a grin on his face. 'There is room for all, if ye mind not the crush! Thank you sir – pass within... Thank you...'

The coins fell into his hand like rain. Thomas smiled, his own curiosity aroused. He was about to see something truly unusual, as Paulo had promised. *Where was the old mountebank?* he wondered idly, allowing himself to be carried along in the crush. His glance strayed to the small side tent, from where his keen ears picked out muffled sounds. Then he was face to face with Kit, and reaching for his purse.

'Nay, falconer.' The young man stayed him. 'Master Paulo bade me admit ye freely. He is a man of his word.'

Thomas murmured his thanks and passed inside the tent, where the excitement was at fever pitch. Yet to his surprise, there was neither stage nor painted backdrop. Instead, the benches, placed so close together that there was little leg-room, faced an empty tent wall. Torches lit the rear. Peering round, Thomas saw a hole had been cut in the canvas, in the centre of the back wall, and covered by a flap. Behind it was the little side tent, but no light showed from within.

He took his place among a group of young chattering fellows. Glancing round, he saw the faces of many he knew. There was Ned near the front with his mother, father and sister, having arrived early to get a good seat. Behind sat Giles Frogg with his wife, the burden of office forgotten for the evening. And behind Frogg, among a coterie of outsiders from East Garston and Great Shefford, sat John Flowers and his labourer Tom Brazier. Of Ambrose Fuller there was no sign until, glancing towards the entrance, Thomas saw him pushing his way in, among the last to leave the inn.

It was soon plain that the show-house was barely large enough. Folk called to others to make way and to shove up, though already every bench was crammed from end to end. Children sat on the grass at the feet of parents and grandparents, while young men hurried to show gallantry by giving up seats to village girls. Soon the tent had filled so that its walls bulged and the heat rose from sweating bodies, and still latecomers pressed in at the rear. Finally, when worried looks were being exchanged, there came a call from somewhere, as if in signal. The entrance flap dropped abruptly and at once a hush fell, for the lights had been extinguished, so quickly that some murmured in alarm. The tent was almost dark.

There was a faint sound and, craning his neck, Thomas saw the little flap in the rear wall lift. The next moment he blinked, for there came the shriek of some wild animal that he knew not, and a lurid picture glowed suddenly, a fuzzy-edged circle on the bare wall opposite. The crowd drew breath as the image slowly came into focus, several feet high, followed by cries of amazement as everyone saw what it was: a dense forest of huge, garishly coloured flowers and strange, tall trees from which ragged vines hung. And from the vines apes were swinging: some like Kit's own creature, others larger and fiercer. Then, as the folk of Chaddleworth stared in disbelief, the sounds began.

There was an animal shriek as before, then another. Then came the cry of a bird, though none that was known to Downland folk. The calls were repeated, multiplying until they rose and melded into a raucous chorus, as if a horde of wild creatures were vying for attention. The din had become a cacophony, and Thomas knew what the constable back in Wantage had meant, when he told him how the show had frightened folk: for this audience was terrified.

Small children howled, and had to be picked up; older children whimpered and pressed close to each other. Men tied to look brave, while their wives and sweethearts screamed and covered their ears. Thomas looked round. Most were staring at the outlandish picture. If this was but the beginning, what would come next?

Then, mercifully, the din abated, until only a single bird call was heard. Instead, from out of the gloom somewhere to the rear, a deep voice rang out, 'Behold the fearful jungles of Afric, where wild lions tear the bodies of deer larger than horses! Where striped tigers and great spotted cats devour the wildmen who wander from the paths; where birds the height of a man, too heavy to fly, stalk the grassy glades; where apes hold sway from the treetops, and insects bigger than sparrows rend a man's flesh, and send him mad!'

The crowd let out cries of terror, but they were mingled with anticipation. The voice – Paulo's, Thomas assumed, perhaps distorted through a horn or similar device – had at first unnerved them, but now it reassured them: this was, after all, a show, and not some devilry – though how it was achieved, none could tell. And if the image on the tent wall wobbled at times, and if the sounds came and went as if being made by two or three very skilled voices varying in height and pitch, they cared not to notice. They merely listened to the storyteller, and gazed in wonder at the glorious, cunningly painted vistas that passed before their eyes: the gleaming white walls of Greek temples, where semi-naked maidens stood with great jars upon their shoulders; the incredible palace of the Great Sultan, its onion domes glistening in the sun, guarded by moustachioed janissaries wielding scimitars; the vast red deserts of Africa, where impossible creatures with huge humps walked, led by dark men in flowing robes. And with every image came a new tapestry of sounds: the mournful strains of a single flute, or the cries of tribesmen; the boom of a deep drum, or the washing of waves on a distant shore (which, to Thomas's ear, sounded like pebbles rolling on a tray); the clash of cymbals and the roar of some caged beast in the Sultan's palace. Finally, to general delight, came a song in two-part harmony, in some foreign tongue, accompanied by a tabor. This complemented the last image, which drew a gasp of recognition from the crowd: that of some great, golden-crowned king of old, seated on a high throne surrounded by knights, courtiers and ladies, while minstrels sang at his feet. Then as the audience gazed spellbound, the image shifted and disappeared, to metamorphose into the same scene, yet with a different figure at its centre. Seated on the throne, in a vast high-collared and jewelled gown trimmed with ermine, was the most splendid portrait of their own queen: Gloriana, Elizabeth Tudor herself. The crowd rose as one, some weeping, others shouting their approval, as the image slowly faded. The applause that broke out was deafening, and still they stood, facing an empty wall. Behind them, lights appeared again as torches were suddenly lit, though by whom was unclear. Then folk gazed about at the familiar faces of their fellows, as if unable to believe that they were still here, in a tent in Chaddleworth. It was over.

The flap was open, cooler air blew in and animated conversation broke out on every side. Thomas made his way out, looking for Ned but failing to see him in the crush. He stood on the green in the dim light, as folk surged past him to the Black Bear, where the ale would soon be flowing.

Idly he gazed up at the half-moon, then froze as a low voice spoke in his ear and something sharp was pressed against his back.

'Ye've grown careless, pikeman. Back in the low countries, you'd have been stone dead by now.'

9

Thomas turned around slowly and gazed into a face he had not seen for almost a decade. The dark hair was longer, the beard greyer than he remembered and the lines about the cold blue eyes deeper, but the short snub nose was the same, as was the half-smile of amusement mingled with wariness.

Thomas let out a sigh. 'Will Saltmarsh...'

'*Sergeant* Saltmarsh!' the other hissed. The poniard was still held against Thomas's back. A few yards away folk passed by, talking excitedly about the show.

'Did you think you would need that?' Thomas signalled with his eye. After a moment the other lowered the blade, though his face retained its hard look.

'I knew not,' Saltmarsh answered, looking Thomas over. 'Are you not overjoyed to see an old comrade?'

'It depends,' Thomas answered.

'On what?'

'On what he wants of me.'

Saltmarsh gave a snort. 'Same prudent Thomas Finbow. I

hear ye've a place now, and a soft bed to lie in at nights, with a comely red-haired jade to warm it.'

Thomas remained silent.

'Wasn't always thus, was it?' The other sniffed and ran a hand across his runny nose. 'Time was you'd have been glad of a horse-blanket under a hay-rick, and a—'

'No,' Thomas snapped, cutting him short.

He felt the years falling away, and knew that he had no wish to travel down the murky path of memory with this man. Some were brutalised by soldiering; others were brutes before they ever took up arms. Will Saltmarsh, to his mind, fell somewhere in between: one who was not wicked by nature, but was prepared to do terrible things to survive – and to anyone who stood in his way.

Saltmarsh fell back, into the shadow of a tree. Most of the lanterns had gone out. Against his will, Thomas took a step until they stood at the edge of the green. From the Black Bear came a loud hubbub, and voices rose in song.

'What troubles you?' Saltmarsh watched him closely. 'Woke a few devils, have I?'

'What do you want of me?' Thomas asked. 'And how did you know I was here?'

'I knew not whether you were alive or dead, until a few days back,' came the reply. 'I was here to seek another, only he's gone. He and I were blood-comrades, Finbow. Fought together, shared our last scraps... He'd not turn me away, if he were here.'

'Who is he?' Thomas demanded. When the other gave him the name, he nodded. 'Gaddy Butler, from Welford? He could never settle to anything after he came back. Went to seek work, I know not where.'

'So I've learned,' the ex-soldier said shortly. 'Then I remembered you and he hailed from the same dung-heap, or one like it...' He glanced around. Thomas followed his gaze to see Paulo Schweiz emerging from the show tent. The conjuror straightened himself, looked about, then seemed to stare directly at Thomas.

'Master Paulo!' Thomas called out deliberately, and the other began walking towards him. He turned back to Saltmarsh. 'I ask again, what do you want of me? I've little money—'

'I want not your money!' Saltmarsh growled. 'Is your memory so poor, or have you chosen to forget what we once were, what we shared...' He broke off as Paulo drew closer. 'Damn your heart,' he muttered.

Thomas hesitated, then said, 'Tomorrow – take the road for Petbury, then turn north towards Wantage. You'll meet the Ridgeway going west. Wait for me a mile further on, at sunset. I'll bring you what I can.'

The other looked hard at him, then dropped his eyes. 'Tomorrow.'

Paulo approached in time to see the other man move away beyond the trees, into the night. Thomas turned to him, concealing his relief.

'Master Paulo, what a rare treat you gave us...'

But Paulo was not wearing his smile. Dismissing Thomas's praise, he placed a hand quickly on his arm, saying: 'It is as I feared, my friend: both those men were poisoned – and by the same hand.'

* * *

They stood inside the now-empty tent, while Kit Page moved about, taking benches off their trestles and stacking them. The ape watched from a corner.

'I ordered Kit to catch me two mice,' the showman explained. 'Then I fed a little of the dead man's porridge to one. After your boy gave me that costrel, I washed out the inside with a little clean water and gave some to the other mouse to drink.' He paused, his piercing eyes fixed upon Thomas. 'Both creatures fell sick at once, suffered convulsions, and they were gone – so!' He snapped his fingers. 'The toxin was swift and deadly. A terrible way to die.'

Thomas frowned at the grass, trodden flat by the crowd. 'How can you know it was by the same hand?'

Paulo gave a snort. 'Plain logic, my friend! This strong poison is wolfsbane, I am sure of it. Made from the roots of a blue flower which grows in the mountains, in countries like mine. It's known since Roman times – once, it was sprinkled on dead carcasses to kill wolves. We know it under other names; some call it monkshood...'

'Friar's cap.' Thomas's frown cleared. 'I have heard of it. Yet in England, it would be hard to obtain...'

'*Ita prorsus!* Exactly, my friend – it is difficult. This poisoner knows his trade.'

Kit approached him. 'May I stop now, and go to the inn?' he enquired. His doleful look was back, Thomas saw, as if he only came to life for the duration of the show.

'We will all go.' Paulo turned to Thomas. 'You will sup with me, my friend? We can talk more.'

Thomas accepted. As they left the tent, he could not help but look towards the opening in the back wall. 'Your pictures,' he began. 'You made them come out of the little tent, did you not? And the noises too?'

But Paulo smiled and shook his head. 'A showman never reveals his secrets, Master Thomas.'

Thomas followed him outside. Then, as they crossed the green towards the Black Bear, they heard shouts. A group of men could be seen by the light that spilled from the windows, gathered about some commotion to one side of the building. Thomas guessed at once what it was.

'A fight. I wonder who's drunk more than he could take?'

But drawing closer he heard names shouted, and stopped just as some of the watchers fell back, the two combatants in the centre stumbling against them. And into plain view came Ned Hawes and Tom Brazier, locking arms, each trying desperately to topple the other. As Thomas and Paulo watched the two parted, fists whirling. Then Brazier, who was the taller, swung his right arm and fetched Ned a crack on the jaw that was audible from twenty yards away. The watchers groaned as Ned staggered and swayed dizzily, his arms falling to his sides, before he sank to the ground in a heap.

Thomas walked over. Seeing who he was, the crowd stepped back. Most began to walk off, some chuckling. As he knelt to examine the boy's injury, he saw Brazier standing his ground nearby. 'Settled the business of this morning, have you?' Thomas asked grimly.

'He brought it on himself,' the other said breathlessly. He had not escaped hurt: his cheek bore a red bruise below the eye that would soon darken. His shirt was torn and stained from the grass.

Ned moaned and opened his eyes, focussing on the familiar face. 'Thomas...?'

Brazier sniffed. 'Naught wrong with 'ee,' he muttered. As he moved off, he threw his parting shot. 'Tell him to watch his great mouth, or he'll end up like—'

'Like what?' Thomas asked. 'Or mayhap I should ask, who?' But the other walked away.

Paulo helped get Ned up the stairs of the Black Bear, to the simply furnished chamber where he and his assistant lodged. There he cleaned Ned's hurts, which were not many, and dabbed ointment on his split lip. After a mouthful of some spirit which the conjuror proffered from a bottle, a chastened Ned murmured his thanks and said he would go home.

'Mind you're in sharp, Monday morning,' Thomas told him. Somewhat shame-faced, Ned took his leave.

Paulo wore a wry smile. 'Mistress Ann will have a supper for us, in the parlour,' he said.

Thomas followed him out and down the stairs. Yet if either man thought there had been enough excitement for one May night, he was about to receive another shock. For no sooner had they sat down at the table in Dillamore's tiny back parlour than cries came from the larger room. Paulo was about to rise, driven by his natural curiosity, but Thomas remained seated. 'Another fight,' he muttered. 'I'm staying here.'

But an anxious Hugh Dillamore appeared in the doorway. 'Thomas, have you seen Giles Frogg?' He asked. When Thomas shook his head, he added, 'Old Nick Gee the shepherd's took sick – just like Kirke! We need a healing-man, or—'

He stepped back in alarm as Thomas and Paulo Schweiz stood as one, knocking their stools over, and pushed past him.

* * *

The old man was lame, and had not worked in years. He lived with his wife, both of them bent and white-haired, in a poor cottage on the edge of Chaddleworth. His sole pleasure was a mug of cheap beer, usually bought for him by a neighbour, taken at the Bear of a nighttime. He had spent his evening seated on a log outside the inn, watching events pass before him. He had not been to the tent show; to him even a penny was a large sum.

Now he was laid out on the grass, surrounded by a different crowd from the one that had witnessed the recent fight. Folk were not merely shocked – they were afraid. Two women knelt beside the old man, but even as Thomas and Paulo drew near they saw it was too late for any homespun remedy – or indeed, any remedy at all. And at once, they knew that the same poison was at work. Only now, along with the horrified villagers, they were able to observe its effects at close hand.

Nicholas Gee was conscious and could speak, though he shook like a leaf. Sweat sheened his face, and saliva dribbled from his mouth. 'Lord God, 'a mercy upon me,' he mumbled. 'I'm pricked with needles of fire...'

One of the women was trying to force a flask between his lips, but the old man spat the liquid out. 'Leave me!' he cried, then inexplicably added, 'Tis like stone!'

To the displeasure of everyone he gagged and began to vomit. The sour smell of beer mingled with stomach acid made some turn aside, but Paulo Schweiz was not dismayed. There were mutterings as he was recognised, giving way to protests as he stepped forward and dropped to the ground beside the sick man, almost pushing the woman away.

'Give him nothing!' He placed the back of his hand against the old man's cheek. Then, to everyone's surprise, he grasped him by the shoulders and shook him. 'Can you hear me?' he cried, pushing his face close to Gee's.

But Gee merely retched and vomited more liquid down his threadbare shirt. Paulo turned a haggard face to Thomas. 'It has done its work,' he said. 'He grows stiff like a board. Feel...'

Thomas knelt on the opposite side of the dying man. Taking his arm, he found that it was indeed rigid.

Gee was making choking sounds now. 'His breath fails,' one of the women cried. 'What may we do?'

Paulo shook his head. 'There is naught to be done,' he said quietly. Gently he laid the old man back on the grass. A hush fell.

As everyone watched, Gee's frame shook from head to foot. One hand flapped feebly and dropped. Later, some would swear the rapid thudding of his heart was audible. Then it stopped.

Paulo bent and put his ear to his chest. Then he rose, leaned back on his haunches and sat in silence.

There was a scream. Heads turned to see Agnes Gee hobbling across the green on the arm of a woman who had summoned her. Like waves, the Chaddleworth folk parted to let her through.

Thomas stood and walked a few yards off, to find himself staring up at the moon again, now at its zenith. Behind him, the old woman's voice cut through the night air, an owl-like shrieking that chilled the blood.

* * *

It was almost dawn before most of the Chaddleworth folk went to their beds. The body of Nicholas Gee had been taken to his cottage, whereupon his widow, crazed with grief, slammed and barred the door, refusing to admit anyone. Giles Frogg, when he heard the news, left her alone. Instead, he summoned Thomas and Paulo Schweiz to his house, and demanded they tell him all they knew. This done, the three went their own ways. Thomas would speak with his master and the high sheriff, who as far as he knew, was still a guest at Petbury.

He accepted the offer to snatch a couple of hours sleep on the floor of Paulo's chamber; the walk back to Petbury seemed long, by the time the village at last fell silent. Yet he knew that few slept; he had seen the fear in their eyes, as Gee expired on the green in front of them, and only a day after the death of William Kirke. And he had seen the way they scattered into groups, talking among themselves before going to their homes. He did not need to hear words like *sickness* or *pestilence*, but it troubled him more to overhear some talk of sorcery, or a curse come upon them.

The Sabbath, Thomas knew, would find the entire population crammed into St Andrew's, to hear old Doctor Scambler offer what words of comfort he could. But he had no time, for the high sheriff and his master must know what had occurred, and the falcons needed his care.

* * *

The gathering took place in the afternoon. Thomas had spoken with Martin in the morning, and then with Sir Robert who was less than pleased at being woken early. But when the news was known, he sent word to the high sheriff's chamber at once. It was Ward who ordered all those who knew anything of the recent deaths to assemble in the Great Hall. And that order was extended to the only other landowner close to Chaddleworth: Sir John Mountford.

It was perhaps a year since Thomas had seen the reclusive Mountford, known as an embittered recusant who still mourned the death of the Queen of Scots five years ago, and along with it, his hopes of a Catholic monarchy restored.

The master of Poughley Manor was a taciturn man, rough-bearded and always shabbily dressed for one of his station, in contrast to his wife: everyone knew Lady Sarah was a gentle soul, deeply religious, who always strived to appear neat – no small achievement since it was said she did much of the family's needlework herself.

Mountford was ill-tempered at being summoned to Petbury, a place he had no wish to enter. He sat in silence at one end of the long table, accompanied by a single attendant, a scrawny,

balding man named John Kydd. Besides Sir Robert and
Richard Ward, Martin the steward was present, as were two or
three trusted house servants. Thomas stood respectfully apart
with Giles Frogg, who appeared stiff-necked and uncomfortable in his best jerkin. But the most bizarre member of the
assembly was Paulo Schweiz in a heavy black gown, looking
like some don from one of the universities. Far from being
intimidated by the company, the showman seemed to be
enjoying himself. Thomas had been amused to hear how he
rode his sway-backed nag through the Petbury gates and
announced himself to a speechless Martin as if he were an
honoured guest.

And more, it was Paulo who would prove the most important
witness.

Ward was sober-faced as he took his seat, glancing round the
Hall. Sir Robert nodded to indicate that all were present, and at
once the high sheriff took charge.

'Sirs...' He inclined his head respectfully towards Mountford,
who merely stared, then addressed the room in general. 'It seems
there is a murderer among us.'

There was an intake of breath. But having created the stir he
intended, Ward went on, 'I meant not, of course, in this room...'
He paused. 'But somewhere hereabouts. One who has killed,
seemingly by poison.' He looked directly at Thomas. 'Or so I'm
informed by one whose word is respected. Falconer?'

Thomas stepped forward and made his bow.

'For the benefit of Sir John, will you tell what you have seen –
and more, what you have gleaned from it?' Ward asked.

So Thomas drew breath and spoke of what was already
known to most in the room: the deaths of Haylock and William
Kirke, and now that of Nicholas Gee, which he had witnessed
himself. But when he came to the manner of their deaths, he

looked to his master. 'Might Master Paulo be permitted to speak, sir? His knowledge is greater than mine.'

All eyes followed Sir Robert's to rest on Paulo Schweiz, who stood aside, calmly sipping from a cup he had taken off a side chest. Nobody spoke, though Mountford expressed his distaste for the fellow with a loud sniff. Paulo lowered his cup and looked directly at the sheriff.

'Tell us what you know,' Ward said after a moment. And it seemed to Thomas that from that moment forth, he rarely took his gaze off the conjuror. For when Paulo spoke in his clear, resonant voice, it was impossible not to listen.

He told them of his meeting Thomas (omitting mention of the stocks); of seeing him again in Chaddleworth on Friday last, and of their going to the house of William Kirke after his wife discovered his body. Candidly, and in good English, he expounded his belief that the man had died from a poison which had been mixed into his porridge. Seemingly heedless of the growing unease in the room, he moved on to his conversation with Thomas, and the matter of Simon Haylock's costrel, which he now knew was also poisoned. Furthermore...

'Enough!' Sir Robert looked angry. And when Paulo fell silent and turned his keen eyes upon him, the knight spoke sharply. 'Why did you not go to the proper authorities?' he demanded. 'You are a foreigner, a visitor to our country—'

Paulo bristled. 'I am no vagabond, *Meister*,' he replied. 'I have a license to travel, and to give shows in all—'

'You have no rights in this!' Sir Robert retorted. 'If you suspected murder had been committed on my land, you should have spoken at once.'

'Sir Robert, if it please you?' a mild voice broke in. Heads turned, as Giles Frogg bowed awkwardly.

'Constable.' Sir Robert gestured him forward impatiently.

'He did speak with me, sir,' Frogg stated. 'As did Thomas –
Master Finbow. He, Master Paulo, I mean, made an experiment
to discover the poison. At first I was loathe to believe him sir, but
now...' He hesitated. 'I beg you will hear him out.'

There was a short silence. Ward threw a glance at Sir Robert,
then nodded to Paulo, who resumed as if he had never been
interrupted. He told of how he had fed some of Kirke's porridge
and the washings of Haylock's costrel to mice, which quickly
died. He mentioned his modest knowledge of poisons, picked up
in a lifetime's travel in many countries; he did not claim to be a
man of science, but an informed amateur. He spoke of wolfsbane,
mentioning other names by which it was known. Then, with
every man's eye upon him, he added his final piece of information, which was not even known to Thomas. Last night, after the
tragic death of the shepherd, Nicholas Gee, unnoticed by anyone
Paulo had taken the mug that lay near the old man's body. This
morning he had subjected its dregs to the same test, using a field
mouse caught by his assistant. And the result was plain: Gee's ale
had also been poisoned. Having delivered the sting, the mountebank bowed ironically, raised his cup and availed himself again
of the refreshment Sir Robert had provided.

The silence was brief before Ward, with a nod towards Paulo,
broke it. 'Well, sirs, let us surmise that for now, I am prepared to
believe this man's testimony—'

'And I am not!'

Mountford, the colour rising to his cheeks, was glaring
fiercely round the table. His hand shot up and pointed at Paulo;
he had not even bothered to remove his riding glove. 'You would
take the word of this wandering juggler?' he cried. 'This rogue,
little more than a beggar?' He turned to Sir Robert. 'I am amazed,
sir, that you allow him to drink your wine as if he were a guest.'

'He *is* a guest, Sir John,' Sir Robert said, with a rare display of mildness. 'Any man who enters Petbury at my bidding is welcome to slake his thirst.'

'Even so!' the other snapped. 'I'll not listen to the tall tales of a conjuror – and a German at that...' He broke off, having said more than he intended. Ward was about to reply, but it was Paulo who spoke first.

'Your pardon, sir: I am not German, but Swiss,' he murmured, meeting Mountford's angry look unflinchingly. 'Yet perhaps that troubles you more, for you will assume I am a Lutheran, raised on the Geneva Bible. Is it not so?'

The colour was fading from Mountford's cheeks. Beside him, his scrawny servant Kydd gulped and looked at the floor.

'Master Schweiz!' All turned to see that Ward too, was indignant. 'You forget your place. You do not speak to a knight of the realm in such fashion.' He faced Mountford. 'The man will make redress, Sir John.'

'I want naught from him, or anyone else here!' Mountford retorted. 'Indeed, I expected little else, in this house...' Refusing to meet Sir Robert's eye, he added, 'I know not why you have called me here. These deaths have not occurred on my lands. Only the widow Kirke is my servant, and she shall be given succour. You will oblige me by letting me go.'

Ward sighed. 'I invited you as a knight of the shire and a neighbouring landowner, for courtesy's sake,' he said. 'Poughley adjoins the parish of Chaddleworth, does it not? Do you not wish to be informed of murder committed here?' Looking round at the company, he added, 'I said when I began, and now I say it again, with even greater conviction: there is a murderer abroad. Does any man now doubt it?'

No one seemed to, and none wished to be first to speak.

Finally, Martin the steward gave a polite cough and addressed Ward.

'If it please you, sir, the riddle that tugs at me is this: if these men – Simon Haylock, William Kirke and Nicholas Gee – were indeed murdered, and by the same hand, then why? Apart from the fact that they were of the same parish, and known to each other, what is common to all three?'

At that, Thomas caught Sir Robert's eye and took his brief nod for permission to speak.

'I've turned the matter over, sirs,' he said, 'and I believe there may be a common thread.' As all eyes rested upon him, he continued, 'If rumour may be believed, both Haylock and Kirke had money hidden away, though I know not how much. Yet if there is one who thought – however unlikely it seems – that Gee too had some secret hoard, might not that be an inducement?'

A sudden noise startled everyone. Mountford had got abruptly to his feet, thrusting his chair back from the table.

'I, for one, cannot fathom such a cause that would drive men to these foul deeds of wickedness,' he said harshly. 'Satan moves them, to his own deformed purpose. The murderer shall reap his just reward, as must we all.' He turned to Sir Robert. 'If there is aught I should know, sir, will you send word? In the meantime, I will lend what aid I can if called upon – as any true Christian man would do.'

If the barb were aimed at Paulo Schweiz, the other made no response. Inclining his head towards his host, Mountford then acknowledged Ward briefly, and without looking at anyone else strode to the doorway. John Kydd hurried after him. A Petbury servant opened the door and bowed, but Mountford barely noticed. As he disappeared, his own servant threw a furtive look behind, as if he half-expected to be called back – and Thomas saw it: the fearful look in Kydd's eyes.

The man was plainly terrified.

10

There was a silence, but it was mainly of relief. Ward turned to Sir Robert.

'Is there aught you would add?'

Sir Robert waved a hand helplessly, picked up his favourite silver cup and took a welcome draught. 'What must I do, post men-at-arms all over Chaddleworth?' he muttered. 'In any case, the first death was down towards the valley, at Boxwell.' He frowned and glanced at Thomas. 'Had Haylock not been pulled from the barn, the fire would have consumed his body, and none would have known about the poison. No doubt that was the intention.' He turned to Ward. 'The killer set the fire, to cover the deed.'

Ward eyed Thomas, who looked sceptical. 'Yet, he made no attempt to hide the others,' he observed.

Martin added his voice. 'Whatever the cause, Sir Robert, we must show vigilance. Your other tenants along the valley – at Betterdown Farm, and South Wilby – have been sorely affrighted by what happened at Boxwell. There is talk of pestilence.'

Sir Robert looked round at Giles Frogg. 'Does no one else

know of the poison, save those who have been in this room?' he asked. When the constable, after a moment's thought, signalled his assent, the knight turned to Ward.

'Here's a quandary, master sheriff. Which would cause greater fear: the coming of some deadly plague, or the notion that a murderer stalks the countryside?'

Ward's face was taut. 'I will not cause panic,' he began, then glanced at Paulo Schweiz. 'Though I fear that, in times like these, folk may look askance at any strangers that have come into the parish...'

At that, Frogg stepped forward, somewhat agitated. 'Truly, sir,' he said. 'I wished to speak of that matter myself. There's been frightened talk in the village, and it turns to anger, as fear will do.' He hesitated. 'I believe master Paulo will bear the brunt of it, should he stay in Chaddleworth.'

All eyes turned to Paulo, who remained silent.

'Some accuse you already,' Frogg told him bluntly. 'They're plain folk; they mistrust a man like you, with your powers. If you wish for my counsel, it would be to roll up your tent, pack your cart and be gone.'

'Nay, that will not do.' Ward shook his head. 'It would give cause for thinking he had something to hide. Moreover, I do not give you leave to quit the parish, Master Schweiz. Not until this matter is solved.'

Paulo's eyes widened. 'You suspect me, sir?' he asked. 'When it was I who showed you the means by which those men were killed?'

'If I suspected you, you would be in chains by now,' Ward answered grimly. 'Yet, I wish you to stay.' With a glance at Sir Robert, he said, 'Like Master Finbow, Master Schweiz too has a keen eye, and is an accomplished logician.' He turned his gaze on Frogg, who wore an expression of pained resignation, as if he guessed what would come next. 'Master constable, I place him in your charge.'

Frogg drew a breath. 'That lays a severe burden on me, sir, for Dillamore told me today that he wants him out of the Black Bear. Ape and all, he said.'

A wry smile spread over Paulo's features, but Frogg had not finished. 'Hence, there's naught else for it. Since we've no lock-up, Master Paulo shall stay in my house for the present. His servant and ape too.' He turned to the sheriff. 'I spoke to my wife on the matter, sir, and she is agreeable.'

Sir Robert seemed to be hiding a smile. Agreeable was not a word that was widely used when discussing mistress Frogg's character. But he said, 'Your charity does you credit, Constable. And if the parish will not bear the cost of your housing such guests, I will do so myself.'

Frogg bowed and held his peace. The assembly seemed to be over, but little had been resolved. Thomas saw it in the faces of every man present, whereupon Sir Robert voiced a thought that had occurred to him.

'Surely our friend here is not the only stranger who has wandered on to the Downlands of late, master sheriff,' he mused. When Ward turned to him, he added, 'There is the Queen's mapmaker, for one.'

* * *

In the evening, having walked out to feed the eyasses and tended the other birds, Thomas went to his cottage. There he looked out some clothes: hose, a shirt and jerkin, an old pair of boots, a girdle with a good iron buckle that would fetch a sixpence if sold. He stowed them in a sack, then sat by the chimney to think.

In the past days, events had moved somewhat too quickly for

his liking. Violent deaths were rare in this remote quarter of Berkshire. Martin had formed a watch, mainly of grooms and gardeners, along with Thomas himself, though how they were supposed to guard Petbury – let alone the entire parish – from a murderer armed with poison had not been explained. And there was another matter that troubled him: he had made no mention to his master, or to anyone else, of the fact that there was at least one other stranger wandering the Downlands – and one whose behaviour was less predictable than most: Will Saltmarsh. His hope was that after he had met him and given him what he could, the man would depart at once. His presence unnerved Thomas. Clearly, life had not treated him well in the years since he had last seen him. More, Thomas knew what he had once been capable of... But this? He shook his head, not liking the notion, and went out.

Since there was never a time when the Petbury kitchens were quiet, he was obliged to go straight to Nell and ask her for a few provisions: loaves, perhaps a capon, and whatever else she could spare. She stood in silence while he made his request. To his relief and unspoken gratitude she asked no questions, only told him what he might take.

Having filled the pack he had brought, he made as if to go, then hesitated near the yard door. Nell was chiding the scullion about some minor oversight, but catching Thomas's eye, she sent the lad away and walked over.

'I heard what happened,' she said. 'Once again you are become watchman, and I know not what else.'

Looking upon her fair, well-shaped face with its cluster of freckles, the deep green eyes, he wished for nothing more than to take her to his bed for the night, and forget all else. Yet, as so often nowadays, it seemed it was not to be.

'They'll ride out tomorrow,' she said suddenly. 'Sir Robert

and Lady Margaret. Mistress Ann is come home, with Master Daniel.'

He frowned. Sir Robert, like some of his station, had a tendency when some serious matter demanded his attention, of riding off to hunt or to some other pleasure, as if to escape his responsibilities. For her part, Lady Margaret stood increasingly aloof from most things. Their daughter Ann, to be married later this year, had been staying at the home of Sir William Stanton, the father of her betrothed, at his manor beyond Newbury. Now, it seemed Thomas must put all else aside to serve tomorrow's hawking party.

'Eleanor was looking for you,' Nell said, eying him.

'It must wait,' he said absently. Slinging the pack over his shoulder he made to go, even as Nell turned sharply on her heel and moved away.

* * *

It had been a clear day, and the sunset was a lake of rose and pale gold, in which flat purple clouds lay like islets. Thomas walked up the hill above Petbury using the track he had worn over the years with his own boots, topped it and continued north towards the Ridgeway. Striking the ancient path, he glanced to left and right but saw no one. In all directions, the empty Downs stretched away. Crows wheeled, stark against the sky.

Dropping the packs he sat down to wait, but almost at once a figure rose from the long grass not ten yards away and started towards him. Hurriedly, he got to his feet.

'I told ye – the soft life has made ye careless,' Will Saltmarsh said. As he drew close in the fading daylight, Thomas was better able to note the man's appearance. The sergeant had indeed lived the hard life since his return. His jerkin was rough-patched with scraps of leather, the breeches mended in half a dozen places. The boots looked as if their uppers would part company with the soles at any moment. Over the whole he wore a heavy woollen cloak tied at the neck, a little too good for the rest of his attire, though few who knew Saltmarsh would have dared enquire where it came from.

'There's some food and clothes.' Thomas nodded towards the bags beside the path. 'The buckle would fetch something, if sold.'

'Charity.' The word flew from Saltmarsh's mouth like an oath. But he stooped to pick up the smaller bag, weighing it in his hand.

'Side-meat and loaves, with some dried plums and jellied carp,' Thomas said, and could not resist adding, 'The bread will taste familiar, mayhap.'

Saltmarsh frowned at him. 'Why would it?'

Thomas looked away. 'I'll not ask if you have sought work, for I know you have.' He sighed. 'There's no grateful populace back home, like they told us, is there?'

'Was there ever?' Saltmarsh's mouth had a bitter twist. 'What's a man fit for, when he has lived as I did?'

Thomas shook his head. 'What will you do?'

The other gave a snort. 'You think there are choices?'

'Is there none you can call upon to speak for you?' Thomas persisted. 'Even a labourer's wage is better than life under the stars.'

'It may well be.' Saltmarsh had untied the sack and was rummaging among the clothes. 'Only I don't intend to test the notion.' Drawing out the boots, he sat down at once and began to pull off his own.

'I thought you had family,' Thomas said, causing the other to grimace.

'*Had* is the truth,' he muttered, dashing his hand roughly across his nose in the manner he had. 'Then, I'm not the first soldier to come back and find himself given up for dead.' He grinned slightly. 'You're talking to a dead man, Finbow. There's my widow down in Portsmouth to prove it. Only she's not a widow any more, she's married to a ship's chandler who said he'd swear out a warrant and have me jailed if I didn't quit the town by nightfall.'

Thomas sat down, suddenly fatigued. He watched as Saltmarsh threw aside his worn-out boots and pulled on the new ones. Then he stood up, stamping his feet, and gave a grunt of satisfaction.

'I thought we were near the same size,' Thomas said.

'They'll serve,' Saltmarsh allowed, and looked up at the darkening sky.

'If I offered a bed for the night, and you swore to be gone at dawn...' Thomas began, but the other shook his head.

'Nay, I won't tarry here. I came on a fool's errand...' He broke off, peering at Thomas. 'You knew Gaddy Butler, you said. What scared him away?'

Thomas shrugged. 'Naught that I know of. He was one of those who couldn't settle to his old life.'

'Nay.' Saltmarsh was firm. 'All he wanted was here – he said so when I saw him.'

'You saw him?'

'Three, four years back.' His gaze wandered towards the horizon. 'He had no reason to take off. He was forgetting... the things we all want to forget.'

He turned his blue eyes upon Thomas. 'Something caught at him, snagged him... wouldn't let him go. Something he'd done, he wouldn't even tell me of.' He frowned. 'Not something from back there. Something closer to home.'

Thomas shook his head. 'Then I know naught of it. I barely knew the man.'

Saltmarsh shrugged, then picked up the bag of provisions and slung it over his shoulder. 'I should thank you,' he said, 'but I've run low on niceties.'

Thomas remained silent.

'If you hear of a Portsmouth chandler, died of some excess or other, send word,' Saltmarsh said, though his grin was far from pleasant. 'My wife was always a woman of vast appetite. Mayhap she'll wear him out.'

Then seeing the look in Thomas's eye, he grimaced. 'Don't waste your pity on me, pikeman,' he muttered, and catching up the sack, trudged off eastwards along the path.

Thomas watched until he was out of sight. Then he looked down at the man's ruined boots, lying in the grass. For a moment he considered taking them away, then he thought better of it and turned towards home.

Nell did not come to the cottage, but then he had not expected her. Casting himself upon his pallet, he fell into an exhausted sleep, to be woken by familiar dreams. Sitting up in the dark, he cursed Saltmarsh for stirring up his demons, as he had known he would.

* * *

The day was warm and humid, and a grey blanket of cloud sat upon the Downs. Thomas rose and stumbled from his sleeping-loft, realising it was past dawn and, rarely for him, he had over-slept. Then there came the noise of the latch, and the door opened to reveal Ned Hawes standing sheepishly outside.

'I seen to the eyasses,' he said. 'Didn't know if I should come by...' He met Thomas's eye, and dropped his gaze.

Thomas gestured him in. 'If you're hungry, there's curds in that bowl.' He pointed to the table.

Ned shook his head. 'I'm all right.'

'Are you truly?' Thomas eyed him, bringing a flush to his cheeks.

'I've said I am.' He sought to change the subject. 'Can't say that for Chaddleworth folk after what happened to old Nick Gee – right after Kirke, too. I never knew such a thing.'

Thomas put on his jerkin and found his boots. Leaning against the table, he took a crust of hard bread from the platter. 'What were you and Brazier fighting about?' he asked. 'Or might I ask, who?'

'Twas naught.' Ned moved towards the door, unwilling to speak further. Thomas shoved the crust in his mouth, then pulled on his boots.

'We've a party to serve,' he mumbled. 'Best get busy.' He hesitated. 'Have you and Eleanor quarrelled?'

Ned stopped, his hand on the latch, and gave a nod.

'What about?'

The boy paused. 'Someone – twas Alice Latter, I wager, as had it from her sister – told her I was sweet on Mistress Mead. The mapmaker's girl.'

'And are you?'

Ned met his eye. 'I was,' he admitted. 'Only, I know 'tis a fool's notion... She's beyond my reach.' His brow furrowed. 'I did tell Eleanor that!'

'You said that to her?' Thomas asked, exasperated. 'And you wonder why she's angry?'

'If Brazier hadn't blathered to half the village, she'd never have known of it!'

But with a sigh, Thomas shook his head. 'You're learning how to handle falcons well enough, but you've much to learn about women.'

For a moment, Ned looked as if he would make a retort. *You're a fine one...* But seeing the look that came over Thomas's face, he turned and went outside.

* * *

The morning passed swiftly, and it suited Thomas to busy himself. Sir Robert and Lady Margaret rode out with their daughter and Daniel Stanton, each with a bird on the wrist, but today there was no sign of Richard Ward. Thomas sought for a chance to ask his master about it, but none came; instead, he was obliged to attend Lady Margaret.

She had reined in, and sat her fine Neapolitan mare, watching the merlin hover above. When Thomas came up she called, so he walked over and made his bow.

'I hear you are playing intelligencer again.'

He gave a smile. 'It seems that way, my lady.'

'Does it please you?'

He blinked. 'I will serve Sir Robert, in any way he wishes...'

'An answer, Thomas, if you will.' She had no time for his evasion.

'It would please me, my lady,' Thomas replied, 'to see this murderer caught, so that we may all rest easy once again.'

She sighed and glanced to where Ann Vicary and her betrothed sat their horses, close together. 'They make a pretty couple, do you not agree?'

He smiled. 'They do, my lady.' But as she turned her gaze deliberately upon him, he knew what would follow.

'Why do you make Nell wait?'

He swallowed, struggling to form an answer, whereupon Lady Margaret nodded slowly. 'Poor Thomas.'

He looked aside; Sir Robert was riding towards them. 'I'm surprised the high sheriff is not here, my lady,' Thomas ventured, striving to conceal his relief.

'He left early, to ride home,' Lady Margaret replied. 'A great deal of business has accrued in his absence, he says. Or mayhap he finds our Downland weather a little turbulent for his liking.' She glanced downwards as her husband approached. 'I'm fatigued with telling Eleanor that this foolishness between the two of you must be mended,' she said in a low voice.

He swallowed. 'As you wish, my lady.'

'Well, do you not wish it?'

He nodded. 'You know she has her mother's stubbornness.'

'Her mother has been dead for nigh on a decade,' Lady Margaret said. 'Can you not cease looking backwards?'

'I will try...' He broke off. Sir Robert had reined in sharply.

'Thomas!' he called. 'Can you get yourself horsed this after-noon, and be ready to ride with me? I will ride down the valley and speak with the tenant farmers. I want a man with some tact alongside me.' He frowned and jerked a gloved hand over his shoulder. 'I fear it will be a long while before we may describe young Ned in such terms.' Turning to his wife, the knight said, 'Seeking but to put him at ease, I told him that at hawking men were only as good as their birds – as in another way, it's said all men are equal between the sheets. And can you believe, he goes red in the face and tells me he's still got a deal to learn about women!'

Thomas smiled politely and looked away.

11

When Thomas and Sir Robert drew rein in the yard at Boxwell Farm that afternoon, they found only Ambrose Fuller at work on the barn. On seeing the master of Petbury, the thatcher was obliged to descend his ladder and make a clumsy bow. He threw a sour look at Thomas, who sat his borrowed horse some yards off, but addressed Sir Robert readily enough.

'John Flowers is gone with the boy, to fetch palings and reeds, sir,' he mumbled. 'They ought 'a been back afore now.'

Sir Robert looked around. 'And farmer Ames?'

'Out in the fields, all of 'em.'

Fuller looked impatient to get back to his work, and did not hide his relief when Sir Robert dismissed him. 'We'll water the mounts, and wait a little while,' he said. He and Thomas dismounted and led their horses to the trough.

Fuller was climbing the ladder, a bundle of reeds on his shoulder. As he neared the top, he glanced round, shielding his eyes, and called down. 'Cart's coming!'

He pointed along the track that led east to the Hungerford Road. Sir Robert frowned suddenly. 'I forgot something yesterday: to enquire of Mountford why he took it upon himself to take charge of Simon Haylock's body.'

'It sat curiously on my mind too, sir,' Thomas replied.

They turned, hearing the rumble of wheels. The cart came into view, where the track bent round an oak. Flowers held the reins, while Brazier sat in the back among a pile of thatching reeds. As they pulled into the yard, Sir Robert left his horse and stepped forward, Thomas close behind. On seeing them, Flowers hauled at the reins, but as he clambered down both men were struck by his manner. He looked highly agitated.

'Sir Robert.' The young man came forward and made his bow. 'There's terrible news from the village… Great Shefford, that is. Another man took sick and died, shaking and retching.' He turned to Brazier, who had climbed down from the cart and stood beside it, subdued. 'Tom here says it was same as with the Chaddleworth men, Kirke and Gee.'

Sir Robert stifled an oath and glanced from Flowers to Brazier and back. Then he turned aside to Thomas, and spoke under his breath. 'So it's not merely men of Chaddleworth that our killer has in his sights. Must we have eyes in every hamlet in West Berkshire?'

Soon they stood silently in the yard, and let the young builder and his labourer tell their tale. The dead man, it transpired, was Thomas Rawlings, the brewer at Great Shefford – a less humble figure than the three who had died thus far: Haylock a labourer, Kirke a joiner and Gee a shepherd. Rawlings was well-known within a radius of ten miles or more, a church-warden and respected elder of his village. His ale and beer supplied a dozen inns, as well as being sold by the barrel or jug at his brewery. Today he had been at his work as usual. Nothing untoward had happened until mid-morning, when he began to complain of feeling unwell. In a very short time he had fallen to the floor and been unable to rise. He was sweating and salivating, and had difficulty speaking. Workmen ran to fetch a healing-woman, but to no avail: in less than an hour, the man was dead.

A grim-faced Sir Robert heard Flowers out, then issued his instructions. Thomas was ordered to ride at once to the brewery in Great Shefford and discover what he could. Sir Robert would return to Petbury and send word to the high sheriff. Sir John Mountford too, would be informed. When he had finished speaking, he turned to John Flowers.

'Rawlings' body – has someone taken charge of it?'

Flowers nodded. 'His wife, sir... I should say, his widow.'

Glancing up at the barn roof, Thomas saw Fuller, motionless at the top of his ladder. His face was averted, but he was hanging on every word.

Sir Robert spoke briskly to the young man. 'I'm obliged to you for giving me such a thorough account, John Flowers.' He walked towards his horse, saying over his shoulder, 'I will let you return to your work.'

Flowers bowed, turned to Tom Brazier and gestured to him. Without looking around, Brazier moved to the cart and began unloading it.

Thomas had taken up the reins of the Petbury gelding he rode. As he put his boot to the stirrup, he caught Flowers's eye, and saw the discomfort in it.

'I'm sorry for what happened between Tom and Ned,' he said.

Thomas shrugged. 'It's their quarrel – you and I did not make it.' Then he added, 'My master and the sheriff will seek the cause of these deaths, and put an end to them.' Flowers nodded. But as Thomas shook the reins he saw the sombre faces of both he and his labourer, and guessed that neither was reassured by his words – any more than he was himself.

Sir Robert rode away northwards, urging his mount to a gallop, while Thomas turned south.

* * *

He found Great Shefford in near uproar.

Folk of all ages stood in the street, talking animatedly. The village lay beside the Lambourn river, its small timbered houses clustered about St Mary's Church. Beyond was the bridge, leading to the crossroads where the Hungerford Road met the east highway to Newbury. Though the manor belonged to the Bridges family, Thomas soon learned that master Anthony was away in London, and authority had devolved for the moment to a few frightened village elders, most of whom were still gathered about the brewery. When Thomas reined in they looked askance at him, seeing a man in plain dress riding a rather fine horse. Even when he had dismounted and explained whom he served, they remained suspicious. But he was permitted to enter the brewing-house, and look about for himself.

It was the oldest journeyman, Rawlings' most trusted helper, who agreed to show him where the master brewer had died. Shaking his head, the old man led Thomas to a corner, near one of the vats. The warmth of the place, along with the stench of fermenting hops and malted barley, was already making him light-headed.

'Twas most fearful,' the man muttered. 'He was spry as a hare this morning – always is on Mondays.' He grunted. 'Or was...' He turned a watery eye upon Thomas. 'I never seen sickness come on a man so quick,' he said.

Thomas looked about, though there was little to see. It was a place of work, and a cramped one. Men moved to and fro as if in a daze, knowing not what else to do but continue their tending of the vats. Sacks lined two of the walls, barrels of all sizes filled the space between. At Thomas's feet was some straw, which someone had thrown down to lay Rawlings on while they watched him die.

Keeping his voice low, he began to ask the questions he had formed during his short ride. 'Do you know what Master Rawlings ate this morning?'

The brewer's man stared. 'Same as all of us,' he answered. 'We started soon as 'ee was light, then stopped for a bit of breakfast. Bread and porridge, and a mug...'

'Where are the mugs?'

'On the shelf.' With a frown, the old man pointed. 'We dipped into yon keg – 'tis watered, weak as piss. Master wouldn't let us drink as we please, else.'

Thomas stared. 'You may drink your fill, at any time?'

The man nodded. 'Only from yonder keg, though.'

'And nobody else has fallen sick?'

The other drew breath suddenly. 'Hark ye, there's naught wrong with our beer! Never caused a day's illness to anyone, all the years I been journeyman here.'

Thomas managed a reassuring smile. 'I know it – I've drunk Master Rawlings' beer many times.' He glanced about, thinking the answer he sought did not lie here. And if he breathed in the heady fumes much longer, he would likely be half-drunk. He faced the old man again. 'Did your master always drink the same beer as his men?'

The other nodded slowly. 'Save when he's tasting, of course.'

'Tasting...?' Thomas echoed, at which the old man's gaze grew contemptuous.

'Can't brew beer without tasting, can 'ee? I thought everyone knew that.'

But Thomas's eye had fallen on a horn dipper, that hung by

its handle over the side of a nearby vat. 'Is that the master's tasting mug?'

'No, it's mine,' came the reply. 'Master and journeymen each got their own – we don't let no one else use them. Tasting's a mystery – takes years to learn 'ee.'

'Then where's Master Rawlings' mug?' Thomas asked, somewhat sharply.

The old brewery man looked puzzled. 'What do 'ee want that for?'

'The inquest,' Thomas told him. 'Will you show it to me?'

'Inquest?' The other looked uneasy. 'Master was took sick, is all. Who'll be doing with inquests?'

'The high sheriff will,' Thomas said. 'And I'm charged with aiding him. Will you show me the mug?'

The old man hesitated, then pointed to a hook on the wall from which hung a little pewter tankard. At once Thomas went over, took it and started to walk out. Then he stopped.

'Were you close by your master, before he died?' he asked.

'I did cradle his poor head in my arms,' the other mumbled.

'Did he say anything?'

But at that, his informant's lower lip jutted out. 'If he did, 'tis a matter between friends – not for ye!'

Thomas sighed. 'You may be called upon to speak under oath, at the inquest.'

'Well see now, we left mistress Elizabeth alone with master at the end,' the journeyman growled. 'And I wouldn't go troubling her in her grief!'

Signalling that the conversation was over, he shuffled off. Aware that a silence had fallen, Thomas glanced round to see the entire work force of nine or ten men standing in a body, staring at him with unconcealed hostility.

With a heavy heart, he turned and went outside.

* * *

The house was quite large, and stood on the edge of the village beside the river. Thomas tethered the horse to a tree near the front door and knocked. It was opened by a tiny servant woman who stepped back fearfully at sight of this tall man looming over her. When he stated his business, the woman looked alarmed.

'It isn't the time, Master...' She faltered. From within, Thomas heard female voices, though there was no sound of weeping. But almost at once, someone called out.

'Let them come – we'll turn no one away.'

The servant stood aside, and Thomas entered the darkened house. Minutes later, having explained his business, he was left alone with the brewer's widow.

They sat in a small front parlour, well-furnished but thankfully devoid of the corpse of the deceased. Elizabeth Rawlings was a large woman of middle years with a hard eye and a commanding manner. She would be no weeping mourner, Thomas saw. Already she had taken charge of her late husband's house, as no doubt she would of his business.

He refrained from asking to see the body. Not only would it have met with a refusal, but he knew it would tell him little he did not already know. But when he came, as tactfully as he could, to the matter of the death, the woman stood up.

'He's barely cold, and you wish me to speak of what passed between man and wife?' She glared. 'You are a storm-crow. Leave my house!'

Thomas stood up slowly. 'I will, Mistress,' he answered, feeling shamed. 'Were it not for my master's orders, I would not have troubled you at such a time.'

The woman remained standing. 'I cannot assist you, in any case,' she said sharply. 'For he spoke but one word to me before he breathed his last, and it meant nothing.' And when Thomas hesitated, to his surprise the widow seemed to relent.

'For what use it may be, I'll tell you the word,' she said. 'Rather it was a name, and one I do not know. Then I'm not born here, being his third wife, and one of few years' standing.'

Thomas waited. 'The name was Walden,' she said.

He frowned. 'You are certain it was that?'

'It was but a whisper,' she answered. 'Yet I'm sure as may be, that was the name he spoke.'

She seemed to shudder, almost forgetting Thomas's presence. 'So many times did he shut me from his affairs,' she mused. 'Even, it would seem, with his dying breath.' Then she regained her composure and moved to the door.

Thomas murmured his thanks, and left her house of mourning.

* * *

He did not return directly to Petbury. Having free use of the gelding, he took the Wantage Road and rode at once to Chaddleworth. Arriving in the village, he dismounted and was about to lead the horse to Giles Frogg's house when a thought struck him. Tethering the animal to a tree on the green, he walked into the Black Bear and found Hugh Dillamore.

'Has Master Paulo moved out yet?' he asked.

Dillamore was rolling a new barrel onto its cruck. Seeing the look in Thomas's eye, he had the grace to look ashamed. 'Ann was fretting, after what happened Saturday. There's been a lot of talk...' He trailed off.

Thomas watched him settle the heavy barrel. Finally, the innkeeper straightened himself, faced his friend and gave a shrug. 'Foreigners bring sickness, Thomas,' he said. Receiving no reply, he added, 'Mayhap you choose not to remember last time the red plague came here... We were young then, and less weighed-down with our cares. But Ann don't forget, for it took her mother and father both.'

Seeing Thomas's expression soften, Dillamore took a step forward. 'I've naught against the fortune-teller,' he allowed. 'I like him, even if that boy of his never spoke a civil word. But Ann wanted him gone. They're settled at Frogg's, and there's an end to it.'

Thomas was about to go, then stopped himself. 'You'll hear soon enough, so I'll tell you now,' he said. 'There's another dead in the same manner, down at Great Shefford. Tom Rawlings, the brewer.'

Dillamore's jaw dropped.

'But sickness is not the cause.' Thomas eyed him grimly. 'I shouldn't speak further of it, and I ask you too to keep silent. I tell you as my friend, to ease your fears.' He hesitated. 'I pray the matter will break asunder soon, and all will know the truth.' Without waiting for a reply he went out, and a few minutes later he stood in the tiny back garden of Giles Frogg's cottage, face to face with Paulo Schweiz.

The conjuror was glad to see him. He had kept himself busy, dismantling his tent and packing it away in his cart. Kit was walking the Downs, since the ape disliked it here and was fretful.

'A man like me may always find occupation,' Paulo said with a smile. 'There are some who beg me to tell their fortunes, despite all else...' A glint came into his eye. 'They bid me visit while their husbands are away in the fields.'

Thomas sighed. 'You court danger, more than any gamester I've known,' he said. 'Have you forgotten what happened to you in Wantage?'

Paulo raised his eyebrows. 'I see no stocks here.'

With a shake of his head, Thomas reached into his pouch and drew out the small tankard, catching Paulo's attention at once. When he told him about the death of Thomas Rawlings, the conjuror listened intently.

'Four!' he exclaimed. 'Four dead by the same hand...'

'Let's not swear to it yet,' Thomas broke in. 'Will you do your experiment once more, and tell me if this vessel too was poisoned?'

'I will!'

Thomas thanked him, and to Paulo's disappointment took his leave somewhat abruptly. To his mind, the showman seemed to relish the task a little too much.

* * *

He returned to Petbury by the end of the afternoon, and having returned the gelding to the stables, walked up to the mews to find Ned at his most conscientious. He had fed and exercised all the birds, swept the floor and now sat outside working at the little board they used for cutting leather. Seeing Thomas approach he sprang to his feet.

'Thought I'd get some practice in, making jesses,' he said. He held up the narrow strip, its end tapered to a neat point, with a slit for the leash.

Thomas showed his approval. 'It's a weight off my shoulders,' he said, 'finding how good a learner you are.' Then he told Ned what had happened at Boxwell.

The boy was thunderstruck. 'I knew something was afoot!' he cried. 'Sir Robert came back in a vile temper, shouting at the stable-lads...' Then he remembered. 'I was supposed to tell you to go to him, soon as you got home.'

Thomas nodded. 'Finish here when you like, and go on home yourself. I'll look in on the birds later.'

He walked with heavy steps towards the house. As he went, he wondered what further part his master would charge him with in untangling what was become, after all, a pestilence of sorts.

Though one borne not on the wind, but caused by human wickedness.

12

He stood in Sir Robert's private chamber. The light was fading and candles had been lit. His master sat at his writing table, scattered with a profusion of papers.

'The high sheriff will likely return, as soon as he receives my message,' he said. 'I have offered the Great Hall as a meeting place, should he wish to use it again.' He frowned at the hearth, where a small fire burned. 'That name, Walden. Does it mean aught to you?'

'There was a Richard Walden in Chaddleworth, a long while back. More than ten years, I'd say,' Thomas recalled. 'He died... I remember not the cause. His widow was broken by the loss. She left the parish soon after, and never returned.'

Sir Robert was nodding. 'I recall something of it. Martin would know more...' He looked up. 'Can it have any bearing on the brewer's death? Or even, if your friend Schweiz discovers traces of poison again – might it have bearing on all the deaths?'

Thomas shook his head. 'I know not, sir.'

Sir Robert showed his irritation. 'When word of what happened at Shefford gets out, there will be near panic.' As if suddenly fatigued, he rubbed at his face and beard. 'Is there naught comes to mind, Thomas?'

There was one thing: he had thought of it on the short ride back to Petbury, though it promised little.

'This poison, sir,' he said. 'The plant doesn't grow in England, as far as my knowledge goes. Master Paulo says it is difficult to obtain. I could go to Halliwell, the apothecary in Wantage. If anyone knows aught of it, he would.'

'Indeed!' Sir Robert seized on the notion. 'Will you ride there tomorrow?'

'I will, sir.' Thomas waited to be dismissed, but Sir Robert's mind was moving in another direction. 'There have been no more thefts, have there?' he enquired. 'I mean, from the bakehouse, or...'

'No, sir,' Thomas answered quickly. 'I believe the culprit was merely passing by, and has gone.'

But Sir Robert's reply shook him. 'Mayhap he has not gone far,' he said with a grim look. 'Martin says someone has broken into Poughley Manor.' He grunted. 'Not that there's much to steal at Mountford's seat.'

Whereupon the knight cleared his throat and dismissed Thomas, who bowed and made a swift exit, his thoughts swirling like hayseeds.

* * *

To his relief, Nell came to his cottage after nightfall.

She was tired, and their coupling was brief and somewhat hasty on Thomas's part. Truly, he thought wryly, they were as husband and wife now... And yet he was at peace as they lay in the pitch dark in his bed, hearing the nightbirds beginning their discourse.

He had resolved, since seeing her the previous night in the kitchen, to try to forge a better understanding. He had been harsh, he thought; she was faithful and kind despite her sharp tongue, and deserved more than he had given. But she it was who spoke first.

'I cannot make your mind up for you.'

'I know, and—'

She interrupted him. 'Yet you must decide, for I'll not wait beyond the summer's end.'

In the dark, she heard his steady breathing. 'You would leave Petbury?'

'I might.'

'Then...' He hesitated. 'If it comes to that, it will be because I have failed you.'

'Failed?' She put out a hand to touch his face. 'How so?'

'I met a woman today, newly widowed... She said her husband always shut her out of his affairs. I would not wish that to be said of me.' When she said nothing, he went on, 'I would have you know what's in my heart—'

'No, forbear that. For I have not told you all that is in mine.'

He waited, but she turned on her side, saying she would sleep.

For a while he lay in the dark, until at last he too slept.

* * *

A long walk to Wantage the next day might have given Thomas time to order his thoughts. However, Sir Robert had supplied a horse to speed him on his errand, which meant that the morning was still barely advanced when he found himself once again at Halliwell's shop in Wallingford Street. But this day it seemed fortune had forsaken him, for the door was locked and the shutters closed. A small hand-written sign in the apothecary's neat script hung on the door-handle.

Master Daniel Halliwell begs his customers' indulgence. He is called away on physician's business until tomorrow.

A phrase had been added as footnote.

Halliwell's bespoke worm remedy now in stock, for the benefit of all falconers.

Thomas turned away and retraced his steps.

The square was busy with townsfolk, but he barely noticed. Having recovered the gelding, he was leading it along Newbury Street, preparing to mount and ride home at once, when a tall figure detached itself from the press of folk entering the town from the south. Thomas halted abruptly, causing his horse to jerk its head. Across the street, Christopher Mead was leading his own horse – worn-out, by the look of it. And this time, seated upon it was his daughter.

The mapmaker himself was surprised to encounter Thomas here – more, he looked displeased. His ironic smile quickly in place, he paused as they drew level.

'Falconer.'

'Master Mead.' Thomas inclined his head, then acknowledged the rider. 'Mistress Grace.' He had forgotten how fair she was. Her face was shadowed by the broad-brimmed hat she wore against the sun, yet its beauty was undimmed.

Mead shifted impatiently from one foot to the other. 'Though it pains me not to pass the time of day with you, I fear we're in some haste,' he said.

Thomas kept his eyes on Grace Mead. Was it his fancy, or was

it more than mere shyness that made her look away at once? He
turned deliberately to Mead.

'Have you finished with the Lambourn Valley, then?' he
enquired. 'The river here flows north, into the Thames.'

He surprised himself by his boldness. *I am in a poor humour
indeed,* he thought, even as he saw the anger on Mead's face.

'My affairs are my own, Master Finbow,' the mapmaker said.
'And not to be expounded to falconers.'

'Then forgive my poor attempt at conversation, sir,' Thomas
replied. 'My mind was elsewhere.' On impulse he added, 'There
is turmoil at Great Shefford – but then you will know of it,
lodging nearby.' He was watching Mead's reaction, and realised
at once that the other knew it. 'A man dead, sir,' he added. 'So
sudden, it appears unnatural...'

But Mead spoke quickly, cutting him short. 'We are no longer
at those lodgings,' he snapped. 'They were cramped, and served
us poorly.' When Thomas raised an eyebrow, Mead added, 'Now
we'll attend to our business, and let you attend yours.'

The dismissal was plain, as the man jerked at the reins. But
even as his horse took a plodding step forward, Thomas said,
'There is to be an inquest at Petbury, at the high sheriff's bidding.
It may be that you too, sir, will be called.'

Mead stopped dead. The horse stopped too.

'What do you mean, fellow?' The mapmaker had flushed to
the top of his large forehead. 'What have I to do with this death?'

Thomas showed surprise. 'Surely you have heard, being in
the environs? This death is but the latest of four, in the space of a
week.'

Mead blinked. 'I am not concerned with...' He took a breath.
'Then, mayhap there is some sickness abroad. And hence, I'll not
stay here and put my daughter in danger.'

Thomas glanced at Grace Mead. It struck him then, that the

tale of her being unwell that day might not be false – there was a frailness about her that he had barely noticed when he and Ned had first encountered her, almost a week ago.

Then it struck him: the softness of her flesh, the fullness of the breasts, the way she sat the horse... Had he forgotten how Mary had looked at such a time?

The girl was pregnant. And Tom Brazier's words from three days ago, came to his mind: *You don't truly believe she's his daughter...?* He realised then, that he did not.

'Indeed, sir,' he said in a measured tone. 'If sickness be the cause, it would be wise not to place any woman in danger... more so, should they be at risk for any reason.'

And from Grace, he got the reaction he expected. Though she concealed it well, there was no mistaking her alarm. His bolt had struck home.

Mead drew a sharp breath, and Thomas turned to find himself fixed by a look he recognised well enough. Had he not looked murderous anger in the face before? Yet he spoke calmly.

'I wished not to alarm you, sir. But is it not best that you know what has occurred?'

But Mead merely tugged again at the rein and led the horse off towards the town square, without looking back. Neither did the young woman look anywhere but directly ahead.

* * *

In the afternoon, Thomas left Ned to tend the falcons and sought audience with Sir Robert, but was told his master was occupied and would see him at supper time. Hence he took it on himself to go at once into Chaddleworth, and seek out Paulo Schweiz.

He found Giles Frogg's house deserted. Frogg himself was absent, as were the showman and his entourage. So Thomas walked to the end of the little row of cottages, which backed on to the church, heading for the Black Bear, whereupon there came a shout. Paulo, in his black gown, was striding across the green towards him.

'My friend!' The conjuror looked glad to see him. And, pleased as he was to see Paulo too, Thomas thought later, he let his guard slip and betrayed himself. Or was it rather, that the man truly had powers that few others possessed? Whatever the cause, he was brought up short when the other stopped, peered into his face, and said, 'These two paths – you cannot delay forever. You must take one or the other, and soon.'

Thomas said nothing, but Paulo made no apology this time.

'You still do not trust me entirely, Master Thomas,' he said, with a shake of the head. 'Yet that matters not. You know what I speak is truth.'

Thomas looked away. 'If it is, it's my affair, and I must make my choice.'

'Indeed! I never tell folk what they must do – I but tell them what I see,' Paulo answered. He sighed. 'I was called to the house of the old man that died here on the green...' He pointed. 'His widow is in such turmoil, it is feared she will lose her wits.'

Thomas frowned. 'Could you not help her in any way?'

Paulo shrugged. 'I am no physician. And if I were, folk would not trust me to attend upon them... Still some believe I have brought bad luck, or sickness.' He hesitated. 'Yet I did calm her a little. An odd thing: she has a notion there is a fortune hidden in her house, and that it will be stolen. She trusts nobody.'

Thomas drew breath so sharply that Paulo could not help but notice.

'So...' He nodded slowly. 'She is perhaps not so distracted as folk think? I thought such.' He paused. 'Mayhap this thief that they speak of, and your murderer, are one and the same?'

And when Thomas gave no answer, he took a step closer. 'The little mug, from the brewer... It was as you feared,' he said quietly.

Thomas's eyes narrowed. 'You are certain?'

Paulo nodded. 'I washed out the dregs... Poison was there, as before. The bottom of the mug had still a coating of it. When the man filled it with beer and drank, there was likely enough in a mere mouthful to cause death.'

'I must tell my master,' Thomas said. 'I fear that you will be called to give testimony before the high sheriff.'

Paulo gave a shrug. 'I will enjoy that. I find little opportunity to exercise my wits here...' He stopped. 'My friend, forgive me! Your village, your folk...'

Thomas dismissed the matter, gazing absently about the village which was almost deserted in the late afternoon. His father's house still stood, barely a hundred yards away, though no Finbow had lived in it for more than a decade.

'These two paths,' he said after a moment. 'Is there one which looks steeper or stonier than the other?'

At once he regretted his words, but Paulo was staring. 'My friend...' The showman shook his head, and gave one of his sudden explosive shouts of laughter. 'You cheer me, like a glass of fine wine!' And clapping Thomas hard on the shoulder, he turned and walked off towards the Black Bear, still laughing.

Thomas made a wry face, and took himself home.

* * *

Sir Robert summoned him before supper, and the two of them took a turn about the gardens. When Thomas had told all, his master appeared in more of a quandary than ever.

'Well, the matter will out tomorrow, come what may,' he

muttered. 'The sheriff returns in the morning, and intends to hold an open inquest on all four deaths, here in the Great Hall.' Seeing Thomas's surprise, he added, 'Ask me not if this is common practice, for I'm no lawyer. Yet I can understand if he wishes to deal with the matter in one swoop, and restore some calm to the Downlands.'

Thomas kept his own thoughts private. Instead, he told his master something of the fearful atmosphere in Chaddleworth.

'I will see what can be done for the widow Gee,' Sir Robert said. 'As for the German—I mean, the Switzer...' He shrugged. ''Til tomorrow.'

Thomas made his bow and watched him walk off. He was thinking that for a man who wished not to cause panic, Richard Ward was going an odd way about it. More likely he would arouse even more alarm than existed already.

13

Word of the deaths had spread far and wide, and this time there was no difficulty in recruiting a jury for the inquest at Petbury. Indeed, folk flocked to the Great Hall as if to a fair, so that by the Wednesday afternoon it was filled with those of every station: from Sir Robert and the high sheriff as well as a sour-faced Sir John Mountford, to the humblest cottagers from Chaddleworth, Great Shefford and neighbouring hamlets. A clerk sat near the sheriff to record the proceedings.

The old custom had been observed of calling the finders of each body, as well as the neighbours of the deceased, but in fact no one who had an interest, no matter how slight, had been turned away. Hence the Shefford brewers rubbed shoulders with John Ames and his sons, and with drinkers from the Black Bear. John Flowers was there, sitting with Ames. And two of the widows were present: a pale-faced Jane Kirke, who sat beside Mountford's servant, the weasel-faced John Kydd; and Elizabeth Rawlings, a solid figure in well-cut mourning clothes, flanked by her late husband's journeymen. Agnes Gee had refused to attend, had refused even to open her door to Giles Frogg, who had not pressed the matter. He sat stiffly beside the now-famous showman, Paulo Schweiz. Kit and the ape, to the disappointment of the curious, had not been called.

And there would be further disappointments, for the high sheriff's reasons for holding such an inquest, open to all, soon became plain to Thomas: if there were some way to play down the events and restore calm to the Downlands, Ward sought to find it. Indeed, the stark choice Sir Robert had outlined a mere three days earlier, between arousing fear of pestilence or fear of a murderer on the loose, seemed to have been side-stepped: the high sheriff, it appeared, intended to discourage both. Hence to the surprise of Giles Frogg, Thomas and others, the matter of the poison was not mentioned and Paulo Schweiz was not even summoned as a witness. Instead, after all concerned had testified to the time, place and manner of the deaths, a physician nobody knew, dressed in a sober gown and skull-cap, stood up at the sheriff's behest and announced that all four men appeared to have died of heart failure, brought on by some unknown sickness. That given the circumstances, contagion was unlikely; there were no tokens of plague, nor was any pestilence known which produced such symptoms. Hence, the cause might be construed as death by misadventure.

There was some consternation in the hall. Thomas caught Sir Robert's eye, but his master looked away. He then looked at Paulo, who wore no expression at all, but gazed upwards as if admiring the fine hammer-beam roof.

'Silence, I pray!' Martin the steward, at his most officious, quelled the muttering that had risen.

'Our thanks, good doctor,' Richard Ward said loudly, 'for coming such a distance to assist us.' With a stiff bow the man moved off and took a seat near the door, as if eager to be gone.

Ward faced the jury of sixteen men drawn from the parishes, sitting in a tight group looking somewhat bemused.

'Masters,' he began. 'You have heard full accounts from the witnesses of the manner of each of these sad deaths, and all matters pertaining thereto. Hence I trust you will wish as I do, by God's will, to bring matters to a conclusion; to let each man lie in peace, that their widows may grieve, in the sure and certain knowledge that—'

'Master sheriff, I beg you!'

Heads snapped round in surprise. It was a woman's voice, loud enough to echo to the rafters, which had presumed to interrupt the high sheriff's attempt at summing-up. And Thomas felt a surge of admiration for the doughty Elizabeth Rawlings who was on her feet, somewhat flushed, gazing directly at Richard Ward.

'Mistress...' Ward glanced at his clerk, and faltered a little. 'You have already given your testimony...'

'Not in full, sir, for I was not permitted to!' The brewer's widow stared hard at the sheriff, then at the jury, every one of whom shifted uncomfortably; here was a woman to be reckoned with.

'Mistress Rawlings,' Ward said more loudly, flushing a little himself. 'While all allowance is made for your loss and for your distress, we need hear no more—'

'Yet you shall, sir!' There was something akin to a gasp from all sides at the woman's boldness. And having taken her stance, she would not be cowed.

'I have sat, sir,' Mistress Rawlings began, 'and held my peace, and listened to a tale that is already known to many here. The sudden deaths, so close together, of Haylock, and Master Kirke, and Gee, coupled with my own affliction... Such a thing has not been seen hereabouts, sir, since the plague visited us, as those of

my years will recall.' She paused, seeing she had the ear of
everyone in the room, then pressed her advantage. 'Yet the
doctor, that you saw fit to fetch all the way from Reading... This
doctor speaks truly in that the cause of this is neither plague, nor
any pestilence known to us. Hence, some believe it is some
foreign sickness brought in by newcomers...' She trailed off, and
her gaze strayed across the wide room towards Paulo Schweiz,
who was looking directly at her.

Thomas felt his pulse quicken, but he was surprised when
the widow looked away from Paulo to face the sheriff and added,
'I am not one who believes that, sir. For I knew my husband, as
well as any wife knows her own, and though he sought to keep
matters from me, I was aware in the last few days that he was
troubled. Now, it seems to me that he was in fear for his very life.'

'That is enough!' Ward had risen at last, and his angry
expression stayed even the stout widow. 'You overstep yourself,
Mistress. Whatever your husband's fears, he died as the others
died – at his work or in some public place, away from the hand of
any evil-doer. You yourself watched him expire!'

The widow blanched, but remained silent.

'And in any case,' the sheriff continued, 'it is a matter for the
jury now to determine whether there has been foul play. And I
for one will not prejudge their finding!' He glanced around as if
daring anyone to challenge him. None did, but Thomas,
concealing his own discomfort at the way the meeting was being
steered, caught one or two expressions that mirrored his own
feelings. One was that of Giles Frogg, close by, who clearly
showed his unease. Another was Paulo's, though he appeared
calm, stroking his thick beard like some Old Testament sage.
And then, there was Sir John Mountford.

Thomas looked, then shifted his gaze before the master of
Poughley Manor could read his surprise. For unless he was

mistaken, Mountford was afraid – almost as afraid as his servant Kydd had been, the last time they were in this very room. Indeed, Kydd himself looked much as he had done then, and sat gripping his knees as if they might be seen to shake.

Sir Robert was staring fixedly at the table. But feeling Thomas's gaze upon him, his master looked up and signalled with his eyes: *Hold your peace, and wait.*

Ward was still on his feet. 'I have said all I wish to,' he stated firmly. 'Unless any man—' he pointedly ignored Elizabeth Rawlings '—has further testimony to add, we shall let the jury retire.'

There was coughing and scraping of boots, but nobody spoke. Within minutes the jury had filed out, and it was little surprise when they returned a short time later and delivered their verdict: that Simon Haylock, labourer, William Kirke, joiner, Nicholas Gee, shepherd and Thomas Rawlings, brewer, had each died through mischance, taken by the same sickness but one unknown to any save Almighty God, and not by the hand of any other party. And might the jury be reimbursed for loss of their afternoon's earnings?

It was over. With some haste, Sir Robert's steward summoned Petbury servants and began clearing the Great Hall. A hubbub rose as folk thronged the doorway and the outer passages. Among the last to leave, Thomas saw, were the two widows, now side by side. Jane Kirke was weeping, but Elizabeth Rawlings walked erect and stony-faced, supporting the smaller woman as if she were a sister.

Thomas made his farewell to Ames, John Flowers and others, eager to go to his work and collect his thoughts. But catching his master's eye, he understood that he was to wait. When the last of the villagers had departed, the doors were slammed and a silence fell. Those who remained were the high sheriff, Sir

Robert, Mountford, Martin the steward, Giles Frogg, and Paulo Schweiz.

'Thomas.' Sir Robert waved him forward, bidding the others gather round the far end of the long table. But Mountford remained pointedly in his seat.

'Sir John?' It was Ward, with eyebrows raised, who gestured to the chair at his side. Still Mountford did not move. Only when the silence had grown uncomfortable did he rise, his expression one of hostility.

'What game are you playing, master sheriff?' he asked icily.

There was an intake of breath.

'No game, sir,' Ward replied, calmly enough. Now that the inquest had gone as no doubt he intended, he had relaxed visibly. 'Sir Robert and I wished merely to touch on certain matters in private...'

'By the Lord, mistake it not – I know what you do!'

Mountford's eyes blazed. Now that he was among his own class, apart from a few servants who would not dare to question their masters, he gave free rein to his frustration. Thomas guessed that the man had sat and squirmed through the entire inquest, knowing as only a few others did that it was little more than a comedy, and a poorly plotted one at that.

'You have played upon all, like a pair of virginals!' Mountford snapped. 'The verdict is worth less than a cartload of dung! This poison, that was talked of last Sabbath...' He flicked a hand at Paulo. 'Now, it is not even mentioned! Nor is this juggler, in whom you appeared to set such store, called as a witness.'

Turning to Sir Robert, he added, 'And you, sir, I deem a willing party to this pageant, this varnishing of truth...' He was beginning to splutter. 'But then, what should I expect of a Vicary – another of the new nobility who garnered their fortunes from the loot of broken monasteries. Calvinism, sir, is not a proper religion for a gentleman!'

He had gone too far. There was an ugliness in the room, that had more than a whiff of the bear-pit about it. Ward fell back, as Sir Robert rose from his seat. Even old Martin seemed poised to hurry to his master's side. Frogg stood apart, clearly out of his depth, while Thomas had stiffened from head to foot, and had to stop his hand from wandering towards the poniard at his belt.

'You are under my roof, sir,' Sir Robert said, keeping his voice low as Mountford had failed to do. 'Hence I will not act. But mistake not: should we meet elsewhere, you and I—'

'You and I?' Mountford echoed. 'You and I are men of separate worlds, sir – riding the same air current, yet no more alike than an eagle and a bat!'

He turned a bleak gaze upon the other men. 'Do your worst. Lay your plots, and reap what rewards ye may – and as God is my judge, I will reap mine!'

And turning on his heel he walked the length of the room, for the second time in a matter of days, without looking back. When he was gone, and the door shut hard upon him, a wave of relief was felt by all that remained.

Ward broke the silence. 'Sir Robert... might these men be permitted to ease their thirst, as well as you and I...?'

Sir Robert gave a short laugh, letting his anger escape with it, and gestured to the jug of wine which stood on a side table. 'Indeed, I think we have all earned it,' he answered, and turned to Martin. 'Master steward?'

Martin nodded, and gestured to Thomas to assist as impromptu server. Soon every man had a cup of good claret in his hand, and at Sir Robert's bidding, drank freely. In a very short time the atmosphere had lightened considerably.

'Falconer, Master Frogg – and you, Master Schweiz.' The

sheriff looked at each in turn. 'What may follow is to be kept in strictest confidence, do you mark that?' When the three signalled their assent, he turned to Sir Robert.

'Mayhap it is best that he's gone,' he said quietly.

Sir Robert made no reply, but turned briskly to the others. And though he addressed them all, he was looking at Thomas in particular. 'The high sheriff has sought to allay fears by his action today,' he said. 'Yet you, and you alone, know how those men died. More—' he glanced at Paulo '—we know now that the death in Great Shefford was caused in the same manner.' He raised an eyebrow. 'Your trials bore fruit again, Master Schweiz.'

Paulo made a slight bow. Seeing the baffled look on Giles Frogg's face, the knight added, 'The brewer's tasting mug was also poisoned.'

Frogg spoke up, frowning. 'Sir, these events trouble me greatly, for word may out, in some fashion. And should there be another death – God forbid it – then the verdict of that jury won't matter a scrap. Folk will be even more afeared than they are now.'

The high sheriff spoke. 'We are not unmindful of the danger, master constable...' He eyed Sir Robert. 'And now, I have a mind to air the matter you and I talked of earlier.'

Sir Robert gave a nod, though the notion did not cheer him. To Thomas he said, 'That name that the brewer spoke before he died – Walden. Have you thought more upon it?'

Thomas shook his head. 'Nay, sir. I went to the apothecary's at Wantage – a fruitless errand, for he was absent—'

Ward was impatient. 'One matter at a time, falconer.' Turning to Frogg, he asked, 'Do you recall the death some ten years ago, of a man from your village, named Walden?'

Frogg stared, and something in his manner made the others stiffen; the constable had paled in the space of a moment.

'Well... that I do, sir,' he muttered finally.

Ward frowned at him. 'Then speak, man.'

Frogg took a gulp of wine, as if he expected to have it taken from him and be shown the door. 'Richard Walden,' he began. 'He was churchwarden at St Andrew's... Dug graves, and minded his own bit of land, and worked the farms at times.' Seeing the sheriff's impatience, he added quickly, 'His death was sudden, 'tis true – but it were deemed an accident.'

Now Thomas drew breath, berating himself for forgetting. Of course – it would be around the time he had left for Holland. When he came back Mary was sick, and he was in turmoil, and had no time for aught but his own troubles... He looked up to find Sir Robert's eye upon him. But under the sheriff's stern gaze Frogg was speaking, nervously now.

'He was a humble man, a devout man, was Walden,' the constable said. 'Too honest for his own good, some said...' He looked down at his cup. 'His wife Rebecca took off with her child, after he died—'

'The death, constable.' Ward eyed the fellow grimly. 'Tell me how he died.'

Frogg gulped. 'He were found in the woods near the old Poughley priory. A fall, mayhap.'

'A fall!' Ward's patience had evaporated. Putting his cup down on the table somewhat loudly, he said, 'He was beaten to a carcass, was he not?'

Frogg looked so forlorn, it was difficult not to pity him. 'The body were broken, sir, and bloody, 'tis true...'

'Aye.' Ward glanced at Sir Robert. 'Bloody, and broken in half a dozen places, from what I heard. And yet the jury's verdict was not unlike that of today: death by mischance. An accident.' The last word was accented.

There was silence, until Sir Robert, perhaps feeling his status as principal landowner coming into question, said, 'But there was naught to be done, master sheriff. The verdict was clear and nobody questioned it, not even the man's family. Walden was laid to rest in St Andrew's churchyard, and lies there still.'

'Then mayhap it is his ghost which takes revenge,' Ward said grimly, at which every man looked uncomfortable. 'You see now,' he went on, 'why I was so hard upon the brewer's widow, lest she blurt out what I feared. For she told Master Finbow here that her husband uttered a name before he died: the name of Walden.'

Frogg's jaw fell open, but was quickly closed again.

'And now we hear, she believed her husband was in fear of his life,' Ward added.

Sir Robert was frowning. 'Do you touch on revenge? Is that the way your mind moves, master sheriff?'

For answer, Ward kept his eyes upon the hapless Giles Frogg. 'Well, Constable?' he enquired. 'Would you like to speculate for us?'

Throwing caution to the winds, Frogg took another gulp from his cup before facing the sheriff. 'I would guess you mean revenge upon the... Upon those who, if Walden were killed unlawfully as you maintain, who might have done it.'

'I do.' Ward replied, and glanced at Thomas. 'Falconer – you're a Chaddleworth man like Frogg here, though one blessed, I believe, with somewhat sharper powers of deduction. Which way would your mind move?'

Thomas took a moment before answering. 'I thought, sir, since Haylock and Kirke – and mayhap Gee too, if his widow be believed – had money hidden away, and that robbery was what drove the killer. Yet the brewer's death troubles me, for it does not sit well with the others.' He frowned. 'As for Walden... If he were murdered ten years back, how could anyone know who did such? And if the one who killed Haylock and Kirke and the others is taking revenge after all these years, who is he? And how does he know they were a part of it?' He shook his head. 'It makes no sense, sir. Nor do I believe those men capable of such savagery. Moreover, Walden hadn't an enemy in the world, nor had he money to tempt thieves... Why would anyone wish to kill him?'

'My question, too,' Ward nodded. 'Do you recall aught that sheds light upon it?'

Again Thomas shook his head. 'My memory of those days is poor, for I was gone from England for some of that time.'

Ward caught Sir Robert's glance, and chose not to pursue the matter. Instead, he turned deliberately to Frogg. 'Well, Constable – can you not assist us further?'

But to Thomas's sharp eye, a flicker of what might have been relief passed across Frogg's broad features. Looking up at the sheriff, he gave his answer with as much finality as a plain man could muster.

'I cannot, sir,' he maintained. 'I was not Chaddleworth constable back then – nor do I intend to be again. Now with your leave, might I return to my duties?'

Ward let out a sigh of exasperation, picked up his cup of claret and waved the man away.

14

That evening Thomas supped in the kitchen with Paulo Schweiz. Sir Robert had given permission in recognition of the service the conjuror had rendered. Glad of the opportunity to eat well, and free of Mistress Frogg's company for a night, Paulo was eager for conversation. But when the meal was finished, and he saw Nell and Thomas exchange glances, he grew thoughtful.

'So, she is a part of your *Schwierigkeiten*,' he said. 'A very attractive puzzle indeed.'

Thomas blinked. 'I begged you a good supper,' he said. 'Now I'll thank you not to try telling my fortune again.'

Paulo shrugged. 'What must I do then, if she should ask me?' But seeing the look of alarm that came over Thomas's face, he gave his habitual snort of laughter. 'My friend, be not amazed, for I would not hurt the man who aided me as you did in that market square.' He paused. 'Now, before I return to rejoin my servant, will you allow me to view your falcons?'

Thomas showed his surprise, but rose from the bench. As they went outside he glanced over his shoulder. Not merely Nell, but serving-men, the kitchen boy and wenches alike were staring at the disappearing form of the showman, word of whose *Mundus Peregrinus* had now spread throughout every home on the Downs, from the greatest houses to the humblest of hovels.

He bade Paulo keep quiet as they approached the mews, but the man needed little instruction. He had known falconers, he reminded Thomas, as he had told him on the road back from Wantage. Together they entered, hearing the birds stir on their perches. Paulo stood back, admiring Sir Robert's prized creatures, while Thomas inspected each and saw that Ned had put enough food and water out.

Yet soon his mind was elsewhere. The revelations of that had day troubled him. He felt as though the explanation for what had occurred lay somehow close by, yet hidden from his gaze. As always, he wished for the eyesight of a falcon gentle, to soar and see all that lay below, as a map...

The mapmaker. He had forgotten to mention to Sir Robert his encounter with Mead and his daughter – or rather, the young woman he was now convinced was not the man's daughter at all. Though how significant it was, he did not know. That the man had things to hide seemed obvious. Was he in more urgent need of ready money than Thomas had thought? He recalled the deadly look Mead had given him in the street in Wantage, and wondered.

As he surveyed the birds, his thoughts wandered. Before taking leave of his master he had learned the reason for Sir John Mountford's removal of Simon Haylock's body, which seemed innocent enough: Haylock, it was recalled, had worked for the master of Poughley at times as a day labourer; and as with Jane Kirke the laundress, Mountford meant to fulfil his responsibilities and offer some succour to his servants. Yet Thomas could not forget the man's anger that afternoon, and the fear that seemed to lie behind it. There was more here than the snobbery of an impoverished landowner, even one from an ancient family...

He came out of his reverie, to see Paulo gazing at him with amusement and affection. 'Would that I had travelled so far as you, in such a short time,' he said.

Thomas gave a wry smile. 'I'm so used to being alone here, I forget when there is company.'

Paulo's gaze rested upon the mighty Tamora, erect upon her perch, who was staring at him with unblinking eyes. 'In the Italian states I have seen many like her,' he murmured. 'The lords have stone towers upon the barren hills, where falconers mind their charges day and night. Some have a hundred birds or more – eagles, too.'

'I've heard of such,' Thomas nodded. On impulse he said, 'I have shown you my work. Will you tell me nothing of yours?'

Paulo's eyebrows went up. 'But you have seen it already!'

'I've seen what your audience believes it sees,' Thomas replied. 'I would know more of what it is we really see.'

The other paused. 'Still you do not trust me.'

Thomas met his eye. 'I do trust you,' he said finally. 'Though your boy Kit, I find hard to fathom.'

'There is naught to fathom,' Paulo said with a shrug. 'Unless it be what passes betwixt him and the ape.'

* * *

The next morning Thomas walked out on the Downs to the nursery mews, aware that Ned had gone before him. As he approached, he found the boy waiting for him before the hut. At sight of Thomas he raised a hand, and walked to meet him.

'The chicks are growing fast,' he said. 'When do we begin to train them in earnest?'

'When the summer draws on.' Thomas gazed across the empty Downs, where larks twittered and hovered. Ned was right; the eyasses would soon be claiming more of his attention. He caught the look on the boy's face. 'What troubles you today? Seen a ghost?'

But he showed surprise as Ned swallowed and said, 'Not me. But Jane Kirke did yesternight – and she is near out of her wits!'

* * *

After they had finished their work, Thomas took him back to his cottage where they shared a breakfast mug while Ned told his tale. And though it discomforted Thomas to hear it, he realised he was not entirely surprised, for in a place like Chaddleworth the matter was bound to surface quickly. In later times, Giles Frogg would always maintain that he had held his tongue as the sheriff ordered him – but no such instruction had been given to Elizabeth Rawlings. She it was, who had told Jane Kirke of her husband's nervous demeanour in his last days, and of the word he had spoken before he died – and hence, a matter that folk had been somewhat too ready to forget, rose to haunt them. And the notion of the ghost of Richard Walden rising to avenge his murder ran through the village like a blizzard.

Swearing Ned to secrecy in his turn, Thomas told him the gist of what had occurred the previous afternoon, upon which Ned voiced the same doubts Thomas had raised.

'I was only a little eyas myself, back then, and I don't recall much – but I know Will Kirke would never have done such a thing! Nor old Nick Gee – he never hurt so much as a fly, in all his days. Even Haylock, though he liked a drink, and maybe got into a brabble now and then... But to beat a man to death?' He shook his head. 'Don't make no sense to me.'

'Jane Kirke always had a powerful streak of fancy,' Thomas observed.

Ned eyed him. 'You don't believe she saw it?'

'What does she say?'

'She was walking back from Poughley last night – she went there after she'd been to the inquest. And she saw someone on the path – a dark shape it was, she said – and he growled at her! And she ran home screaming, straight into the Bear, and told everyone.'

Thomas paused. 'That was all?'

Ned nodded and drained his mug. 'Then she's not the only one newly widowed, who's took leave of her senses. Agnes Gee walks about the village like a fey spirit herself, muttering and whining.' He sighed. 'I know one thing: something wicked happened to those men, and the shadow hasn't passed yet.'

Thomas hid his unease; he would not tell Ned of the poison. He would fret for his family's safety – and moreover, he would be unable to hold his tongue. And then there would truly be a panic, as Sir Robert feared.

He drained his own mug, and stood up. 'Let's take Tamora and Caesar out, and forget our troubles for a while,' he said. A thought striking him, he added, 'Have you made your peace with Eleanor yet?'

Ned flushed. 'I haven't seen her for days.'

* * *

A day of low cloud passed slowly, as they made several forays onto the Downs, exercising the birds and bagging up game for the kitchen as they went. By evening Ned was dog-tired, and made his farewell in half-hearted fashion. As they parted outside the mews, he said, 'I near forgot! The conjuror, Master Paulo, said to tell you he's going to petition the sheriff to let him leave. Tired of being stuck at Frogg's, I reckon – and who'd blame him?'

'Not me,' Thomas admitted. 'He and his helper are travelling folk, after all. Need to set up their tent somewhere else.'

Ned clapped a hand to his brow. 'There's more – I forgot, with so much going on! Yon mapmaker's been poking around again.'

'Poking around?' Thomas echoed.

'At Poughley,' Ned told him. 'He was seen leaving there yesterday, took the path for Brickleton. Mayhap he's been paying his respects to Sir John.'

'Was he alone?'

Ned hesitated. 'If you mean was Mistress Grace with him, I didn't trouble to ask.'

Thomas smiled at the boy. 'You've worked hard today. Go on home.'

With a half-wave, Ned turned and trudged away downhill.

Thomas looked in on the falcons at nightfall, and was about to go to his bed when he was hailed by a shout from below. Lights showed at the windows of the Great House, where no doubt Sir Robert and Lady Margaret were still at table with Ann and Daniel. Richard Ward, it seemed, had ridden home soon after the fraught little council that had followed the inquest. Now a groom appeared out of the gathering dusk, calling up the hill to him.

'Thomas! You're to wait upon master at once!'

Thomas called back. 'Do you know what he wants of me?'

The fellow was turning away, but stopped long enough to shout, 'There's mayhem at Poughley – Sir John Mountford's dead!'

* * *

He stood close to his master and Martin the steward in the small fire-lit chamber, his thoughts whirling. But any conclusions he had leaped to concerning death by poisoning were quickly destroyed. In a tense voice Sir Robert announced, 'Sir John Mountford has been slain – stabbed through the neck and heart. He was found in his chapel...' With distaste, the knight went on to speak of the shocking discovery by Lady Sarah herself, when she had gone to join her husband for evening prayers and found him lying in a lake of blood. No intruder had been seen, going in or out.

'Word has gone to the sheriff,' Sir Robert went on. 'Yet I need hardly say that the magnitude of this death consigns the others to oblivion. The man was a knight of the realm; the lord lieutenant must be told...' He broke off irritably. 'God knows Mountford had few friends and even fewer admirers. But this?'

He raised his hands helplessly. Martin, his face haggard in the half-light, spoke up.

'Sir Robert, I beg you not to distress yourself. The hard words that passed between you and Sir John were of his making – we have witnesses aplenty to that. More, anyone could see that the man was troubled and short of temper. You speak of a dearth of friends and admirers – one may more easily speak of his enemies, who have been numerous, given...' He coughed nervously. 'Given the matters of his religion.'

'No.' Sir Robert shook his head vigorously. 'He is but one of many, in Berkshire as anywhere else, who make little secret of their faith. Though it is true we have fanatics enough in England, he has always lived as he has. Poughley is not a fortress – any man bent on such a deed could have done such long ago. I fear this has some other cause, perhaps related to the robberies that have taken place, at Poughley as here.'

He put a hand to his head, whereupon Martin spoke again.

'The high sheriff saw yesterday how things stood. Let him mount what enquiry he will – I'll ensure that the proper degree of mourning is shown at Petbury. We were neighbours to Sir John, when all is said. And Lady Sarah will need whatever aid we can provide.'

Sir Robert seemed to collect himself. 'You do well to remind me of my duty, master steward,' he said. 'In the morning, I'll ride to Poughley myself and offer what service I may. Lady Sarah shall not be left to bear such a burden alone... unless she wishes it.' He glanced up. 'You will come with me, Thomas.'

Thomas made his bow, and soon after was dismissed.

* * *

Poughley Manor stood a mile to the east of Chaddleworth beside the brook that bore its name, and a little north of the old ruined priory; a relic of an older England, when abbots ruled with more power than many lords, and monks and nuns trod the well-worn paths, even on the Downlands of Berkshire. The rambling house was built mainly of timber infilled with brick, but one wing was of grey stone taken from the priory rubble in the turbulent days after the Dissolution. Hence, Sir John Mountford was fond of proclaiming to those of his own faith, the old religion lived on unbroken in the walls of his small chapel. And here it was, kneeling at his devotions, that he had met his terrible end at the hand of a nameless assassin.

Thomas and Sir Robert stood in the doorway the following morning and contemplated the scene. Finally, Sir Robert turned to Thomas, wetting his dry lips. 'Mayhap our killer could not gain access to any of Mountford's drinking vessels – or has merely run out of poison.' Somewhat bitterly, he turned aside.

Thomas was looking about. Mountford's body had already

been taken up, washed and dressed in his best clothing and laid out in a coffin draped with black cloth and hung with branches of yew. Candles burned on the altar. But though most of the blood had been washed from the floor, nobody was keeping a vigil. Indeed, most of the household, it appeared, had hidden themselves away when Sir Robert and his servant rode in. Only a white-faced John Kydd, nervous as a hare, had appeared to greet the visitors. At their request he had shown them to the chapel, though he himself would not enter.

He was waiting outside when the two men emerged, closing the door behind them. He bowed to Sir Robert. 'Lady Sarah will receive you, sir.'

Sir Robert was ill at ease. 'I have no wish to disturb her, in her grief.'

Kydd swallowed. 'Sir, I think she would welcome a visit from one of her station. Indeed, none but you has sent even a word of condolence.'

There was an imploring look in his eyes, that Thomas did not yet understand. But Sir Robert nodded, and bade the man lead the way.

If Thomas had seen little of Sir John Mountford over the past decade, until recent events had brought him to Petbury, Lady Sarah he had not seen at all. Indeed, Chaddleworth folk said that in earlier times she would have been a nun, and joked about her bringing forth around a dozen children in her twenty years of marriage. Only half of the children had survived their early years. The oldest youth had disappeared, and was said to have run off to Rheims to train for the priesthood. The others were schooled at home, and kept apart from those outside their faith. Indeed, seldom was anyone from Poughley seen, so that the manor had become a secluded place, forgotten if not shunned by most of the nearby inhabitants.

They walked through unlit, stone-flagged passages, chilly even in the mild May weather, past closed doors, until they climbed a flight of steps to the Mountfords' main receiving chamber. It was not large and the furniture was old and worn with over-use, but a good fire burned in the chimney, beside which sat the Lady of Poughley in her mourning clothes. As Kydd showed the two men into the room she rose to make her curtsey.

'Sir Robert... Be assured, you are welcome.'

Lady Mountford's appearance always occasioned surprise. She was straw-haired and doll-like, so slight that she looked incapable of bearing children, let alone of keeping in good health. In the tautness of her grief, her pale face was composed and dignified, even wearing a faint smile of welcome. A single woman-servant in plain black stood at her side, stony-faced.

Sir Robert bowed and approached the table, where wine and cups had been set out. Thomas remained near the doorway. When his master turned he made his own bow, and the two men exchanged glances. Thomas understood that he was to make a polite withdrawal, which would afford him the opportunity to look around, even ask questions – provided he could find anyone who would talk to him. But as if in answer, there was John Kydd loitering outside. As Thomas emerged from the main chamber and descended the steps, the man flinched.

'By Jesu...' He caught his breath, peering at Thomas with fearful eyes from a ravaged, pock-marked face. Thomas gazed at him, recalling the man's demeanour on both the occasions he had accompanied his master to Petbury. If he was certain of anything, it was that there was no better place to start looking for answers.

'Master Kydd, I ask pardon for startling you.' He kept his eyes on the man. 'It's a dark day for your mistress, if not for—'

But Kydd was not listening. He took a step forward, with a furtive glance to either side like some stage conspirator.

'For the Lord's sake, Finbow,' he blurted, 'I ask your help – for all of us!'

Ignoring the surprise on Thomas's face he added, 'Twill out now – it does already! You are trusted at Petbury. I beg you to intervene, to ask your master to protect us, else we're all dead men, like the others – like my master...' He broke off, close to tears. Snivelling like a child, he wiped his nose on the sleeve of his threadbare doublet, and to Thomas's dismay fell upon his knees, clasping his hands.

'God's mercy, Finbow... Let Sir Robert take us under his wing, for there is nowhere to hide! The avenger knows who we are – he snuffs us out one by one! Only now he shows his hand, and cuts off the head itself, to proclaim that none shall escape, no matter their station!'

Tears welled up, and somewhat awkwardly Thomas bent to raise the whimpering fellow to his feet. 'I don't follow,' he muttered. 'The head itself...?' He frowned. 'You said, *we're all dead men, like the others...* What others?'

With a sniff Kydd got slowly to his feet, avoiding Thomas's eye. Then in a hoarse voice, he spoke the words, 'The Devil's Jury.'

15

THE DEVIL'S JURY

It was never spoken of, that dark chapter, buried in the collective memory of the folk of Chaddleworth and its surrounds for ten years. Locked away until, it was hoped, it would wither and die, as those implicated in its work died, until it had faded for ever.

But it would not fade, not now. Having dragged the words from Kydd's mouth, Thomas steered the scarecrow of a manservant – the title of steward seemed to sit poorly upon him – out of the house and into a kitchen yard. Sounds from a half-open door meant that the business of the household continued in some fashion, though no other servants were in sight. There they stood, and once Kydd realised Thomas would do nothing until he had told him all, reluctantly he spilled the tale.

'You would needs throw your mind back ten years,' he began. 'When the Queen began to squeeze men like my master. Recusants, I mean...' He shook his head. 'For saying mass, a man faced a year's gaol and 200 marks' fine... Anyone who even heard mass faced gaol. Moreover, landowners like he would have the value of their lands assessed by jury. If they did not, or could not pay the fines, they would forfeit two thirds of their wealth.' He shuddered. 'You cannot know what a fog of terror there was back then, after the Jesuit Campion was captured at Lyford – here, in Berkshire! – and taken off to face torture and execution. My master had seen him but days before... He had heard Campion say mass himself! As had all the family, and those servants that share his faith...' Kydd's gaze had wandered; now he turned sharply to Thomas.

'I am not one of their number, yet I'm loyal both to my master and mistress. 'Tis but that...' He hesitated. 'Sir John began to search his heart, after he went up to London, to the synod of Southwark, and heard Father Parsons rouse the faithful, proclaiming that even a token attendance at a parish church would be regarded as an act of impiety. What was he to do? He tried to live lawfully, yet the fines for not attending church crippled him. The thought of losing all he held dear – he, the proud scion of an ancient and noble family. It was too much to bear!'

Sensing that Kydd was coming to the nub of the matter, Thomas nodded his encouragement. The man swallowed, and continued. 'Thomas Bullock was high sheriff, back in 1582. When he appointed the jury that would assess Poughley's worth, words passed betwixt he and Sir John. I know not what, but I may say this: by the time we sat – for I was one of those picked – every man there had been seen in private, and given to know that if the jury valued the lands far below their worth, he would receive his reward.'

Thomas stared. 'Mountford bribed you? Every one of you?'

'He was not the only one!' Kydd cried. 'Many juries undervalued the lands of their local gentry, for like reasons... Some were merely threatened. My master can be a hard and bitter man, but he would not do such...' He looked away. 'What do the details matter? We knew what our task was, and we took what seemed the easiest course and did as we were bid.' He broke off, then added, 'Save one...'

'Richard Walden.' Now, in a moment Thomas saw it. Fixing Kydd with a hard look, he said, 'He was the only honest man among you. He refused to take a bribe, and his body was found soon after!'

Kydd's voice shook. 'None of us would have done such! We deplored it, as did Sir John! Nobody knows who killed Walden...' He turned aside. 'Unless it be this avenger. But nay, he himself knows not: he assumes it was one of the jury, and...'

Thomas was piecing it together. 'Your speech wanders, John Kydd, but the fog clears a little. You, and Haylock and Kirke and Gee, all sat on that jury, yes?' Taking the little man's silence for assent, he frowned. 'But Rawlings the brewer – he was from Shefford.'

'He was a juryman too,' Kydd admitted. 'He owned land here-abouts, hence he was entitled.' He lowered his gaze. 'Walden was the one whose conscience was too strong... He would have held out against us all. And he paid for his piety... By whose hand, I know not.' In great agitation, he added, 'And I say again, this avenger knows not: he merely snuffs out the jurymen, one by one – and now he has slain Sir John himself, as instigator of it all...'

He looked close to tears again, but Thomas had little sympathy for him. His mind working rapidly, he said, 'So the inquest jury who sat soon after, and pronounced Walden's death an accident—'

'Was the same sixteen men!' Kydd cried. 'The Devil's Jury... Now you see how the name was born.'

'It was well-named,' Thomas said, as the notion sank in. 'And had I been part of the life of the village in those years, I might have asked how a man beaten in such manner could have been pronounced dead by mischance.' He took a breath. 'So it's not robbery that drives this murderer at all, but vengeance. He assumes one of the jury did the foul deed, and he destroys you one by one in certainty that he will have his revenge.' He paused. 'But then who is he, and what was he to Richard Walden?'

Kydd shook his head. 'That concerns me not!' he cried. 'Will you not think of the remaining jurymen? Like me, they're in fear for their lives – as Rawlings was, before he perished! They know it was no pestilence that killed Haylock and Kirke and the others... though what means was used to make them sick I know not. I only know that not one of us has slept in days...' He broke off as a bleak smile appeared on Thomas's face. 'You think this a matter for jest?' Kydd snapped.

'Nay, but if they're like you, I can imagine how they must be quaking in their beds of a night.' He paused. 'So, who are the others? How many are you?'

Kydd looked away. 'Some have died in the years since. Others have gone away. Some could not rest easy in themselves, after...'

'Men like Gaddy Butler?'

At once Will Saltmarsh's tale leaped to Thomas's mind, causing Kydd to show surprise. 'Butler was one... yet there are still four who remain hereabout: Robert Clements, the tanner; Thomas Friar; John Palmer; and Francis Ball, the maltster.'

The names were all familiar enough to Thomas. 'And you too,' he said.

'And me,' Kydd echoed.

There was a stack of firewood beside the yard wall. Having made his confession Kydd sat down upon it in some despair. Thomas gazed at him, but the man would not meet his eye. Finally he looked up and asked, 'Now will you speak with your master, and beg us leave to ask sanctuary of him?'

'I will try.' Thomas looked towards the house, not needing to hear more. 'I can lay the matter before him,' he added, 'but he will make his own judgement.' Another thought struck him. 'Your mistress – does she know she the whole of this sorry tale?'

But John Kydd had got up and was moving away. A shambling figure, he disappeared through a doorway with the gait of one who would look over his shoulder for the remainder of his life, however long or short that might be. Thomas had no chance to voice another question that rose to his lips: *Whatever Mountford paid you, do you still believe it was worth it?*

* * *

As he and Sir Robert rode back to Petbury together, he told him the whole tale. By the time he had finished they were already in the stable yard. A groom appeared to take the horses, and stood waiting for the master to dismount.

But Sir Robert sat his horse, staring at the cobbles.

'I have heard of such cases,' he muttered at last. 'A few crowns spent on bribes to jurymen is a goodly investment for a landowner who could lose thousands...' He glanced at Thomas. 'I never had much time for Mountford, yet for all his faults I always believed him an honest knight.' He frowned. 'Lady Sarah is one of the most virtuous women I've known. I would wager she knew little of what happened, for her conscience would trouble her greatly. Despite the shock she has suffered, she is calm in her grief, trusting that what happened is somehow the will of God...' He shook his head. 'I find it hard to maintain such faith.'

The knight drew his leg from the stirrup and swung his body across the horse's back. Thomas too dismounted, and stood waiting while his master handed the reins to the groom.

'I will ponder what's to be done,' he said in a low voice. 'The high sheriff should arrive soon, then we may decide some strategy.' He eyed Thomas. 'The Devil's Jury,' he muttered. 'Whatever was their wage, I venture those that survive have had ample time to regret taking it.'

* * *

It was late evening before Thomas was summoned to attend his master again. While at his work alongside Ned that afternoon, he had kept matters to himself as ordered. But his mind ranged freely over the events, now that Kydd had told his story. He wondered still at the way this murderer had moved so swiftly and cunningly, to poison four men in the space of a few days. Yet the man's boldness in entering Poughley and killing Mountford in such a savage manner troubled him even more. What certainty was there that the same hand was at work? Was it possible there might be more than one? Even so, the question remained: who was it, after a decade had passed, who was bent on taking such a terrible revenge?

The family...? He recalled that Rebecca Walden had left the parish soon after her husband's death. Could it be she? Surely few others would be driven to take such risks to exact revenge than the widow of a murdered man. Yet though his memory of her was vague, he recalled she was a pious woman, of a gentle nature... And there was a further puzzle. Whoever the avenger was – and it was no ghost, of that he felt certain – who was it, ten years back, who had killed Richard Walden?

He entered the house at nightfall after finishing his evening tasks, and was sent at once to his master's private chamber. Richard Ward, he learned, was here and had already supped with Sir Robert. Entering the room he made his bow, and as expected found only the high sheriff, his master and Martin the steward present.

'Finbow,' the sheriff greeted him, though his tone was less than friendly. 'You, it seems, have been the vehicle for this pretty tale. Your master has spoiled my digestion with the telling of it.'

Thomas waited until Sir Robert spoke up. It appeared to him that whatever discourse had taken place before his arrival had not been entirely cordial.

'We have turned the matter about from all sides,' Sir Robert said. 'And I see no other course, as neighbouring landowner, than to offer these frightened men the shelter they crave, here at Petbury.' Raising an eyebrow, he added, 'It seems they had already gone in a body to Mountford and begged his protection, on the very day he was killed.' He paused, frowning. 'He refused them.'

There was a silence, wherein Thomas sensed there were things between his master and the high sheriff that Ward was not prepared to air before him. And though he had questions aplenty, he held his peace. As if to answer him, Ward spoke.

'The murder of Sir John Mountford has thrown all into disarray, falconer. Its implications are wider than will concern you. Yet we may take some small comfort from the fact that his death does not appear to be linked to the others – those men of humbler rank who, as we in this room know, were poisoned. Indeed, I would ask you to put from your mind much of what you were told by Sir John's servant. He's a canting knave, who will tell any lie to protect his own skin.'

Thomas caught his master's eye, read the warning and held his peace. But the next moment, the sheriff's words came as a blow.

'And you may know now that a man has been apprehended this afternoon on the Newbury Road, who is a known rogue. It is my firm intent to charge him with the murder of Sir John Mountford.' When Thomas froze, Ward added, 'I can think of few who would fit the bill better than a vagabond, with stolen goods in his pack, some of which may come from Poughley Manor; more, he's a former soldier, who hates papists and has served in the Low Countries against them.' He wrinkled his nose in contempt. 'His name—'

Is Will Saltmarsh... Thomas silently mouthed the words to himself alongside the sheriff's, even as his heart thudded. He stood rigidly, keeping expression from his face. Then seeing the other men watching him, he tried to make some response.

'Has this man admitted to the killing, sir?' he asked, to which Ward gave a very grim smile.

'Not yet, falconer,' he replied. 'But he will.'

* * *

A short time later Thomas left the room, having been instructed to help settle the five men who formed the living remnant of the Devil's Jury, when they arrived at Petbury that same night. He had learned nothing further, save that Will Saltmarsh had been put in chains by the sheriff's men and was being held in an empty barn at Great Shefford, thence to be transferred to Reading gaol for questioning. The name struck fear into his heart, for he had little doubt that given time, even a man like Saltmarsh would be broken, and ready to confess to anything. For it seemed clear to him now that Ward wished to play down the murder of Mountford, as he had encouraged the inquest jury to reach a verdict of mischance concerning the other deaths. He claimed to be forming a strategy to apprehend the murderer secretly, so as not to cause further alarm; meanwhile, men like Thomas should look to their own business.

But had he known Thomas better, Ward might have been disconcerted to learn of the resolve he had formed to seek a private audience with his master, the moment the business of receiving the jurymen was over.

There was not long to wait.

They arrived on foot in the pitch dark, which was somehow fitting: five men in workaday hats and capes, carrying few possessions. Martin the steward received them, and along with Thomas and James the head groom, conducted them to the stable yard. There, in the light of a single torch, they stood in a silent, fearful group to learn that since there had been no time to prepare any better accommodation, they were to be put in the hayloft, where pallets had been laid out.

Kydd, it seemed, would be spokesman. Facing Martin, he asked, 'You are certain none outside of Petbury knows where we shall lie?'

Martin, whose distaste for the whole business was obvious, answered the man in a tone bordering on contempt. 'As far as I am aware. And Petbury folk, at least, are trustworthy.' When no reply followed, he added, 'Mayhap you should enquire among your fellows, as to their own discretion.'

Nobody spoke. Thomas, standing some distance away beside the groom, felt the fear that emanated from these villagers, most of whom he had known all his life. Yet how little had he known them, he reflected. Here was Francis Ball, the ruddy-faced maltster who had lately passed the business over to his son, and now spent most of his days fishing. Here was elderly John Palmer the shepherd, a childless widower noted for his taciturn ways. Clements the tanner was the youngest, a man in his early forties, always somewhat vain about his appearance; now he looked ill at ease, his gaze shifting nervously from one face to another. The last of the five was Thomas Friar, a grey-haired farmer from north of the parish, near Brickleton, whom Thomas barely knew at all.

The five men listened in silence while Martin proclaimed the rules Sir Robert had laid down. They must remain in the stables for the present, while somewhere more spacious was sought in which to house them. Food would be brought from the kitchens. When any man needed to go outside he should go alone, dressed in plain clothing like a groom or other servant, complete whatever task he must do, and return at once to the hayloft. Exercise might be taken at night, in pairs, but only as far as the paddock, and only so long as one or more Petbury servants were present. Sir Robert may wish to speak with the men later, but in the meantime...

'We are as prisoners.' Ball, bolder than the rest, voiced the notion for them all.

Martin turned to him with a bland look. 'You are free to return to your homes at any time.'

The others shifted their feet, with one or two irritated glances at Ball for his ingratitude, whereupon Martin pressed home his point. 'I deemed it unnecessary to remind you, that it was you who asked shelter from my master,' he told Ball. 'But if the arrangement displeases you—'

'Nay.' The maltster looked away. 'We are humbled by Sir Robert's charity.'

And without waiting he picked up his small pack and walked into the stable. The others followed.

Thomas climbed the ladder to the hayloft, staying only long enough to see the men bestowed in their new quarters. None addressed him, not even Kydd, who seemed intent on avoiding him. With a final glance he came down, left the stable and went at once to the house. But to his chagrin he was told by Martin that both Sir Robert and Lady Margaret had retired, not to be disturbed. There was nothing for him to do but go to his bed and try to gain a few hours' sleep, without the consolation of Nell's presence, before the dawn birds began their discourse.

But in the morning his spirits rose a little, for word came that Sir Robert would ride on the Downs, and Thomas should get himself mounted and be ready to accompany him. Somehow he knew that his master wished to be free of Ward's company for a while, which suited him well. There were matters he wished to unburden himself of, and quickly.

An hour later, as the sun rose at their backs, the two of them were riding west across Lambourn Down, Sir Robert bearing Tamora on the gauntlet. Reining in, he unhooded the falcon, raised his arm and let her soar at once until she floated on the breeze, far above. Then at last he turned to Thomas.

'Well, now,' he asked. 'Who, pray, is this Will Saltmarsh?'

16

Sir Robert could at times be more perceptive than folk allowed, and he knew his falconer and had caught the look on his face when Ward spoke the name. So with some relief Thomas told him, omitting nothing – not even the possibility that it was Saltmarsh who had seen fit to appropriate a few items from Petbury and elsewhere, to meet his needs. But, he maintained, theft of a few loaves and bed-sheets was one thing; murdering Sir John Mountford at his prayers was quite another. And this, he maintained stoutly, was not something the Saltmarsh he knew would have done.

Sir Robert listened in silence. Finally he said, 'I am inclined to agree with you.'

Thomas let out a sigh.

'I've not seen the man myself,' his master continued. 'Yet though he may be a rogue, you know him and have the measure of him... and like you, I see no likelihood that he would risk all by entering Mountford's chapel and committing such an act of savagery.' He grimaced. 'Yet luck has deserted him now, for he was close enough to Poughley to be taken on suspicion – and he will be sore put to plead his innocence.'

Thomas kept calm, sitting stirrup to stirrup with his master. Leaning down to pat the gelding's neck, he murmured, 'I ask pardon, sir, for not telling you of him sooner.'

Sir Robert waved a hand dismissively, as if matters of greater import weighed upon him. 'Ward will do naught to apprehend the poisoner.' When Thomas showed surprise, he added, 'Indeed, it would suit him to see the survivors of that cursed jury picked off to a man, until there be none left to tell of it.'

'How can that be?' Thomas asked.

Sir Robert gazed upwards, to where Tamora hung on the breeze. 'You have recalled, or been reminded, who was the high sheriff ten years back,' he replied. 'Have you wondered at the extent of his involvement?'

In fact, Thomas had begun to do just that. And when he turned over John Kydd's tale of the day before, it seemed to him likely that Thomas Bullock had been a party to Mountford's strategy of bribery – indeed, he could have profited from it. After all, it was he, as fitted his office, who had appointed the jury...

'Is he a friend of Master Ward's, sir?'

The question prompted a short laugh from Sir Robert. 'That he is, Thomas. And our worthy high sheriff would do much to preserve the good name of his friend – whether or not that friend had been a party to any wrongdoing.'

So it was plain: Bullock had been a willing accomplice in the stratagem. No doubt he had appointed those jurymen who appeared amenable, and who in their turn had recommended others. Where his judgement had failed, with tragic conse-quences, was in the selection of Richard Walden.

'Once again, Thomas, the matter rests upon your shoulders,' Sir Robert said.

Thomas shrugged. 'Yet I know not what I might do, sir.'

'Find out what you can, is all I ask,' his master told him. 'Use even your mountebank friend, if he will aid you further.'

'I hear he means to ask the sheriff's permission to leave,' Thomas recalled.

Sir Robert frowned. 'In view of what has transpired, I think Master Ward will be only too glad to grant such... But no matter. Go where you will. At least now that we appear to know who the other intended victims of this avenging ghost were, we can keep them safe under our roof.'

At which a thought occurred to Thomas. 'Might the danger be greater now, sir? I mean, should the man learn that we have all his chickens cooped up in one pen...'

Sir Robert's frown deepened. 'Indeed. They must not be left alone, day or night.'

Thomas's next words jolted him. 'Yet, might we not try to gain a step ahead of our ghost?' he mused. 'I mean, let it be known where they are, and hence—'

'Set a trap!' His master smiled suddenly. 'God's truth, Thomas, as a hunting man you thrill me to the heart!' His eyes gleaming, he added, 'Would that not be a masterly stroke, for a plain country knight to take the prize, where a man like the high sheriff has failed? Then the whole tale shall out!'

He clapped his falconer on the shoulder. 'Concern yourself not with my reputation,' he said. 'Suffice it to say, Master Ward looks to the future, when he is likely to be called to the Court, and to return as Sir Richard. He covets the favour of the lord lieutenant, along with other men of influence.'

Thomas said nothing. Though Sir Robert's reputation had grown in recent years as a man of honour, his standing among the great families of Berkshire was, as always, dubious. He would never be lord lieutenant; he knew it, and had come to accept it. Perhaps Ward's ambitions remained higher...

Thomas's smile was warm. 'You know that I will do all I can.'

'I do.' Sir Robert's manner grew brisk, as it was wont at such times. Shaking the reins, he urged his horse forward. Yet Thomas had not finished. Drawing alongside his master, he asked, 'Might I visit the prisoner, sir? I mean, Saltmarsh.'

Sir Robert turned. 'Is that wise?'

'I know not. Yet if you could arrange it, I believe I may learn something.'

His master considered a moment, then gave a nod. And touching spurs to the horse's flanks, he rode off to follow his favourite falcon.

* * *

Thomas found Ned at the mews that afternoon, and spoke at some length with him. It was fruitless now to keep the tale to himself, for news of the five men hiding in the stable-loft had run through Petbury like stubble-fire. And though many details were unknown to the boy, he had guessed more than Thomas expected.

'What will you do?' he asked, the gravity of the matter only now dawning on him.

'Learn what I may, then wait a while,' Thomas answered. 'It's Saturday after all, and I may take a mug in the Bear, and talk with whom I like.'

Ned threw him a hopeful look. 'You would do better with my help,' he said. 'I know Chaddleworth and its folk as well as you.'

'True,' Thomas said. 'Yet I need you to mind the birds, and serve Sir Robert should he wish to go hawking.' Seeing the

disappointment on the boy's face, he added, 'Yet, there may well
be a part for you in what lies ahead.'

That was enough to cheer Ned. He shook his head, and
exhaled. 'Poisoned... Who'd have believed such? So there is no
pestilence, no curse...'

'And no ghost,' Thomas finished. 'Only something far more
dangerous.'

In silence then, bent to their own thoughts, the two went
about their work.

* * *

The first person Thomas encountered when he stepped through
the door of the Black Bear that evening was Giles Frogg.

'See now, I got business with you,' the constable said. A
stolid figure in his black jerkin, he waited while Thomas called
for a mug, then guided him to a corner. The Bear was filling up
already. As he moved among the familiar faces, acknowledging
a greeting here and there, Thomas caught a few odd glances,
not all of them friendly. How much, he wondered, was known
about the men now cowering in the Petbury hayloft? It was
foolish to think that their sudden absence had passed
unnoticed.

Frogg's voice was unusually sharp. 'You must aid me,' he said,
'for it seems he'll listen to none but you.' Seeing the puzzled look
on Thomas's face, he added, 'Master Paulo, I mean. He's got leave
to quit the parish, he says, but he won't go. And Mistress Frogg is
making my life a purgatory!'

Thomas frowned. 'He won't go...?'

'Not yet,' Frogg replied. 'Mayhap not until he's seen you. Now
master sheriff has set him at liberty, he don't see any need to tell
me his plans. Only he's packed his cart ready for off, I know that

much. And it can't be soon enough for us – him and his servant, and his foul ape!'

Dillamore appeared with a brace of mugs in each hand. Nodding to Thomas, he muttered, 'There's rumours flying about thick and fast here. Mayhap you can set me straight on a few things?'

Thomas took the beer. 'Later,' he said resignedly. 'Seems I'm wanted elsewhere...' He turned to the constable. 'Mind if I down my mug first?'

Frogg nodded glumly.

A short time later Thomas entered the constable's small cottage, and began to understand, for the place was in disarray. The ape, it seemed, had been misbehaving with greater frequency, the longer the conjuror's party stayed here. Today it had run amok, pulling Mistress Frogg's things from shelves, tearing linen and upsetting a cauldron of pottage. Then it had run away, with Kit in pursuit. Mistress Frogg, reaching the end of her tether, had taken herself off to her sister's house and refused to return until the unwelcome guests had departed.

Thomas looked about, and seeing the look on Frogg's face, hid a smile. 'Where is he?' he asked.

For answer, the constable gestured through the window. In the fading light, Thomas looked out and saw that Paulo had set up his smaller tent in Frogg's garden, among the beehives. 'I thought you said he was ready to leave,' he said.

'Save for that little booth,' Frogg grunted. 'He been telling fortunes, here in my house – when he swore he wouldn't!'

'I'll speak with him,' Thomas said.

But when he entered the tent, it was empty. There was nothing but a little table and two stools. He came out again.

Frogg was standing by the back door. 'He was in there when I left,' he said, frowning. 'And Mistress Kirke with him.'

Thomas started. 'What would Jane Kirke want of him?'

Frogg's brow puckered. 'Same as the rest want,' he retorted. 'They go in to have their fortunes told, and come out all aglow – some straightening their skirts!'

He found Paulo on the edge of the green, watching his old horse cropping the short grass.

'My friend!' The conjuror's face lit up as he drew near. Seeing his expression the smile faded a little, though his eyes sparkled. There was an eagerness about him.

Without preamble Thomas repeated what Frogg had told him, causing Paulo some amusement. Rubbing his ample beard, he snickered.

'Master Giles has been a true friend,' he said. 'And he will be rewarded for his trouble before we leave – which will be at dawn tomorrow. But first, I would speak with you.'

'And I would speak with you too,' Thomas said. When the other raised an eyebrow, he summarised as best he could the events of the past three days. But he soon realised that little of what he had to say came as news to the showman.

'The death of this lord has filled the village with fear,' he said. 'And yet...' He trailed off, and gazed about at the huddle of cottages. 'Chaddleworth intrigues me,' he added. 'More than many places I have visited. So many secrets hidden away... and others yet to be uncovered.' He smiled. 'You know I read lips at times, and I have learned much, from those who come to have their fortunes read.'

'From what I hear, it's not only fortunes you deal out,' Thomas said wryly.

Paulo showed a flicker of impatience. ''Twas ever so,' he said. 'There is a class of folk, mostly women, who are dissatisfied with their lot. They look for more, hence I try to brighten their lives, using whatever skills I possess.' Smiling archly, he added, 'Some come to me for divination, then realise their needs are somewhat more immediate. Others make it plain the moment they are alone with me, what it is they truly want.'

Thomas nodded. 'As at Wantage?'

Paulo shrugged. 'What am I to do, my friend, when a fair lady opens her gown to me, and bids me do my will? What would you do?'

'I hope mistress Frogg was not one of them,' Thomas murmured.

Paulo's shout of laughter rang out across the green. Night was upon them now, and the windows of the Black Bear glowed. 'Even if she were – and she was not – I would not have abused Master Giles's hospitality so! What kind of man do you think me?' His eyes glinted. 'Mayhap despite all you have said, you still find it difficult to trust me.'

A moment passed.

'The letter you seek,' Paulo said. 'It will be found.'

'Well, then,' Thomas said, after a moment. 'That's the first time your conjuring has given me hope, rather than filled me with unease.' He raised an eyebrow. 'Since you're leaving tomorrow, will you take a farewell mug with me this night?'

But Paulo shook his head. 'I have much to do,' he said. 'And though I will be gone in the morning, it is not farewell. That is what I wished to speak of.'

He bent closer, and though there was no one nearby, lowered his voice. 'It was no ghost, that mistress Kirke saw.'

'This I know,' Thomas replied, but the other stayed him.

'Yet, there is an evil stalking these hills,' he said.

Thomas frowned. 'Our poisoner?'

'Ah yes, he...' Paulo looked uneasy. 'But there is another with him.' When Thomas merely stared, he went on, 'I cannot see the true picture, for it is very dark. The two are known to each other, and yet they are not.'

'I don't understand,' Thomas said.

'In truth, nor do I – but I fear that what your master has done, will be of little help.' Seeing Thomas's expression, he added impatiently, 'I told you, I have learned much from the people who have sat before me. And guessed a little more.'

'Then you know that Sir Robert had no choice but to offer those men the shelter they sought,' Thomas said.

Paulo nodded. 'But now they have become a target, *nein*?' Taking Thomas's silence for assent, he added: 'So you will try to snare him, when he comes.'

Thomas paused. 'I said once before, you are a dangerous fellow.'

Paulo broke into a mischievous grin. 'But that is where I may help, good Master Thomas,' he said. 'Seek me in Great Shefford, in two days, and we will devise a strategy.'

He clapped Thomas on the shoulder, strode briskly to his horse, caught up the reins and began leading it away.

* * *

His mind busy, Thomas went back to the Bear and called for a mug.

The crowd was thick now, as was the pungent blue cloud from cheap smoking-weed, tobacco mixed with shredded willow bark. Yet on all sides the talk was subdued, for recent events had brought a chill to the entire parish. Thomas withdrew inside himself, forming a resolve to leave soon rather than be drawn into discourse. For it had become plain to him that the plan to protect the five surviving jurymen, by housing them at Petbury, was doomed almost before it had started. Not only were the men conspicuous by their absence, he thought wryly, but the entire village seemed to know where they were.

He stood by the barrel while Dillamore poured him a mug, and took it gratefully.

'For my part,' the inn-keeper was saying, 'I'll be sad to see yon showman leave. He was a lively fellow, and good for business. And though she once mistrusted him, Ann will miss him, since he told her fortune so skilful well, she says. She's been back for more, and more again.'

Thomas was taking a pull from his beer, and almost choked on it.

'Have a care,' Dillamore said. 'That's first of the new barrel.' He watched Thomas recover, then banged him on the back when he coughed. 'What a time this has been, Thomas,' he sighed. 'Folk don't know which way to turn...' He frowned. 'You've kept a few things close to your chest, I warrant.'

Thomas let out a breath. 'I was ordered to hold my peace,' he muttered weakly.

Dillamore shrugged, and turned to acknowledge a call for three more mugs. Taking them from the pegs, he added, 'We've a new guest lodging above, in the room the conjuror had. Gentleman, too – though one who's mighty unwilling to dip into his purse.'

Thomas took another drink and listened.

'Proud of himself, too,' the inn-keeper went on, 'and a little too sharp-tongued for my liking. He says he's the Queen's mapmaker.'

Thomas swallowed, narrowly avoiding another bout of near-choking.

17

On the following morning, the Sabbath, Thomas rode out of the Petbury gates on the gelding borrowed from the stable, heading south onto the Hungerford Road.

It was a fair day, with a strong wind blowing from the south-west – too windy for flying falcons, which gave him respite from his normal duties. On the ride to Great Shefford, he could now turn over the matters which had kept him awake for much of the night. This, he thought ruefully, on a night when Nell had come to the cottage. She had been so tired, however, she had fallen asleep the moment she got into his bed and had snored until dawn.

When he ordered his thoughts, he found that first among them was the reappearance of the mapmaker. Casual questioning of Hugh Dillamore had revealed that Mead was lodging alone, and whatever had happened to Grace Mead (if indeed, that were truly her name) was dark to him. The man appeared still to be engaged in his work; folk had seen him south of the village, bent over his wondrous dioptra. To all enquiries he answered the same, with some irritation: he was mapping the Lambourn valley, working his way south-east to Newbury.

As he rode, keeping a leisurely pace, Thomas's thoughts turned to Paulo Schweiz. Dillamore had told him that the conjuror intended to give another tent show soon, in Great Shefford, drawing crowds from the villages in the lower valley before moving on. Thomas had affected surprise at the news. He recalled that Paulo would leave Chaddleworth at dawn today, hence he would likely be at the village already. He frowned to himself: the man's ruminations on the identity of the poisoner, let alone of the murderer of Sir John Mountford, were fresh in his mind, yet they had told him little. Indeed, they merely added to what Paulo always referred to as 'the puzzle'.

Mountford's funeral was being held today – a private affair, with burial in the family's own vault. None of the other landowners, not even Sir Robert, were invited. Thomas's thoughts drifted to Lady Sarah, standing like a pale wand before his master, but two days ago. Despite the lady's good reputation, he could not let go the notion that she must have known something of the activities of the Devil's Jury. He almost smiled to himself: had his own master ever been involved in such dealings, the thought that Lady Margaret might not learn of it was laughable.

He sighed, and faced another matter. In the pocket of his jerkin was a letter bearing Sir Robert's seal, requesting that the men holding Will Saltmarsh permit his servant Thomas Finbow to question the prisoner about possible thefts from Petbury manor. Richard Ward was making arrangements to move Saltmarsh to Reading, which would be done soon – perhaps even later today. Not only would Thomas have little time, but as yet he had not formed any idea of how to proceed.

* * *

The village was quiet, most of its inhabitants crammed within the confines of St Mary's Church. Thomas rode on southwards and crossed the Lambourn by the old bridge, passing Elizabeth Rawlings' house where he had been almost a week ago. At the bounds of the village, he stopped before the only empty barn he knew of on this side of the river. As he drew rein a tall man, russet-bearded like himself, wearing old Spanish breeches and a heavy jerkin, got up from a tree-stump and challenged him. Unhurriedly Thomas dismounted, stated his business and proffered the paper.

The fellow frowned and stared at it long and hard, until by the way his eyes remained fixed on one spot, Thomas realised he could not read.

'As you see,' he said with an easy smile, 'it bears my master's seal.'

The man looked up. 'I'm to admit no one. Orders of the high sheriff.'

Thomas hesitated. 'Master Ward himself was a guest of my master when the order was signed. As you see, it bears his name also.'

The man reddened and peered again at the paper. ''Tis not his seal,' he objected.

'Yet he gives permission – there.' Thomas pointed to a line of his master's stout handwriting and waited. In the distance, the bell of St Mary's began tolling for the end of morning service.

'I see it,' the guard retorted, scowling. He looked up, clearly uncertain what to do, and Thomas saw his chance.

'My master will be most gratified, if I learn aught of the fine plate this rogue likely stole from our manor,' he said. 'He will likely commend you to his good friend the sheriff – mayhap even offer some reward.'

It was enough. After looking hard at Thomas for a moment,

the fellow handed back the letter, moved the few steps towards the door of the barn and lifted the heavy beam from its rest.

'I'll grant you a half hour with him,' he announced, 'But I must be present.'

'I am to question him alone,' Thomas said. 'Some of the items stolen were royal gifts, precious to my master – hence, the likely size of the reward...'

The man swallowed. 'Very well. But if I hear voices raised, or aught that troubles me, I'll be in like a terrier.'

The door swung open, and Thomas stepped into the gloom within. He paused, letting his eyes grow accustomed to the dimness. The door was left ajar behind him, but at once there came a shuffling from nearby, and the unmistakeable clank of a chain.

'Finbow...?'

He swung his head, and saw Will Saltmarsh seated against the wall. His arms and legs were chained together.

'Which of us now has grown careless?' Thomas asked, after a moment. 'To let himself be taken prisoner by a couple of Berkshire bailiffs?'

Saltmarsh gave a snort. 'Come to scoff, have ye?'

Thomas moved towards him. Since there was nothing that would serve as a seat, he eased himself down onto the dusty floor. A quick glance round told him that the barn was all but empty. 'I thought you knew me better,' he said.

There was an ugly bruise on Saltmarsh's cheek, and a swelling about the mouth. 'Then why are you come?' he demanded.

Thomas cocked an ear towards the door. 'We must speak low,' he murmured. 'As far as that one knows—' he jerked his thumb towards the door '—I'm here to question you at my master's bidding, about thefts from the manor—'

'I stole nothing from there!' Saltmarsh hissed. 'Nor from any other house. I had naught in my pack when those whoreson rascals waylaid me, save what was freely given to me in charity—'

'Soft.' Thomas glanced towards the door.

Saltmarsh gave an exasperated sigh, but managed to keep his voice down. 'I swear to you, Finbow, I've not stolen from your master, nor any other.'

'Not even loaves from the bakehouse?' Thomas persisted.

'Not even a crust!' Saltmarsh's eyes blazed at him in the gloom. After returning his gaze, Thomas nodded.

'I believe you. But listen now, for it matters not. The sheriff wants a felon, tried and convicted for the murder of Sir John Mountford. And he cares not who it be.'

There was silence, in which he heard Saltmarsh swallow. 'Murder... You think I would do that?'

At once Thomas shook his head. 'I do not. But as I've said, it matters not. There have been deaths hereabout, and the sheriff wishes to put a speedy end to it. He means to sweat you in Reading gaol, until you confess to whatever he wants.'

Saltmarsh drew a deep breath, and at last Thomas saw fear in his eyes.

'Then I'm finished,' he muttered. 'No man can last long at the hands of the Scavenger's daughter... or even a torch, cunningly applied.' He swallowed again. 'And one who has lived as I have of late will likely weaken swifter than most...'

Thomas fixed him with a gaze. 'Swear to me now, that you did not enter Poughley Manor at any time,' he demanded.

'I swear!' Saltmarsh spat. 'I have said already, I took nothing from anywhere!'

Thomas looked away, realising that here was still another

puzzle: if Saltmarsh were not responsible for the recent thefts, then who was?

'Well,' he said finally. 'Then we must find a way to free you.'

Saltmarsh was silent, but in the echoing emptiness of the barn Thomas could hear his rapid breathing. He looked around, but there was neither window nor weak point in the wall, nor any other egress that he could see. Moreover, the locked chains that held the prisoner were strong, and unbreakable for anyone save a blacksmith.

'When will they take me?' Saltmarsh asked suddenly.

Thomas looked away. 'Soon… Today or tomorrow…'

The other drew breath. 'If a couple of stout fellows like you could wait on the road, and—'

'No.' Thomas shook his head. 'I'm too well-known hereabouts. I would be hunted down, and likely taken along with you.' He frowned. 'I will do what I can, yet I know not what.'

Saltmarsh sniffed and began to lift his hand to his nose, before the weight of the chain told. Helplessly, he sat back against the wall.

'It seems I'm in your hands,' he said in a tired voice.

'Have they fed you?'

Saltmarsh nodded towards a bowl nearby. 'I have water.'

Thomas stood up, dusting off his breeches. 'If yon sentry asks, you told me where you hid some plate you took from Petbury. He'll want to know, so that he may claim his reward.' A thought struck him. 'I wonder how deep is his greed?'

But Saltmarsh shook his head. 'He would not take such a risk as to let me go. His place is likely worth more to him.'

'I see you still have the boots,' Thomas observed, glancing at them.

Saltmarsh managed a grim smile. 'They serve well enough.'

He watched as Thomas stepped away and turned towards the door, then unexpectedly said, 'I do thank you, pikeman.'

'I've done naught,' Thomas replied. 'At least, not yet.'

He left the barn, and with a nod to the turnkey outside, went to mount the gelding which stood patiently at the roadside. Having dropped the door-beam back in place, the big man turned around quickly, but Thomas had mounted swiftly and ridden away without a word.

If luck had deserted Will Saltmarsh that windy Sunday, it seemed it had not quite deserted Thomas. For as he rode through the village, now busy with folk coming from church, he saw a familiar cart ambling towards him, drawn by an old sway-backed horse. Two figures sat behind the reins, and as he slowed, one of them raised a hand in greeting.

He stood beside Paulo in an open field east of the village. In the distance, men in shepherd's capes tended their flocks. Kit was already pulling the cart's cover off, busying himself with its contents. The ape sat on the step, watching.

Having summarised his predicament, Thomas waited while Paulo, scratching furiously at his beard, absorbed the information. Finally, a smile began to form.

'My friend,' the showman said. 'Now you set me a fine puzzle! If I can solve it, will it repay you for what you did, when I sat in the stocks that day in the square?'

Thomas gripped his shoulder. 'It would repay me ten times over.'

Paulo beamed. 'Then *noli timere*, master hawksman – for it will be done!'

* * *

That afternoon, with much to think over, Thomas went to the mews to look at the tercel Brutus, now recovered from his ailment. Seeing the bird was frisky, he hooded him and took him out for exercise. But as he headed for the uphill path, there came a call from the direction of the house. To his surprise, Eleanor was hurrying towards him, holding her skirts above the long grass.

'Last time I walked up here, I got half a dozen ticks for my pains,' she muttered, a little out of breath. 'You should borrow a scythe and mow the slope.'

He paused and smiled, prompting a little smile from her in return. His was prompted by her striking resemblance, as each year went by, to her mother; hers by the recognition that this was her oldest memory of him, unchanged and undimmed: standing in the open with a hooded bird on the arm, stroking its tail feathers and watching.

'Has your mistress set you free for the afternoon?' he enquired. 'The day is fair, and I did not intend to walk far.'

She nodded. 'Lady Margaret is taking a Sunday nap. So I have leave to visit my father, who seems to be everywhere but at his work these days.'

Thomas made a wry face. 'Not of his choosing.'

Eleanor took his arm. 'You may tell me of it while we walk.'

With a glow of pride to be in the company of his fair daughter, he led the way.

They talked of the recent events, which had been enough to drive thoughts of the missing letter from their minds – that is until Paulo had reminded Thomas of it with another of his jarring predictions. Now he let the matter rest, for he was eager to hear Eleanor talk. Yet after a while she grew silent, saying at last, 'I have wanted to speak with you, about Ned Hawes.'

He said nothing.

'He is honest and true,' she said. 'And kind, if a little ungainly...' she trailed off. 'There are maids in Chaddleworth who dream of getting him to the altar.'

Seeing her father's eyes upon her, she flushed and looked away. With an easy gesture Thomas drew the hood off Brutus, raised his arm and let the tercel take flight. The two of them watched as he climbed.

'Is it not too windy?' Eleanor asked.

'It has dropped since morning,' he answered. 'But I'll keep him close, and call him down ere long.' He paused. 'You were talking of Ned – or rather, singing his praises.'

She bit her lip. 'I do not love him, father.'

He was silent. 'I guessed as much.'

She started. 'But I thought it was your hope that he and I would...'

'My hope is that you be happy,' he broke in. 'If not with Ned, then with another.'

She drew breath suddenly, and gave a sigh. 'Father...'

He folded his arms about her. When they parted she looked up and smiled anew, as if a weight had lifted from her shoulders.

'I will be a sister to Ned, always. But I cannot be more.'

He nodded. 'Do you wish me to speak with him?'

She considered. 'Do you not recall what my mother would say? Never ask another to do your dirty work.'

He smiled. 'True enough.'

She had grown serious again. 'Do you not know how much Nell loves you?' she asked.

He looked away. After a while she took his arm, and walked a few steps. When he looked down at her, she was smiling again. All had been said.

Then glancing up at the soaring tercel, Thomas was

suddenly alert. Eleanor followed his gaze, shielding her eyes. 'He sees something.'

He nodded and began to walk forward briskly. Hurrying to keep up, Eleanor trotted behind, lifting her skirts. 'He does not stoop,' she called, peering at the hovering bird. On the breeze came the distant tinkling of the falcon's bells.

'I like it not,' Thomas said. He strode uphill to the Ridgeway, not a hundred yards from where he had met with Will Saltmarsh a week ago and given him his boots. Gazing eastwards along the pathway towards the Wantage Road, he shaded his eyes and peered.

There was a horse, standing still, with no rider. And more, he recognised it: the mapmaker's dun-coloured nag.

He began to run.

'Father!' Eleanor called from behind. 'What is it?'

He did not answer, for he had seen the pale shape in the grass with Brutus hanging uncertainly above it. As Eleanor ran, she saw him drop to his knee.

She came up, panting, to find him cradling the head of a dark-haired young woman in a loose gown who was lying by the path, her breast rising and falling rapidly. Sweat ran down her face. Nearby, a wide-brimmed hat lay on the sward.

Eleanor halted, mouth wide in surprise, even as Grace Mead opened her eyes and saw Thomas.

She frowned before recognition dawned. 'You're the falconer...' She closed her eyes, her face taut with pain, and her hands went to her abdomen.

'My baby,' she muttered. 'I fear for my baby...'

18

They managed to lift her onto the horse, and though at first she begged them not to, soon she grew silent and submitted to their care. Thomas, with the hooded Brutus on one arm, led the nag downhill as slowly as he could while Eleanor walked alongside, ready to support Grace should she fall. In a short time they had reached his cottage, lifted her down gently and taken her inside. There Eleanor hurried to make up a pallet while Thomas unsaddled the horse. When he returned, Grace was lying on the makeshift bed, her head propped up on a bolster with Eleanor kneeling beside her. She turned quickly as Thomas came in, closing the door behind him.

'The baby is unharmed – she felt it move!'

He drew up a stool and sat beside them.

'You should not be riding at such a time, Mistress Mead,' he murmured. 'Especially not alone...'

Grace shook her head slightly. 'There has been no difficulty until today... It was but a faint.' She met his eyes. 'Yet I thank you heartily.'

'Where is Master Mead?' he asked, somewhat abruptly. 'I hear he's been lodging alone, at the inn in Chaddleworth.'

An agitated look crossed her delicate face. 'I came to seek him.' Seeing Thomas's eyes upon her, she gave a little sigh. 'You know little of us, Master.'

Thomas opened his mouth, but Eleanor stayed him. 'She needs rest. I will go to the house and make her a posset—'

But Grace put a hand upon her arm. 'You are kind, and yet I cannot stay here. I must find my-my father.' The last word came so awkwardly, she dropped her eyes at once.

'Is he truly your father?' Thomas asked quietly. 'Or the father of your child?'

Eleanor gasped. 'What can you mean—?'

'Please.' Grace was shaking her head. She tried to move, and instinctively Eleanor bent to help her. Taking a few breaths, the young woman sat upright, then looked Thomas in the eye.

'He is neither,' she said.

He waited until she continued, 'He is my father's brother, my uncle, who makes maps for the defence of the realm.' She hesitated. 'Yet, that's not why he is here.'

Still Thomas waited, whereupon Eleanor spoke up with disapproval. 'Will you play the inquisitor now? She needs care – she is near to her lying-in time.'

'It is but a little over five months,' Grace said, turning to Eleanor. 'I did not think to take to a bed yet.' She looked at Thomas. 'If you wish to help me...'

'I do,' he said at once. 'Yet I would like to know who it is I am helping, and what she and her uncle are doing here.'

'Grace is my name,' she answered. 'And it was Mead, before I married.'

'Where is your husband?'

She hesitated. 'In hiding,' she answered. 'As I was hereabouts, until the family took fright after the death of Sir John Mountford, and begged me to leave...' Levelling her gaze at Thomas, she added, 'Can you not guess now, why I am come to this pass? Why I roam the Downs like a fugitive...' She dropped her eyes. 'I *am* a fugitive.'

Eleanor did not understand, but her father was nodding. 'You came to the Downlands to hide away during your confinement,' he said. 'So that when your child was born, you would not have to present it for baptism at a parish church.'

Grace said nothing. Nor did she react when Thomas added, 'Your uncle was taking you from house to house, asking folk of your faith to take you in.' He wore a wry look. 'Only nowadays, even the staunchest Catholics are afraid to run such risks, are they not? Mayhap they remember what happened to Master Yate.'

Eleanor drew a breath. Though she was but a child at that time, she knew as well as anyone of the capture of the Jesuit Edmund Campion at Lyford Grange in the north of the county, more than a decade back. Yate, whose mother had lived recklessly in the house with a group including ex-Brigittine nuns and even priests, was jailed and tormented.

Grace swallowed, biting back tears. 'Since you know so much, why do you ask me?' she asked, somewhat bitterly.

'See now, I care not what is your religion,' Thomas told her. 'Nor do I like the way your uncle left you so readily, without waiting to see you safely housed.' After a moment, he added, 'You may stay here tonight. I'll go to Master Mead and tell him what's happened.'

Eleanor was gazing at Grace. 'How could the family who were sheltering you, cast you out at such a time?' she asked.

'Your father has guessed aright,' Grace answered, after a pause. 'Their memories are long, and since Mountford's murder, none feel safe. They could pay dearly for aiding me.' She bit her lip. 'I do not even know where my husband is... He fled when a congregation hearing mass was raided. Now he too moves from place to place, like a hunted rogue.'

Getting to her feet, Eleanor faced her father. 'We must find a refuge for her.'

He raised an eyebrow. 'If her uncle, who knows the names of the families on whom he may call, cannot find one to take her, then how may we?'

But he grew wary, for Eleanor was wearing her stubborn face. 'Sir Robert gives shelter in his own stables, to a few cowards who lied on a jury and now fear for their necks!' she cried. 'Cannot one young woman be given a place in which to bear her child in peace?'

He glanced at Grace, who was watching the two of them. 'I have said I will seek out her uncle...' he began.

'And if he cannot help?' his daughter snapped. She lowered her eyes, realising how hot she had grown in her anger.

'Eleanor!' Thomas's tone was one of exasperation. 'Think on it. I cannot look after a woman who is bearing a child...'

'No, you cannot.' They turned to Grace, surprised to see her smiling. To Eleanor she said, 'If you will help me up, I believe I can stand readily enough.'

Eleanor bent to assist her, but she needed little support. Soon she stood up, fixing Thomas with a look of respect.

'I know you will do what you can,' she said.

* * *

At nightfall Thomas went to the kitchen door and asked for Nell. When she came out to him, he made his explanation as quickly as he could.

'I thought, if you should come by the cottage and find her there...' he ended weakly.

Nell looked concerned. 'What will you do?' she asked.

He shrugged. 'Get her away as soon as I can.'

For a moment she regarded him, then broke into a smile. 'By the Lord, Thomas...' She shook her head. 'Most folk who take a walk upon the Downs, manage to come back alone.'

He was about to speak, but she leaned forward and planted a kiss upon his mouth. 'When the cottage is empty again, send word,' she said, and was gone.

He walked into Chaddleworth soon afterwards and entered the Black Bear. There were few drinkers present and no sign of Hugh Dillamore, which suited him well enough. Without preamble he climbed the stairs to the upper storey and knocked on the door of the chamber that Paulo Schweiz had once occupied. There was no answer. He knocked again and lifted the latch.

The room was empty. More, there were no packs, nor clothes, nor other sign of occupancy. Christopher Mead was gone.

He came downstairs, to see Ann Dillamore watching him from beside the barrels. 'If you seek the mapmaker, he's forsaken us,' she said as he drew near. 'He only stopped for a night.' She jerked her head towards the nearest keg. 'Time for a mug, have ye?'

He nodded, thinking on what to do. As she worked the spigot she began to talk in her easy fashion, caring little whether he listened or not.

'If 'tis other news you seek, we've plenty. Jane Kirke lost her place at Poughley now Sir John's dead – Lady Sarah will keep to her own now, I guess. Agnes Gee has barred her door again – accuses folk of trying to get money off her. The conjuror's gone... Oh, and Ned was here. Him and that carpenter from Shefford.'

'John Flowers.' Thomas took the filled mug from her.

Ann nodded. 'Seems he's about finished rebuilding the barn down at Boxwell, which means Fuller be out of work again...' She sighed. 'Either way he'll be soused tonight, and trying to skip off without paying the reckoning.'

Thomas took a drink. 'You can deal with Ambrose. There isn't a man in the village you couldn't better.'

She snorted, but was not displeased. 'See now: how are your runagates faring, in the hayloft?'

He swallowed, tried to look puzzled, then gave up. 'I've seen naught of them. I suppose they're well enough.'

Ann smiled at him. 'What of the cook? Yon carrot-head?'

He made a wry face. 'God's heart, Ann, do you seek to tie me in knots?'

'From what I heard, 'tis she done the tying. Only she can't tie the knot that matters, is't not so?' His look of helplessness prompted her to give a yelp of laughter.

'Thomas,' Ann muttered, and wiped her eye with a corner of her apron. 'Why not wed her and be done with it?'

He finished his beer and left the inn. Dusk was falling. Three or four village men walked past, giving him good-night. He wandered to the edge of the green, where he had stood beneath a tree with Will Saltmarsh's poniard at his back, and gazed about. Nearby Paulo had thrilled an audience with his *Mundus Peregrinus*. A large square of grass was still yellowed where the tent had stood.

Two matters weighed most urgently upon him: one was the future of Will Saltmarsh, and whether Paulo would be true to his promise and find a way to help him. The other was a deal closer to home: what was he to do with Grace?

This time he could not tell Sir Robert. His master was preoccupied with the legacy of the Devil's Jury, and as far as Thomas knew, wondering how to seek out the man who had murdered the others. More, he would not be a party to concealing a Catholic woman from the authorities, merely that she might preserve her child from a Protestant baptism – at which, a notion struck him.

There was one place that might provide Grace with a refuge, even if only temporary: Poughley Manor. Though whether he should go there without his master's leave, and ask such a weighty thing of Lady Sarah, troubled him. Still, it seemed the best course; what worse could she do than simply refuse?

He took a lungful of sweet air, hearing a nightjar call in the distance, and set out on his homeward walk.

A half hour later he dropped by the yard at Petbury and found a young stable-lad seated on a stump beside the doors. The boy scrambled to his feet as Thomas approached, peering at him through the gloom.

'Falconer, you near frit me to death!'

'Rest easy, Peter...' Thomas glanced about. 'Are you the only one keeps watch?'

Peter drew himself to his full height. 'I can wield a cudgel,' he said.

Thomas looked to the hayloft above. 'Have any of them been outside this night?'

The boy snickered. 'Only to piss, and I'll wager they'll be doing a deal more of that. Would you believe it? Some kind friend sent 'em a barrel of ale!'

Thomas made as if to go, then stopped dead.

'When?' he demanded, so sharply that Peter stepped back.

'Not long since,' the boy answered, then fell back as Thomas barged past him, shoving the doors open.

His boots on the ladder caused a stirring from above. There were muffled voices, and the scramble of feet. As his head emerged above the floor of the dimly lit hayloft, a figure loomed over him, arm raised.

'Hold!' he called out. 'It's Thomas Finbow.'

There came an outburst of relief. Peering upwards he saw the face of Robert Clements the tanner, tense with anxiety. The man dropped the billet he had wielded, leaned down and offered Thomas a hand. Soon he had clambered onto the dusty floor, and stood amongst them.

Being poorly ventilated, the loft was warm and fetid, and stank of hay and sweat. Close to the walls, some crouching, others seated on their crude straw pallets, the sullen survivors of the Devil's Jury regarded him with little show of friendship.

'I ask your pardon,' Clements muttered. 'We knew not who—'

'The ale,' Thomas snapped. 'Have you touched it?'

There was a silence.

'Where is it?' he asked, looking at each man in turn. 'Did you not think on what happened to the others?'

Clements gaped at him. 'But it came from Dillamore,' he said. 'He wouldn't...' He swallowed, and swung round to face the others.

'How do you know it came from the Bear?' Thomas demanded. 'I was there tonight, and mistress Ann said naught about it.'

'Oh, sweet Jesus...' There came an anguished cry from the corner. The ageing John Palmer was sitting on his bed, holding a leather mug before him and staring at it. As Thomas looked, he turned it upside down to show it was empty.

Francis Ball was on his feet. 'John was thirsty,' he began. 'We cracked the keg and gave him first pull...' He held up his own mug. 'I took but a mouthful...'

'Who else?' Thomas demanded, looking round. The others

were on their feet too, and all had mugs. Following their gaze, Thomas saw the barrel, wedged against the eaves. 'Who else has drunk?' he repeated. 'And how much? Quickly now, else it's likely you're all dead men!'

Fear showed stark on their faces. 'We drew our mugs a little before you come,' Thomas Friar muttered. 'I barely touched mine...' He looked aghast at Palmer.

'Poisoned...?' It was John Kydd who sprang forward in his stockinged feet, trembling.

'Downstairs, quick!' Thomas shoved him towards the ladder-head, then turned to the others. 'Get outside and make your-selves retch. Use a feather, your fingers, anything! Spew all you have, until you can vent no more! It's likely you have only drunk enough to make you ill – though mistake not, you will feel like living carcasses for a while. Move!'

They needed no further prompting. In a very few minutes four men had almost leaped down the ladder into the stable, falling over each other to be first, startling the horses in their stalls. Peter appeared in alarm, but the jurymen thrust him aside and crowded through the door. There in the yard, without cere-mony, they set about ridding themselves of the contents of their stomachs. An unpleasant chorus of coughing, hawking, retching and spluttering began, and soon the cobbles were spattered with vomit.

But Thomas remained in the hayloft, crouching beside the still-seated figure of the taciturn shepherd John Palmer, who was breathing rapidly. Staring wide-eyed, the old man swallowed. ''Tis plain yon ghost has took his vengeance on me, too.' He let out a sob, gazed at the empty mug which was still in his hand, then turned a haggard face towards Thomas. 'Poison... Is that what did for the rest?'

Thomas barely nodded.

Palmer was shaking, and Thomas could only watch helplessly as the wolfsbane did its work. But he drew a sharp breath when the other gave a cry and clutched at his chest. 'Good Lord, forgive me,' he whispered, and fell back onto his pallet. The mug dropped from his grasp and rolled away.

Thomas stared as John Palmer's last breath rattled in his throat, and his eyes closed. Then, he thought he understood. It was as if the old man's body had taken charge, not prepared to wait for a slow death filled with agony and indignity. The shock had made his heart stop.

He came out into the yard, to find a near farcical scene. Grooms and even house servants had appeared, to stand in amazement at the sight of four men gasping and retching, with many a muttered oath in between. Finally the last of them gave up and sank onto the cobbles beside the others, holding his stomach.

'Best fetch them salted water to drink,' Thomas said to James the head groom, who had arrived holding a torch.

James stared. 'What the devil's afoot here?'

Thomas looked past him to see the stooped figure of Martin in his cloak, hobbling into the yard with a frown on his face.

'I'll tell you,' he answered in a tired voice. 'But for now, let none touch that barrel in the hayloft.'

But as he moved away, James muttered in his ear, 'When you do, mayhap you can also tell me whose old dun-coloured nag that be, that has appeared in my stable since this afternoon.'

Thomas ignored him and went to face Martin.

19

Sir Robert was angry.

Instead of withdrawing to his private chamber and ordering Thomas to wait upon him there, he stood before the fire in the Great Hall while the remains of supper were cleared from the table. Lady Margaret sat there also. Martin the steward, having finally dismissed the servants, stood aside while Thomas told his tale. When he had finished, his master exploded.

'The fools! It would serve them aright, had they all drunk their fill and died where they lay! Save that it would reflect ill on Petbury...' He faced Martin. 'It seems this murderer may go where he pleases, even in my stables! Now he strikes another from his list!'

Martin coughed. 'Sir, had the watch been better kept—' here he scowled at Thomas '—rather than left to a mere boy armed with a stick, the delivery of a barrel of ale on a Sunday evening might have occasioned more attention.'

Sir Robert grunted. 'Well, see the watch strengthened at once, until I order otherwise.' He frowned at Thomas. 'Where were you, this night?'

Thomas hesitated, and was relieved when Lady Margaret spoke.

'It will profit us not to berate the servants, nor to tear ourselves with remorse, sir,' she murmured. 'For John Palmer, it is too late. For the other men, we must find a more secure refuge.'

But Sir Robert began pacing about impatiently. 'Who delivered the barrel?' he demanded. 'Do we not even know that?'

Martin looked embarrassed. 'The stable-lad says a man with a cart,' he answered. 'He did not know him, nor did he think to question his tale that the landlord of the Black Bear had sent the men a gift to cheer them. And since it was growing dark, he marked little of the fellow's appearance...'

He turned as the door opened and a serving-man entered. The fellow bowed, delivered his message quickly and went out. Martin turned to his master. 'Sir Robert, it seems that one of the men in the stables begs an audience with you.'

Sir Robert gestured vaguely. 'Indeed? Then let him come in.'

All eyes turned as Francis Ball entered, approached the table and bowed nervously. Being the boldest, he had clearly been elected spokesman. As indeed, it had lately been remembered, he had once been the foreman of the Devil's Jury.

'Well?' Sir Robert fixed the man with a hard look.

'Sir...' Ball fumbled for the words, his face pale in the candle-light. 'We – my fellows and I... The matter is, we cannot stay here.'

'God's heart, man, you think I don't know that?' Sir Robert returned. 'Even now we are debating the matter.' But seeing Ball's agitation, he bade him continue.

'I beg you, sir, not to deem us ungrateful,' the man said. 'You took us in when another, who owed us much, would not. You've likely saved our lives – or most of them...' He swallowed, glanced at Thomas, and added, 'We will not trouble you to seek further shelter for us. We have conferred, and are resolved: we will leave Petbury tonight and scatter, each man taking his chances where he may. We are certain it is the only solution.'

There was a short silence, before Martin's irate voice broke it. 'Do you dare to impugn Sir Robert's reputation, and cast doubt upon the safety of this manor?' he demanded. 'He has already done more than any nobleman would, to save your miserable necks—'

'Master steward,' Sir Robert cut him short. 'You made your feelings towards those men plain when the matter was first aired. Pray hold your peace.'

Martin drew breath and lowered his gaze, whereupon Sir Robert faced Francis Ball again. 'You are free to leave, of course,' he said coolly. 'Yet you've seen how resourceful is this avenger, who it seems will not rest until he has taken the lives of every last one of you. Where do you think to go, where you might be safe?'

Ball's mouth was dry. He coughed, wet his lips and answered, 'Sir, I know not. Yet if we scatter, we at least make his task harder. He cannot be everywhere.'

Though neither Sir Robert nor his servants sought to dispute that, their silence seemed to suggest that if the avenger of Richard Walden could not be everywhere, so far he had seemingly managed to be in all the places that mattered.

Thomas made a sound in his throat, whereupon his master looked round. 'Well?'

'I am minded of our discourse yesterday, sir...' he began, but Sir Robert stayed him.

'So am I,' he said. When Martin looked up, crestfallen that he had not been a party to this discourse, Sir Robert said, 'Master steward, indulge me a while.'

Martin threw Thomas a look, and waited.

'Well, now...' Sir Robert eyed Ball. 'Do you not believe that it would be better to waylay this murderer at his next attempt, and thus see him caught and hanged?'

Ball stared. 'Sir, how might that be...?' He gulped as realisation dawned. 'You mean to use us as bait?'

Sir Robert's silence was answer enough, and now a smile appeared on Martin's face. 'A most cunning notion, sir,' he murmured.

Ball was controlling himself with difficulty. 'But... Sir Robert, might I beg leave to say that this villain is too clever to be caught? When each of his victims perished, by poison or other desperate means, he was either nowhere near – or rather, he made his escape with ease. Small wonder that gullible folk swear they have seen Walden's ghost...'

'Enough!' Martin bent his gaze upon the man. 'Remember your place.'

'Thank you, master steward,' Sir Robert said. Whereupon there was a stir from Lady Margaret, who had been listening calmly.

'What manner of trap had you in mind, sir?' she enquired.

Her husband hesitated. 'I have thought upon it a little, yet not come to any firm decision,' he admitted.

His wife's gaze strayed towards Thomas. There was a brief silence, broken by the falconer.

'I have a notion, my lady,' he said.

* * *

Monday morning dawned warm and sunny, with larks calling from the Downs as Thomas stumbled from his sleeping-loft, looking for his boots. A low voice made him start.

'I have made up the fire. The porridge will soon be hot.'

Grace was sitting by the chimney. Embarrassed, Thomas tucked his shirt into his breeches.

'You forgot I was here,' she murmured.

He managed a smile. 'My helper, Ned, will likely come by soon,' he said. 'Though he has a loose tongue at times, he has my trust...'

She nodded. 'Please, tell him what you will.'

He went outside to make water. Grace had been asleep on the pallet Eleanor had made when he returned late to the cottage, and as yet did not know that her uncle was gone. What was to be done now, Thomas had little idea. He had even thought of placing the matter before Sir Robert last night, had there not been more than enough to concern his master already.

One thing had been decided upon, which both alarmed Thomas and excited him: the surviving four members of the Devils' Jury were to be taken away this night, and housed in the disused barn at Great Shefford, which the village constable as well as the sheriff's men sometimes used as a lock-up. The prisoner Saltmarsh, it was assumed, had been moved by now. And though none would be told directly of the men's removal, enough folk would be permitted to learn of it, for the matter to leak out. What would also become known, was that the men were being held only briefly for their own protection, before being separated – hence, the avenger of Richard Walden would have one further chance to do his worst. The hope was that he would not be able to resist the prize.

Martin, at first, had argued against the location, though relieved that the source of danger would at least be removed from Petbury. Francis Ball was aghast at the scheme, yet bowed at last to Sir Robert's wishes. Thomas had his own fears about using the barn, but since his talk with Saltmarsh, and the lack of opportunity to report what transpired to Sir Robert, he held his peace, particularly when Lady Margaret had raised a somewhat ticklish question.

'Might I ask, sir,' she had enquired of her husband, after a benumbed Francis Ball had left the Hall, 'why you did not discuss this small matter of setting a trap with the high sheriff when he was last here?'

Sir Robert had made no reply. But from the glances which flew thick and fast between him, his falconer and his steward, Lady Margaret began to understand.

'I hope you know what you do,' she had said at last.

That night in his bed, when he had turned the matter about, Thomas had begun to think that hope was all they had: that, and the services he was about to call upon in secret, of his friend Paulo Schweiz. And though much later, both Paulo and Thomas were uncertain who had arrived first at the plan that would unfold, they were in no doubt of the boldness of the measure, nor its ingenuity. What they chose not to dwell upon was its aspect of desperation.

Now, having dashed water on his face from a pail, Thomas went back indoors, and sat at his table to take breakfast with Grace. That was how Ned Hawes found them a while later when he let himself into the cottage, and made both of them laugh at the way his mouth fell open.

* * *

Ned having tended the eyasses, he and Thomas walked upon the Downs with two of the sisters, and let the birds fly where they would. Ned was unusually silent, Thomas thought. Likely the boy was turning the momentous events of the last few days over in his own fashion.

'By the Lord, Thomas,' he said finally. 'What a tale we are caught up in.'

'I have told you all there is,' Thomas said. 'I only ask that you keep silent about, well...'

'About everything, I reckon,' Ned finished. He shook his head, then voiced the concern that was in Thomas's thoughts. 'What will you do with Mistress Mead?'

'She isn't Mistress Mead,' he answered absently, before a thought struck him.

'Have you heard aught of the mapmaker?' he asked.

Ned shook his head. 'Gone from the village, none knows where. John Flowers came in the Bear for a mug, said he saw him Saturday, down near East Garston.' He frowned. 'How could he abandon her... a fair lady like that?'

'He may be looking for her,' Thomas said.

Ned brightened. 'We could take her to the Bear – she could lodge there. Dillamore wouldn't kick her out...' His face clouded. 'But likely, Ann would.'

They walked for a while in silence, before calling the birds down and making ready to return to Petbury. On the way back neither spoke until the chimneys came into view.

'I'll go to the house after my work today,' Ned said then, 'and not budge until Eleanor comes to speak with me.'

Thomas looked away. But when he next turned to Ned, he found the boy's eyes upon him. 'Say naught, Thomas,' he said quietly. 'Let me fool myself for just a day longer, that she will have me.'

Thomas felt Thalia stir on the gauntlet, and stroked her wing feathers as he walked ahead.

* * *

Soon after dark, the first part of the plan was put into action.

The four fugitives, carrying their meagre possessions, left the shelter of the stables and clambered quickly inside the covered cart which had been backed up to the doors. No lights burned in the yard, and only James the groom was there to see them off. The whip cracked, the vehicle lumbered over the cobbles and out into the paddock. In the driver's seat was Thomas the falconer. That in itself would cause no particular surprise, for no one else had the eyesight for a drive of more than two miles in the dark. The reasons for such a journey, however, would be left to folk's imagination.

Sir Robert's servants had not been idle. While the frightened men in the hayloft kept themselves hidden, the body of John Palmer had been removed. Meanwhile a groom had gone down to Great Shefford with instructions to look in at the barn, and perhaps speak with the men who guarded it. And it was there, in the late afternoon, that the man learned of events that had caused the two sheriff's men to scurry about Great Shefford and its surrounds all day in fear for their livelihoods, if not their necks: the prisoner Saltmarsh, an ex-soldier apprehended for theft, vagrancy and perhaps even murder, had escaped.

It was a mystery which had brought the entire village out on the streets in fear, as they had gathered a week ago upon the sudden death of Thomas Rawlings. The previous evening, the prisoner was still there – that was indisputable, for a kindly woman had been permitted to take him fresh water and a little food. His presence later that night had been marked by those going home from the inn, who had heard the restless clink of his fetters. But in the morning he was gone – chains, leg-irons and all – and none could fathom how. There was neither breach in the wall, nor hole in the roof. More, the guard sitting outside swore he had heard nothing. Now, he and his fellow were still scouring the neighbourhood on what it was becoming plain was a fruitless errand.

Thomas had heard the news a little before sunset, when he came into the kitchens for supper. But if his heart rejoiced to hear it, he gave no sign, merely lowered his head and proceeded to do justice to a dish of Nell's best pottage.

* * *

Great Shefford was quiet, though lights showed from the cottages and from the Fox inn, which stood back from the Wantage Road. Thomas passed it, driving at a steady pace through the village and across the Lambourn bridge. Outside the barn he hauled on the reins, and the cart rumbled to a halt. He looked about until a lantern showed, and a figure loomed out of the dark. Clambering down, he faced the same russet-bearded man to whom he had presented Sir Robert's letter the previous morning.

'You!' The fellow's face was menacing in the lantern-light. 'You visited the prisoner yesterday and now he's gone. I'll wager you know something about it!'

Without expression, Thomas drew another letter from his jerkin, one in which Sir Robert took responsibility for the men in the cart, until such time as the high sheriff returned. But when he began to explain, the big man refused to listen.

'A pox on your whoreson paper! I'll not aid you again – more, I've a mind to arrest you on suspicion! Ho there, Will!'

He turned and shouted, whereupon a shorter man appeared from nowhere. The taller one strode to him, and the two had a hurried conference.

Thomas stood beside the cart. From within, a muffled voice asked in agitation what was going on.

'Hold your peace, and wait,' Thomas ordered.

The two sheriff's men looked round, and bore down upon him. They were exhausted from their day's searches; Thomas saw it, as he saw the anger in their eyes. They had lost an important prisoner, and they feared the sheriff's wrath. For want of anywhere better to go they had returned to the lock-up. Thomas smelled drink on their breath. The smaller man took charge.

'Who are you, and what have you come for?' he demanded.

Thomas told him. And as his tale unfolded, as far as it was intended to, he saw the hostility on their faces give way to looks of disbelief. 'Are you a madman?' the small one asked. 'You think our warrant extends to playing nursemaid to these knaves when there's a murderer on the loose?'

Thomas kept his patience. 'Can you not see,' he began, 'that the one who will likely try to come at them is the one who killed Sir John Mountford?' When they hesitated, he pressed his advantage. 'Even if Saltmarsh was a thief, he had neither the courage nor the occasion to kill Mountford. You help us trap this fellow, and you save your own skins. The sheriff will have the true culprit, and the whole of the Downlands will stand in your debt!'

They were silent until the big man growled. 'Downlands,' he spat, and eyed his friend. 'By the Christ, Will, I wish I'd never left Newbury!'

But with relief, Thomas saw that Will's manner had altered. 'This scheme your master has devised,' he muttered. 'How will it come about? How can you know that the killer you seek will appear?'

'It's his last and best chance,' Thomas said. Briefly he outlined what remained to be said, then waited.

'Let's take a look at them,' Will said, after a moment.

They watched as Thomas went to the rear of the cart, untied

the cover and threw it back. The big man with the lantern came forward and raised it, to reveal the nervous faces of Francis Ball, John Kydd, Robert Clements and Thomas Friar. He swore under his breath.

'You think the lives of these frightened rabbits worth preserving?' he asked.

But his companion grunted. 'They're the carrion by which we may catch our wolf.' He turned to Thomas. 'I'll do your master's bidding, and hold them here until tomorrow. But then I'll send to the sheriff as to what must be done.'

Thomas hesitated, then saw the other's expression brooked no argument. 'Agreed,' he said. But the russet-bearded fellow, who clearly disliked the whole arrangement, scowled at him.

'I'd still like to know what was said between you and that runagate cove yesterday,' he snarled.

But Thomas was distracted, for the fugitive jurymen were clambering hurriedly down from the cart. Kydd was tense as a bowstring, and threw him a fearful look. Friar and Clements kept silent, but Francis Ball took a step forward.

'I had a deal of persuading to stop them from jumping off the cart, back on the road,' he muttered, with a glance at the barn. 'Are we to be clapped up like felons now?'

Somehow, Thomas could not find it in himself to be harsh. Whatever the men had done on that ill-fated jury, they were brought to a sorry pass. Their lives were in ruins; they lived a day at a time, knowing not where to turn.

'I will do what I can,' he said, 'as will Sir Robert.'

Ball turned away, and followed his companions into the gloom of the barn. Thomas watched until the doors were closed and barred. The sheriff's men stood apart, talking low. After a moment Will said, 'Better take your cart away, and yourself too.'

Thomas climbed onto the driver's seat, then called down.

'Do you know if Paulo the Switzer has set up his tent hereabouts?'

The other nodded. 'He's got license to give a show tomorrow night, in the east field.' He snorted. 'It'll give these village rabbits something to divert themselves, else they all drop dead from fright.'

Thomas shook the reins and eased the cart forward, relieved to be moving.

20

In the showground east of the village, all stood in readiness for the morrow.

The main tent was raised, the side tent attached. Torches blazed at several points, not to attract customers yet, but to deter incomers: Paulo Schweiz it seemed, was in a cautious mood. Thomas sensed it when he drew up beside Paulo's cart, and found the showman seated by an open fire.

'My friend!' He rose as Thomas climbed down. Nearby, Kit was busy with some task, hunched over a little board. The ape was nowhere in sight.

'Master Paulo.' Thomas found himself glad to see a friendly face. But as he drew near, the showman frowned.

'So...' Paulo gazed at Thomas, but seemed more interested in the empty air about him. Finally he said, 'There is much that lies heavy upon you, *nein*?'

Thomas walked over to the fire and sank onto an upturned basket which served as a seat. 'Indeed,' he answered. 'But first I would thank you, for I am in your debt.' When Paulo raised an eyebrow, he added, 'I hear the prisoner has escaped from the barn, though how it was done seems little short of magic.' He paused. 'I might even say, it is a puzzle.'

Paulo seated himself. 'Indeed, a wondrous occurrence,' he agreed. 'The village is in a state of great anxiousness, if not of fear.' His eyes shone in the firelight. 'Fertile conditions for our show tomorrow night!'

Thomas could not help but smile. Despite the circumstances, he was content to be in the conjuror's company again. 'The show, Master Paulo, is what I would speak with you about,' he said.

Paulo eyed him. 'You have a plan... Mayhap it took form after we last talked together. Am I near the mark?'

But there was uncertainty in Paulo's eyes. 'When we last talked, Master Thomas, I said you were still doubtful whether to trust me,' he said. 'Now, if I do what you will ask of me, and reveal secrets I share with no one, you see it is I who must place my trust in you.'

'I do see it,' Thomas replied.

Paulo met his gaze, then glanced to where, a few yards away, Kit continued to work by lantern-light. There was a scraping, as of some sharp tool. The young man looked up and found Paulo's eyes upon him, then bent to his task again.

'The boy,' Paulo added. 'He too relies on me a great deal.' Then he sat up, took a breath and was his exuberant self. 'Enough. It will be done! Now, I have a flask of Gascon wine we may share before we go to our beds. Will that serve?'

Thomas smiled gratefully.

* * *

The next day was one that he would never forget.

In the morning, having fed the carthorse, he helped Kit Page place seats in the show tent. The young man was taciturn, and barely spoke. When they had finished he went out to rekindle the fire. Paulo was nowhere to be seen.

Thomas stood beside the tent and listened to the sounds of the village, not unlike those of Chaddleworth. Men were already out in the fields, women at their work in the cottages and gardens. Then merely to pass the time he left the showground, walked through the winding street and across the bridge until he stood before the barn once again. Will the sentry sat on the stump outside the door. Beside him was a bottle of ale. He did not get up as Thomas approached.

'All's well within, so you needn't fret. I took 'em in a bit of breakfast an hour back...' He sniffed. 'Least these ones have money to pay their keep.'

'I would speak with them,' Thomas said.

With a resigned air, Will got to his feet and moved to unbar the doors. 'This is a mighty strange way of setting a snare, to my thinking,' he said. 'Are you trying to draw folk's attention?'

Thomas said nothing, only waited until the man had stepped aside and went in.

They had improvised pallets of straw and sacking, against the opposite wall to where Saltmarsh had sat. Each man eyed Thomas as he approached.

'I forgot to ask whether you had armed yourselves,' he said.

Francis Ball stood up. 'We are not quite so witless as everyone seems to think,' he answered. 'We have poniards and billhooks, oak billets...' He eyed Thomas. 'How long must we be a part of this dumb show?'

'Is it not best for all if we catch the one who murdered the others?' Thomas asked. 'He who has driven you from your homes?'

But Kydd was on his feet, jabbing a nervous finger. 'What certainty is there you will succeed?' he cried. Stooping, he picked up a leather mug and dashed its contents across the floor. 'Meanwhile we're afraid to drink a drop, even to eat, for fear of poison!'

'Hold your peace, weasel,' someone growled. Clements was seated in the far corner, glaring at no one in particular.

Thomas sighed. 'I'll draw a pail of water from the nearest well and carry it to you myself, if that will ease your fears,' he said. But Thomas Friar, the stolid farmer from Brickleton, spoke up in a phlegmatic tone.

'Nay, you'd best not come here again, falconer. If your scheme has a chance of succeeding...' He paused. 'I for one won't wait beyond tonight, but leave and take my chances elsewhere.' His gaze dropped. 'Already my family have given me up for dead.'

Having no words of comfort, Thomas left them and walked back to the show field.

* * *

When night fell at last, the excitement in the village was plain. A small crowd had already gathered near the entrance to the field, to find the gateway barred. This time it seemed Paulo did not want inquisitive children peeking under the tent. But torches stood on posts, illuminating the show tent with its fluttering pennants. Kit Page, clad in his bright green and yellow, was on hand to do tricks and stir folk's curiosity, his ape on his shoulders.

Meanwhile in the side booth, all was prepared. And standing at Paulo's side in the cluttered space, Thomas listened in silence as the showman shared his secret.

'I will describe my machine,' Paulo said, 'if you will swear to speak of it to no one.' Thomas gave his word, intrigued by the large box of polished hardwood which stood on legs, tapering horizontally to a curious brass cylinder which faced the flap in the wall. Clearly, when the flap was lifted, the cylinder would point through the hole. But how it sent those wondrous pictures through the air, swelled them up and threw them onto the far wall of the main tent, he had no idea.

In a tone of reverence, Paulo explained. 'This camera obscura was the invention of an Italian, Cardano. I learned much from him...' His voice dropped. 'A man of profound knowledge, was that bold Milanese; an expert in ciphers, an astrologer – he even came to England and cast the horoscope of your boy King Edward, long ago. Later, like so many men of learning...' The conjuror sighed. 'He was called a heretic and jailed. He died many years ago, but not before I had sought him out, that I might study at his feet. He it was who told me how he cast an image into a room full of people. Hence it was but a small step, or a series of steps...'

He turned to a little stand close by, on which stood a wooden case. Opening it carefully he drew out a small square of glass, finer and clearer than any window pane Thomas had seen. It was painted in bold colours, with a curious image. Peering closer, Thomas recognised it: the jungle, with great trees, falling vines and swinging apes, which had appeared on the tent wall back in Chaddleworth.

He turned in astonishment to Paulo, who was nodding. 'Yes – those pictures you saw are but panels of glass.' He opened the lid of the camera obscura, and pointed. 'They sit in that slot there. Behind, is placed a bright flame. The flame shines through the glass, and throws the image onto any screen you place in its path. But the secret by which it is made to grow big, is this: the lens.'

He pointed to the brass cylinder. Thomas looked, and saw a glass disc fitted inside the end of it.

'The lens,' Paulo told him, 'can make things appear bigger. Already learned men are using it to observe the moon and stars.

One day...' He sighed again. 'Would that I might live long enough to see such. But no matter, Master Thomas: you see now what we will do?' When Thomas nodded slowly, Paulo took another pane of glass and held it up, peering through it with narrowed eyes.

'Kit has excelled himself,' he murmured. 'This likeness would afright the devil himself.'

But Thomas had formed a picture of his own: of Christopher Mead the mapmaker, bending over his dioptra, and pointing it at a hill-top. There was no place, he saw, no matter how remote, which in time science could not reach; he felt the vastness of a world beyond his own, and realised how little of it he knew.

The gate was opened and the crowd surged to the tent, where a smiling Kit Page, transformed once again, had launched into his showman's patter. Not that the folk of Great Shefford needed much encouragement: most had heard about the show, ten days back in Chaddleworth, and would have stopped at nothing to see it. All thoughts of recent deaths, of the escaped prisoner, and even of curious coming and goings about the barn where he had been held were forgotten. There had been precious little enter-tainment in months save for the May festival, and few in the village intended to miss this.

Thomas kept out of sight. But peering through the flaps of the side tent, he had ample opportunity to observe those who thronged about the entrance. He was not surprised to see that a fair number of Chaddleworth folk had walked the few miles from their own village, eager to see the show all over again. Giles Frogg and his wife were there, and Ned Hawes behind them; Thomas had expected both. Nor was he surprised to see John Flowers with Ned, the two deep in conversation. What had tran-

spired between Ned and Eleanor earlier that evening, he did not
know. Eleanor had been with her mistress all day, but he knew
she would look in at the cottage; the matter of what to do with
Grace still weighed heavily upon him.

Behind Flowers were Tom Brazier and Ambrose Fuller.
Though he had not been down to Boxwell of late, Thomas
understood that the rebuilding of Ames's barn was finished, as
Ann Dillamore had told. Brazier seemed at ease, his arm about a
young village girl. Fuller, unsurprisingly, had clearly spent much
of the day in the inn. He lurched heavily through the entrance,
caring not who he collided with. But the air of suspense was
such, none paid him any mind; eagerly folk squeezed into the
tent, which was soon filled to bursting point once again. And
once again, it was time.

The latecomers had paid their penny, and since all seats were
taken, stood pressed together around the walls. The entrance
was closed and the torches dimmed, prompting the customary
murmur of alarm. Standing close to the wall of the side tent
while Paulo bent over his projection machine, Thomas was able
to observe matters from a different perspective. He guessed it was
Kit who put out the torches, moving swiftly behind the crowd.
And it was Kit who now slid nimbly under the partition and got
to his feet in the cramped little tent beside Paulo. The ape sat
obediently in a corner.

Kit ignored Thomas; it was plain that he disliked the notion
of a stranger being party to the show's secrets. Leaning forward,
he quickly opened the flap, and at once the hubbub and the heat
of the packed crowd assailed them. Then standing aside, Kit
picked up a small whistle, turned to Paulo and waited his
instruction. The ape, to Thomas's amazement, picked up what
looked like a child's wooden rattle. He turned to peer through
the flap, for in the near-darkness Paulo had struck a flame, and a

shaft of bright light streamed from what Thomas could not help thinking of as the barrel of the camera obscura, over the heads of the crowd to illuminate the far wall. There came a gasp from nearly a hundred throats as the image came into view. Then the sounds began, and Thomas covered his ears against the din that filled that confined space. Thereafter, and for most of the next hour, he continued to keep them covered, amazed at how two men, assisted by the wondrous ape, could produce such a cacophony.

He had been right about some things: Paulo delivered his thrilling oratory through an ox-horn, giving his voice the booming quality that stunned the crowd. Meanwhile Kit and the ape performed miracles: shrieking, shaking rattles, blowing on reed pipes, banging an assortment of tabors and rattling a dish filled with pebbles. Other devices laid out at their feet, some of which Thomas did not recognise, sprang to their hands in quick succession; working closely together, they provided the astonishing array of sounds that had stunned him, back on the green in Chaddleworth.

Meanwhile, Paulo worked his remarkable machine, sliding each glass into place while the trio, well-rehearsed, provided the sound accompaniment. Deftly the showman lifted one panel out and replaced it in the case while reaching for the next – all so swiftly that there was scarcely a break between the pictures. And as at Chaddleworth, the crowd in the main tent shrieked, roared and gasped in astonishment at the *Mundus Peregrinus* of Paulo Schweiz.

After a while, humbled to be a part of it if only as an onlooker, Thomas too was lost in the world that Paulo and his helpers conjured up – so much, that he almost forgot the other purpose of the show. At last, he realised that nearly all the images had been shown. The King on his throne was now in view, leaving only the climactic picture of the Queen in her ermine. He glanced at Paulo, and caught his eye. Sweating and tense from his work, the showman nodded. He and Kit, accompanied by a tabor, had just sung the two-part ballad, both of them so well that Thomas was as amazed at the timbre of their voices as he was at their skills. But now, Paulo slid the penultimate picture from the box and replaced it with the Queen's image. Soon came the shout of recognition from the crowd, followed by cheers and roars of approval. The showman touched Kit on the shoulder, signalling him to be silent.

Thomas waited, his pulse racing, scanning the backs of the crowd's heads. The cheering went on for minutes, causing him to utter a silent oath, for most of the villagers were on their feet stamping and applauding, and it was difficult to see who was where. Then mercifully, as Paulo slid the image out, the crowd began to sit down again. Though it seemed to most that the show was over, the tent wall still glowed with light, and none was eager to leave.

Paulo took the new pane of painted glass, the image he and Thomas had decided upon, and that Kit had prepared especially the previous night. Softly he slid it into the camera.

There were mutterings of surprise, for at first no one was certain what it was. Then Paulo leaned forward to fiddle with the lens, and it grew into sharper focus. Voices rose, then came a gasp from the throats of adults. The children merely stared, scarcely believing what they saw.

Thomas felt a tug on his sleeve; Paulo was handing him the ox-horn. Somewhat shakily he took it, drew a breath and spoke, directing it through the tent flap.

'Behold, the ghost of Richard Walden!'

From all sides came a loud intake of breath.

'Behold,' Thomas intoned. 'An innocent, god-fearing man,

cruelly murdered by night as he walked homewards! Beaten to death, breathing the name of his assailant with his last gasp, before his spirit rose from his body, condemned thereafter to wander the woods until such time as the killer be found, and brought to book for his wicked crime!'

There were cries, and not the delighted screams of folk being thrilled by exotic images but screams of terror. Men and women sprang to their feet; others looked round while some could only stare in horror, rooted to their seats. For the image that shone out was now unmistakeable: the pale, ghostly figure of a blood-stained man, wild-eyed, and pointing an accusing finger at them.

Thomas lowered the ox-horn, sweat running down his neck. Beside him he felt the tension of Paulo and Kit, motionless in their tiny space. In the corner the ape crouched silently, as if even it understood. There came a hoarse shout, louder than any other voice.

Peering through the opening, Thomas saw a heavily built man on his feet, swaying about as if drunk. Heads snapped round, and voices rose: the man *was* drunk. But soon those nearest began to edge away, for there was something unsettling about him. Then as the crowd watched, he raised his arm and pointed to the fearsome image.

'Jesu save me, for I did not mean to kill him!'

Ambrose Fuller, isolated now in a widening circle of staring villagers, turned a haggard face to the assembly.

'Twas only a deer I was after! Who'd begrudge a poor man his supper, even if 'ee steal it from Mountford's wood... I knowed not who it was came on me in the dark. I meant but to knock him down and run!' Spittle ran down the man's chin. He dropped his arm and backed towards the wall. The crowd, silent now, merely stared at him. But Fuller stared back, a frenzied look in his eyes.

'Why do ye gape!' he cried. 'I told ye I meant not to kill the gravedigger – he did challenge me. He brought it on himself!'

He whirled round unsteadily, as if hoping the image might somehow have disappeared, but there it was still. He took one final look, then bolted. Knocking over benches, thrusting men aside, Fuller made for the entrance and none dared stop him. Shouting incoherently, the thatcher pushed his way out.

Thomas emerged from the side booth. A dozen yards away Fuller was lurching towards the gate, even as folk began to spill from the show tent. Paulo appeared at Thomas's side. His pulse racing, Thomas started after the fugitive, ignoring the shouts that broke out. Fuller had reached the gate and blundered out into the lane without looking back. But he was slow and heavy on his feet, and though his face was grim, Thomas knew the chase would be short. Gaining the gateway, he broke into an easy lope, satisfied not only that the murderer of Richard Walden was found at last, but that there was nowhere for him to run...

Then it was, that he realised the shouting came not merely from the show field behind him but from the street ahead too. He slowed, frowning, trying to make out the words, which came from but two or three mouths.

And suddenly, with the retreating figure of Fuller still in sight, he heard and understood, and at once began to run at speed through the village. As he ran, people hurried from the houses, and muttering gave way to shouts of alarm as the fearful cry rang out, as it would in any English village of timbered houses roofed with thatch:

'Fire! The barn is on fire!'

21

He saw the flames shooting up into the night sky, long before he reached the lock-up. With others at his heels he ran over the Lambourn bridge, to halt in dismay before the blazing barn, its walls and part of its roof already a roaring pyre. And at once the words of John Ames from weeks ago rang in his head: *There was no reason for it; no means by which a flame could have been set, save by design...* Then he saw that the doors were barred, and too late, he understood.

Too late... Folk were gathering, shouting for buckets, but it was impossible to save the building. Even as he saw the prone figure of the big sheriff's man slumped some distance away, a mug still in his hand, Thomas understood and cursed the man for his carelessness as he cursed his own. There was no sign of the one named Will. Ignoring the heat, Thomas ran to the doors, and now he heard it, above the roar and crackle of flames: a desperate thudding on the timbers from within, and voices screaming in terror.

He tore off his jerkin, wrapped it about his hands and took

hold of the heavy beam. Burning thatch was beginning to fall about him. Panting, he lifted the bar from its stanchions and threw it aside. Then, his breath coming in bursts, he yanked the doors open and stepped back.

Three figures almost fell over him, clouded in smoke, their clothing blackened. Two dropped at once to their knees, coughing and choking. The third, whose hair and eyebrows were singed, stared at Thomas in terror. It was John Kydd.

'He came!' he cried. 'Someone set the fire. We heard him!'

Thomas grabbed his shoulders. 'Where's the fourth one?' he shouted. When Kydd stared dumbly, he let go of him and ran to the others. Both were on all fours, struggling to breathe. As he watched, one of them turned and lay on his back, coughing uncontrollably. It was Francis Ball. The other was Clements.

'Where's Friar?' Thomas shouted, though the answer was obvious. Clements, burned about the arms, merely raised his blackened face, taut with pain.

A crowd had collected. Buckets appeared, and someone was calling to form a chain to the river, but others shouted that it was too late. Thomas took a step towards the open doors, long enough to glimpse the inferno within before he was driven back. Like the rest, he could do nothing more than stand and watch the barn burn to the ground.

The plan had failed.

Heavily he dropped to his knees beside the dead sheriff's servant and prised the empty mug from the man's hand. How could he – how could all of them – have been so lax? The poisoner had done his work again, but not on the fugitives: that would have been too obvious. He had merely laced the guard's ale, waited until he fell sick, then barred the doors and set fire to the barn. It was the simplest means of disposing of the remaining jurors at a single stroke. There seemed little doubt now that the same hand was at work, that had fired John Ames's barn a fortnight since.

He stood up stiffly, his eyes still smarting from the smoke. Despite Paulo's ingenuity, despite all their plans and preparations, the scheme had fallen short. It had exposed the murderer of Richard Walden, who had promptly escaped in the confusion, but worse, the killer of five – now six – of the former jurymen, as well as of Sir John Mountford, was still at large.

Folk from the show field were arriving, including Giles Frogg and Tom Brazier. They stood in silence, watching the last roof beams fall in with a crash. Sparks flew upwards.

'Are you hurt?'

Thomas turned to see Paulo at his side. He shook his head, then gestured to the body of the sheriff's man, and held up the empty mug. Paulo drew a rapid breath.

'He is still at his work!'

Thomas gestured towards what remained of the burning barn. 'And he has succeeded...' He sighed. 'What might be done now, I know not.'

Paulo placed a hand on his arm. 'Come – you need to rest, drink some water...'

But Thomas shook his head. 'I must return to my master and tell him. What the high sheriff will do when he hears of this, I care not to dwell upon.'

Paulo was about to speak, but there came a shout. They turned as Ned Hawes came running up. He looked aghast at the blazing remains of the barn, and at the three survivors sitting huddled together, exhausted and burned but alive. Relief flooded over him as his eyes fell upon Thomas. 'By the Lord, I thought...' The boy hurried forward. 'I looked for you, but 'tis mayhem everywhere!'

Thomas rested a hand on his shoulder. 'I'm unhurt.'

Ned was breathless with excitement. 'Twas wondrous, what happened!' he cried. 'I always knowed Fuller for a rogue, but none thought him a murderer!' He gazed in awe at Paulo. 'How did 'ee make that picture?'

The showman showed his irritation. 'It's not time to speak of such,' he muttered. 'There are things to be done.'

Recovering his breath, Thomas looked about and saw Giles Frogg watching him. Then another figure appeared, pushing his way through the watchers. The man looked at Thomas, then saw the prone figure of his companion, and darted forward.

'You're too late, Master Will,' Thomas said. 'We are all too late, though three of the prisoners were saved—'

'Them?' Will had dropped to one knee beside the body. He turned to Thomas with a bitter look. 'You think I care a tinker's fart for those rabbits?'

He stared down. The tall man's beard and the front of his clothing were covered in dried vomit, his mouth was twisted into a grotesque smile. Will took his hand, felt it briefly, then let it drop. 'He said not to trust that cove,' he muttered, 'and he was right! Only, he could never refuse a free mug...'

Thomas started. 'Trust who?' he asked.

'The one who brought ale over from the Fox, soon after dark,' Will answered. 'After the rest had flocked to your show...' He looked at Paulo, then at Thomas. 'He played me for a dolt right enough: sent me off on a fool's errand, claiming he saw my escaped prisoner, only there was no one!' He got heavily to his feet. 'I might have got drunk too, and ended up the same...' He caught Thomas's expression. 'Do you know aught of this?'

'He wasn't drunk,' Thomas said. 'He was poisoned.'

Will's jaw dropped.

'Can you describe him?' Thomas asked.

'Who?'

'The one who brought the ale, and called you away.'

Will frowned. 'Young fellow, blond locks and an easy smile... Sort would charm any maid into his bed.'

Beside him, Thomas heard Ned Hawes let out a gasp. He looked round at him, his own heart skipping a beat. 'Where's John Flowers?' he asked sharply. 'Was he with you all through the show?'

Ned gulped. 'We got parted in the crush... He said he'd see me anon.' He frowned. 'I'd swear he was there at the end.'

Thomas swung his head towards Paulo, and saw that the showman was lost in thought. 'I see not one man running,' he said, so low that it was almost a whisper. 'I see two – yet they are not together.'

Thomas put a hand to his forehead. Behind him, flames still crackled and folk still milled about, but he scarcely heard them. For some reason Ned Hawes and Paulo drew closer to him.

Will too drew nearer. 'You know who this fellow is?' he demanded. 'Then speak!'

But Thomas made no answer, as thoughts crowded in upon him: Rebecca Walden had a son, perhaps ten years old – he would now be about the right age; Flowers had only lately come to Great Shefford and had been quick to put himself forward to rebuild Ames's barn – too quick, Thomas thought. And then he saw that the fire was not meant to destroy the body of Simon Haylock at all. If Flowers himself had set fire to it – at one end only, so that it could be saved – then as the one to repair it he would have good reason to be near, to come and go as he pleased, without attracting attention...

He looked up and found the others staring at him.

'He's called Flowers,' he muttered. 'But I think his real name is Walden.'

* * *

The search lasted until dawn, and like the plan that had been the cause of it, that too failed.

Will Ashman the sheriff's servant, Giles Frogg and several of the elders of Great Shefford had listened to Thomas's tale. And though he told it sparingly, his voice hoarse with the telling, no man doubted the truth of it. Frogg in particular, who knew more than most, saw it in its stark clarity.

'He was close by, every time,' he muttered, awe-struck at the murderer's boldness. 'He found chance to poison Haylock's costrel – not difficult, since the man was soused most days. He could've got into Will Kirke's house when no one was there, and poisoned his supper. He drank at the Black Bear, in full view of all Chaddleworth, and poisoned old Nick Gee's mug... Likely it was he who bought it for him!'

'And he was in and out of Shefford all the time, with his cart,' Thomas added. 'He knew the brewery... saw where Thomas Rawlings kept his tasting-mug, that none else would touch. He even sent a keg of poisoned ale to Petbury.'

Paulo Schweiz was standing nearby. 'If this man comes from outside, as you say,' he murmured, 'mayhap he knew where to obtain wolfsbane.'

They had turned it about, and only then had they realised that Tom Brazier was close by, listening to every word.

Frogg and other men went off, bent upon gathering a search party and scouring the village for not one murderer, but two: Ambrose Fuller, and his master, John Flowers. Though the truth at first confounded them: all this while, the young carpenter had employed Fuller as his thatcher, unaware that a decade ago the man had killed his father – as Fuller was unaware that he was working for the son of the man he had killed. And now that

Paulo's show had exposed him, there seemed little doubt that Flowers would hunt the other down before he too was caught. Perhaps, Thomas thought, he cared little about what followed after.

The remains of the ruined barn still burned, but the fire had been contained. Fortunately it was not close to any other building. Folk had brought water to douse the edges of the blaze. The timbers, palings and what remained of the roof they left to burn out. No trace was found of the body of Thomas Friar.

Thomas had not joined the search. Instead, he and a subdued Ned Hawes walked apart with Tom Brazier, until they stood beside the river. Thomas knelt to take a mouthful of water, and to dash some over his face. A short distance away, the crackle of flames was still audible.

Brazier was speechless. Finally, he sat down heavily upon the bank of the shallow Lambourn, and wept in dismay. Ned sat down beside him.

'You scarcely knew him,' he said. 'He only hired you as labourer. How could you know aught of what—'

'Nay, I should have!' Brazier looked round, his long hair falling lank over his ears. 'I knew something wasn't right – not just with Ambrose, but with Master John too...' He stopped. 'Now I don't even know what to call him!'

He looked past Ned, to where Thomas stood. 'He fooled me right enough,' he mumbled, wiping his nose with a sleeve. 'Though he weren't no East Garston boy sent off to serve his prenticeship like he said... He knew a sight too much for that. Let slip once he'd been in London, though he said not why he went.' He turned back to stare at the stream. 'All this while... Him and Ambrose, and neither knew what the other did.' He shook his head. 'It don't make a scrap of sense.'

'Vengeance knows no sense either, but that it must be satisfied,' Thomas said. 'I've never seen one who cloaked it so well, and behind such a handsome visage.'

'Think how I feel,' Ned said. 'I called him my friend, drank with him, joked with him, talked of my sweetheart...' He looked at Thomas. 'How can I see him as a murderer?'

Thomas shook his head. 'Nobody saw. Not I, or you, or those who worked alongside him.'

Brazier sniffed. 'I was with him in the village when we learned Tom Rawlings was dead... He looked as shocked as anyone else.' His brows furrowed. 'Yet, I know what it was, didn't sit right.' He looked up. 'An hour later, it seemed like he forgot it ever happened, whistling like he hadn't a care in the world. Even Ambrose thought something odd about it, though I paid him no mind. Ambrose don't like no one.'

Ned gave him a rueful look. 'Do you know, you and I fought each other over a young woman as wouldn't look twice at either of us?' he asked. 'For one thing, seems she's married. For another, she's five months gone with child...' With a glance at Thomas, he reddened and shut his mouth. But Brazier turned to him with a bleak look.

'You should've ducked quicker, and fetched me a buffet to the head,' he said. 'Might 'a knocked some sense into me.' They faced each other, and to Thomas's surprise Brazier held out his hand. He was less surprised when Ned took it.

'That's well,' Thomas said to him. 'Now you and I have matters to see to.' He looked at Brazier. 'You'd best go home, Tom.'

The young man nodded and got slowly to his feet, though a look of disbelief remained on his face. In later years, Shefford villagers would say that he never quite lost it, as long as he lived.

* * *

The two falconers walked back to the show field and found Paulo Schweiz sitting by his fire. The field was deserted, the tent closed up. No lights burned, and Kit and his ape were out of sight. Since it was late, the return to Petbury would wait until morning. Accepting a cup of wine, both men gave the showman good-night, climbed into the cart and made themselves as comfortable as they could on the wagon bed, where a day earlier the fright-ened jurymen had lain.

The jurymen. Thomas had all but forgotten them. But in that matter also, he was too late: the three survivors had taken what had been their favoured course of action all along, and scattered into the night.

At Petbury the next morning, all was quiet when they drove the cart into the stable yard. As the sun climbed over the roof-tops Ned went off to feed the eyasses while Thomas looked in at the mews. To his relief, someone had put food and water out for the birds. He guessed who, and went at once to his cottage.

Grace sat by the chimney with her sewing. As he came in she looked up and smiled. 'I am glad to see you returned, for I would thank you before I leave.' When he said nothing, she added, 'I have been here three days – folk will notice, if they have not already.' Her smile grew mischievous. 'And then they will begin to talk. I have no wish to arouse the cook's jealousy.'

He sat down heavily, whereupon a look of concern appeared on her face. She stood up, put her sewing aside and began to stir the pot that hung over the fire. 'The porridge is hot,' she said.

He nodded. 'I thank you for tending the falcons.'

She ladled porridge into a bowl and set it on the table before him. As he ate, she watched.

'My husband delighted to fly his goshawk, in happier times,' she murmured. 'I would walk in the fields and woods with him, and along the brooks, for hours.' She lowered her eyes, then changed the subject. 'Eleanor has been most kind to me. I have lacked for nothing.'

He waited, seeing she wished to say more.

'If you have news of my uncle...' she began, whereupon he lowered his spoon.

'I ask your pardon. I have been caught up in other matters. He... It seems he stayed but one night in Chaddleworth, then left. I do not know where.'

Grace was silent for a moment. 'He has abandoned me,' she said.

Thomas frowned. 'Surely he would not do so...?'

She shook her head. 'You do not know him. He thinks of himself now. With each day I grew more of a burden to him...' She bit her lip, and tried to look to her sewing.

'There is someone who might help,' Thomas said. 'Lady Sarah Mountford.' When Grace looked up in surprise, he went on, 'Though she is in mourning, I do not believe she would turn you away, in your time of need.'

Hope showed in her gaze then. 'Your master,' she said. 'He would not brook your helping one like me into hiding. You risk breaking the law.'

'It seems but a small matter, in view of what else I've done of late,' Thomas replied. 'Or rather, what I've failed to do.' But Grace's smile was so warm, he could only return it.

'If I were your husband,' he murmured, 'I would be scouring all England to find you, and care not for the risks.'

Her smile faded. 'For aught I know, he is dead.'

'Nay, don't think it...' Thomas began, but she stayed him.

'What God wills shall be done. I must think of the child.'

After a moment, he nodded. 'Then let's not delay any longer. We'll go tonight.'

But first there was another matter which would not wait. He left the cottage soon after, and sought an audience with Sir Robert.

22

It was almost noon before he was called to his master's private chamber to give an account of what had happened at Great Shefford, hence it did not surprise him to find that Sir Robert had already learned much of the events. And though the knight was displeased, he was not inclined to blame Thomas, to the latter's relief. Rather, he appeared stunned by the implications.

'Two weeks ago that young man came here to Petbury, to bid for the rebuilding of Ames's barn,' he said. 'And ever since, it seems he has come and gone under our noses – all the while bent on murder. Worse, he's yet free to kill again.'

The two of them were alone. Sun lanced through the leaded windows. Standing beside his master's writing table, Thomas said, 'There's only one he hunts. The jurymen that remain are fled, none knows where, and I do not think he'll try to follow them. Now he knows who killed his father, he'll not rest until he finds him.'

Sir Robert grimaced. 'If we could find Ambrose Fuller and hold him, we might set another trap. Save that I have little faith now in such devices.'

Thomas lowered his gaze. 'I was lax, sir, and I rue it greatly.'

'All of Petbury was lax – nay, so was half the county,' Sir Robert grunted. 'As we were over the matter of those thefts…' He looked up, his brows furrowing. 'Your ex-soldier friend: I hear he too made a somewhat remarkable escape.'

'So it appears, sir,' Thomas answered. When Sir Robert said nothing, he added, 'Saltmarsh swore to me he did not break into Petbury, or Poughley either. I believe him, as I believe he did not murder Sir John Mountford.'

'Of course, for surely we now know who did,' Sir Robert said, allowing himself a thin smile. 'It would be a pleasure to watch the high sheriff's face, when he learns of that.'

Thomas was silent. The deaths of the former jurymen still filled his thoughts. He felt certain he was right about John Flowers, especially as the man had now disappeared, seemingly into thin air. What troubled him was the stabbing of Mountford in cold blood, in his own chapel. Somehow, even though the knight had been the cause of all the devilry that followed, he found it hard to believe that Flowers would have taken his life.

Sir Robert eyed him. 'No doubt you wish to be relieved of playing intelligencer as well as pursuer, and to return to your work,' he said. 'Well, so be it. Yet I ask that you be ready when Master Ward returns, to answer some hard questions.'

'Will that be soon, sir?' Thomas enquired.

'He comes here tonight, yet I'll not call you until tomorrow,' his master answered. His expression softened. 'Get some rest, Thomas, before you begin to mimic your birds, and sleep on your feet.'

* * *

He did sleep, late in the afternoon. When he awoke with a start the sun was sinking, and there were voices in the cottage below. Rising from his bed he dressed hurriedly and descended from the loft to find Eleanor seated beside Grace, the two of them at ease like sisters.

'I wanted to wake you, but Grace said not.' Eleanor smiled, rising and coming over to kiss him. 'Are you rested now?'

He nodded, relaxing somewhat. 'Has she said where I'm taking her tonight?'

Eleanor nodded in turn, saying, 'I have spoken with James. He says if you walk by the yard after dark, the mapmaker's horse will be saddled and ready.'

'There's another I should thank,' Thomas said.

Grace stood up. 'It is I who must thank you both,' she said. 'I know not how to repay you. Only swear that, if Lady Sarah will not give me sanctuary, you will leave me and return home.'

'At night?' Thomas frowned. 'Where would you go?'

'I have a little money – I will find an inn for the night, and then in the morning I will return to London. Nay...' She shook her head before either of them could interrupt. 'I'm tired of fleeing. There are people I can go to, who may have word of my husband – or can get word to him that I am well.' She gestured to a bundle beside the door. 'See, Master Thomas, your daughter has helped me pack.'

He returned her gaze. 'Then let us hope Lady Sarah is merciful,' he said. 'Shall we take a farewell supper?'

* * *

When dusk fell and Petbury grew quiet, he looked to the falcons, saw them settled, then walked down to the stable yard. As promised, the old dun horse stood saddled and tied to a post.

There was no one about. He untied the reins and led the animal away, up the slope and around the back of his cottage, out of sight of the house. Grace was waiting, cloaked against the breeze. The moon shone pale above them.

Stooping, he formed a step with his hands so that she might mount, which she did with some difficulty. Then, as he picked up her bundle, he stiffened and glanced uphill towards the Ridgeway. Grace heard it too: heavy footfalls, drawing close – then she gasped.

'Now you have come!'

Christopher Mead emerged from the gloom, striding through the long grass towards them. The next moment he caught both off guard by seizing the horse's reins.

'Mine, I think,' he snapped, with a hard look at Thomas.

But Grace leaned forward and tried to take the reins back. 'Nay – I am no longer in your charge!' she cried. 'He has been kind, and is taking me to safety—'

'Silence, girl!' Mead was seething with anger. 'I've spent the best part of three days combing this wretched heath for you, without even the means to carry my equipment about – my precious instruments, which you left behind for anyone to steal! You think I'm in a humour to listen to your whining?'

He glanced from his niece back to Thomas. 'Get yourself gone, falconer,' he hissed. 'This is none of your affair.'

But Thomas, who matched the other man in height, let the bundle fall and laid a hand on Mead's arm. 'Drop the reins,' he said, 'or I'll take them from you.'

The mapmaker's eyes blazed. 'Do you realise what you do?' he demanded. 'I could swear a warrant, have you arrested for kidnap—'

'I think not,' Thomas answered, 'else my master and others might learn how you sought to hide Mistress Grace with a papist family, so that she need not present her baby for baptism.'

Mead drew breath sharply and threw an angry glance at Thomas's hand, still upon his arm. But he let go the reins, and at once Grace took them up.

'You abandoned me, Uncle,' she said. 'The duty you swore to my father was short-lived, as I knew it would be. I will tread my own path now.'

'You'll what?' Mead almost laughed. 'You little fool. How far do you think you would get without me?'

Thomas took a step forward. 'Enough, Master Mead. I'm taking mistress Grace to Poughley – to Lady Sarah Mountford, who I believe will house her, at least for a while—'

Mead started; now there was not merely anger in his eyes, but anxiety too. 'You will not take her there!' He almost shouted. 'I am her kinsman and her sworn guardian, and I forbid it!'

Thomas eyed him. 'Why would you do that? Have you not tried every other Catholic family in West Berkshire...?'

'You knave! How dare you!' Mead's hand flew to his belt, even as Grace cried out in alarm. But Thomas stepped back quickly, reaching for his own poniard.

'You're not so big a fool as that,' he said quietly.

Mead let his hand fall, and sought a different tack. 'See now, you know not what you do, Finbow,' he said with an effort. 'You'll bring troubles on your own head.'

Thomas's pulse had quickened, but he kept his voice low. 'If we hold this discourse here much longer,' he said, 'we will be heard. The high sheriff dines with my master tonight...'

'I care not,' Mead countered, his anger rising again. 'I say again for the last time, keep out of my affairs!' But Grace tugged at the reins, and instinctively the old horse moved, causing Mead to step back abruptly.

'Follow us to Poughley,' she said, 'and take the horse back. Then go where you will. Your dioptra is safe where I left it. I do not wish for your help any more – or your company.'

There was pride as well as defiance in her voice. Moved by her courage, Thomas reached up to her. After a moment she placed the reins in his hand.

'Well, Master,' he said, raising an eyebrow at Mead. 'What's it to be?'

Mead swallowed, looking from one to the other. 'Listen to me,' he said. 'You cannot go to Lady Mountford. She will not aid you, for I have asked there already, and been refused.'

Thomas narrowed his eyes. But Grace spoke quickly.

'When did you?' When he did not respond, she said sharply, 'You're lying.' And when Mead struggled for words she continued, 'Of late, I have wondered why it is that you did not take me there sooner – as soon as we came here.'

Mead's mouth tightened, and observing the man's agitation, Thomas added his voice. 'Indeed. Sir John's a known recusant and the house is a warren, with hiding places aplenty. Why did you not go there immediately?'

'Mountford is dead!' Mead cried. 'All England knows it now.' He turned to Grace, with almost a pleading look. 'Surely you can see it is not safe to go there?'

But Grace stared at her uncle, and her eyes grew wider.

'He was one of your twilight customers,' she said.

'Hold your tongue!' Mead shot a glance at her, then tried to seize the reins from Thomas. But when Thomas held firm, causing the poor horse to shy nervously, Mead caught him by surprise, striking him on the mouth with his fist.

Grace cried out, then caught her breath as Thomas recovered swiftly. Seizing Mead's arm he bent it sharply, causing the man to cry out. The next moment Mead was thrown to the ground. He made at once to rise, then saw the glitter of Thomas's poniard in his hand, and froze.

'The truth,' Thomas said, in a voice that neither the mapmaker nor his niece expected.

'Enough, please!' Grace begged. After a moment Thomas straightened, breathing hard, and put away the short dagger. Mead sat in the grass, staring upwards. Then suddenly he sagged.

'You stupid jade,' he mumbled. 'Have you not done enough harm already?'

Thomas was looking at Grace. 'What did you mean,' he asked, 'by one of his twilight customers?'

She bit her lip, but kept silent.

Thomas glanced at Mead, then at Grace, the reins still in his hand. 'Tell me,' he ordered, 'or I'll lead you down to my master's stable and make enough of a racket to bring out the entire household.'

She shook her head. 'The maps he makes... They are not always truthful.' Without meeting Thomas's eye, she added, 'He surveys the estates of certain wealthy men, and reports them as being smaller than they really are.'

Mead let out an oath, and lurched to his feet. But Thomas fixed him with a warning look.

'You mean men like Sir John Mountford... Recusants, who face crippling fines, who may lose two thirds of their lands?' He smiled grimly at Mead. 'Mayhap you're not such a poor man, after all.' He reached out to stroke the horse's neck, easing its nervousness as he did so. 'This tired old nag, and your humble clothes – are they but a sham?'

Mead drew breath. But Thomas held his gaze and said, 'A man might even kill, to keep such a profitable scheme secret.'

Grace gasped. But Mead, looking sick in the wan moonlight, addressed Thomas in a tone that bordered on pleading.

'I did not kill him,' he said. 'I swear it, on the sacred memory of my dead wife.'

There was a silence. Nightbirds called from the trees to the east. Thomas turned to Grace, who said dully, 'He's no murderer. I believe that, and so must you.'

'I might,' Thomas said after a moment. 'If you tell me the truth now – the whole of it, and quickly. I've grown somewhat short of patience.'

Mead glanced towards the house below them, where lights showed from the windows of the Great Hall. 'I went to see Sir John almost a week ago,' he said shortly. 'I believed in view of our past associations, he would help...' He lowered his eyes. 'He refused to take Grace in. He was afraid, because of the recent deaths. The whole fabric is unravelling, he said... Our judgement is come. I remonstrated with him – I even prayed with him, in his chapel, as he urged me to. But he was adamant he would take no more risks. So I came away.' Seeing Thomas's eyes fixed hard upon his, he repeated, 'I left him alone in his chapel, I swear it! He was alive when I left!'

He turned to Grace. 'I did not abandon you! I believed you were safe where you lay. I spent two days searching for another refuge, and when I found none, I meant to come back for you. I had no notion you'd been turned out!'

In spite of himself, Thomas was inclined to believe the man. He looked at Grace, uncertain what to do – but it seemed she would make the decision for him.

'For the sake of my unborn child,' she begged him, 'I ask you to take me to Poughley now, as we planned. I believe Lady Sarah will listen to me... or mayhap, she will listen to you.'

Turning to her uncle, she said, 'You can follow us. If Thomas comes away with only the horse, you may take it and go where you will. If he comes away with me still upon it...' She trailed off.

Mead gazed at her, then turned away. It was clear that whatever happened, neither of them could stay here any longer. Nor could the man abandon Grace, here on the Downs.

'Let us go now, and delay no more,' Thomas said.

* * *

The journey was one of a mere three miles, though progress was slow in the dark. While Mead brought up the rear, Thomas led the horse along the Ridgeway until they struck the Wantage Road. But instead of turning south to Chaddleworth he crossed the road and carried on as far as the old path to Brickleton, skirting the village on the north and east. Soon they were among trees, beeches and small oaks, and the gates of Poughley loomed, with a meagre light showing from the manor ahead of them.

Mead would go no further, but would wait beside the path for Thomas's return. Having accepted matters as they stood, he had withdrawn inside himself, though his eyes still showed impatience, if not anger. As they parted, he stepped close to Grace as if he would speak, but she stayed him.

'If I do not return,' she murmured, 'I would only ask that you get word to my husband, where I may be found.'

He hesitated, then nodded briefly. With a final glance at both of them, he stepped away and melted into the dark.

Thomas pulled on the rein, and led the horse the last few yards to the old oaken gates of the manor.

Though the hour was somewhat late, Lady Sarah Mountford agreed to see the two visitors once she had been told the reason for their arrival; or rather, as much of it as Thomas was prepared to divulge to the ageing manservant who greeted them. John

Kydd, of course, was long gone; indeed, if servants had been few when Thomas had last been here, they seemed even fewer now. Though the sober-faced woman in mourning black still stood protectively at Lady Sarah's side, when they were finally shown into her receiving chamber.

Thomas made his bow, summoning some words of explanation. The risks to his own position, should his master learn of what he was doing, he had put aside. But reminded now of when he had accompanied Sir Robert into this very room, he hid his unease and murmured a respectful greeting. Then he saw Lady Sarah was not looking at him, but at Grace. There was a pause before she spoke.

'Please...' She gestured Grace to a chair. 'You should not stand. Moreover, you should not be riding.' Her glance strayed to Thomas, who strove to ignore the woman-in-waiting. She had regarded him with a frosty expression from the moment he entered.

Grace made her curtsey and took the proffered seat with a smile of gratitude. Thomas waited, aware once again of Lady Sarah's apparent frailty. In the firelight, and the light of a very few small candles, she looked more doll-like than ever.

'Master Finbow,' she murmured. 'You are come alone. Will your master not honour us with his presence?'

It was time to tell all, but as Thomas made ready to explain himself, Grace stayed him with a glance. 'If you please, my lady,' she began, 'The falconer has been my protector only. He met me on the road, and because of my condition, begged leave to escort me. He knows not the substance of why I am here, at this time.'

But then she flushed and lowered her gaze. She did not know Lady Sarah, and too late she realised she had underestimated her.

'Then he is not the sharp-eyed falconer of Petbury that I

know him to be,' the lady of Poughley answered, with a little smile. 'Or mayhap you think your own presence in the Downlands has gone unnoticed.' Grace lowered her gaze, whereupon Lady Sarah added in a softer tone, 'Perhaps we should continue our conversation alone.'

'Then, might Master Finbow wait on me outside? He will need to know—'

'He wishes to know whether I will take you into my house, so that you may bear your child in peace,' Lady Sarah finished.

Thomas stood stiffly, keeping expression from his face.

Lady Sarah sighed, and a sadness seemed to descend upon her. To Thomas's surprise, she turned to her servant.

'Leave us.'

An odd look came across the woman's face. 'Is that wise, madam?'

Lady Sarah's eyes flashed. 'I said, leave us.'

Still the woman remained where she stood. 'Think hard on what you do,' she said in an undertone. 'Might I remind you of Sir John's words...'

But her mistress turned upon her with a sudden anger that stunned the watchers. 'Sir John is dead!' she cried. 'And I will not fail in my Christian duty as he did!'

The woman gasped and, without thinking, began to make the sign of the cross. Too late, she stopped herself – and too late, she saw Thomas's expression. For Thomas in turn had received a greater shock: looking the servant up and down, from her heavy black skirts to the hood which covered everything but her face, he knew what she was, and what had puzzled him the moment he first saw her. More than ten years had passed since the Jesuit Campion was taken at Lyford; few still wondered what had happened to the nuns that were caught with him...

But Lady Sarah recovered, and merely said, 'We will speak of it later. Go now.'

Her mouth tightening, the other bent her head and hurried to the door. There was a brief silence, and Thomas found Lady Sarah's eyes upon him.

'Master Finbow,' she said. 'I think you have taken a great risk this night.' When Thomas said nothing she added, 'As, you might perceive, do I. Shall we then, as fellow-conspirators, tell each other the truth and see what may be done?'

Thomas swallowed. If he lied to Lady Sarah, he knew she would see it. But he would not lie. It seemed to him in his plain fashion that he strove only to help Grace, who had tried to shield him in turn. Hope now stirred within him, that something good might emerge.

'It would ease my heart to tell you, my lady,' he answered. 'As it would lift it, to see you give sanctuary to Mistress Grace. She has suffered enough.'

She nodded, and waited. And there in the light of the dying fire, Thomas told her all there was to tell. When he had finished Grace took up the story. She too, seemed relieved to unburden herself.

Lady Sarah listened intently. Then she stood up. 'You will stay here, of course,' she said. 'And bear your child.'

Grace took a breath, her hand going to her mouth. 'May the good Lord thank you, my lady,' she began, but the other held up a hand.

'I want no thanks,' she said, and turned to Thomas. 'You need fear not, Master Finbow. No one will learn of your coming here tonight. As I hope none may hear of the new addition to my household.'

'I swear they'll not hear it from me, my lady,' he said.

With relief he threw Grace a smile, expecting to be dismissed. But Lady Sarah spoke again, as if to herself.

'Evil was done here,' she murmured, staring into the fire. 'In a sacred place, which cannot be used again until it be newly consecrated.'

She turned to them both. 'How many tears have been shed in this house, none could count in a thousand years.' She paused. 'I stood by my husband... even when I suspected he did wrong, deeming it a matter of confession between himself and God. And I stopped my ears to the rumours that seeped through these walls. Now his sins have found him out, I pray he will be judged as merely weak, and not wicked. For he tried, towards the end... I know he did.'

The tears stood in her eyes, and Thomas and Grace could only watch. 'We saw ourselves as an island,' she went on. 'And yet we could not remain such.' She looked at Grace. 'Do you not see that you are my atonement?'

Grace nodded, then sagged wearily – and at once Lady Sarah's expression became one of concern. 'Let us get you to a chamber,' she said.

And then she did turn to Thomas, who met her gaze and made his bow. As he left, he caught the look of gratitude Grace gave him, and was content.

23

He led the horse along the lane from Poughley, until a tall figure stepped out of the gloom to block his path. There was a moment, before Mead saw that the saddle was empty.

'Yours, I think,' Thomas said, and handed him the reins.

Mead took them, and made as if to go without a word. Then he hesitated, and fumbled for his purse. 'You should have something for your pains,' he said.

Thomas shook his head. 'I want naught from you.'

But Mead's eyes showed only contempt. 'Then you are the first falconer I've known who can afford such scruples.'

'Payment from you would seem somewhat close to a bribe,' Thomas said.

Mead met his gaze. 'You would not dare tell your master what you did for Grace. And I'll wager you wish no attention to be drawn to Poughley, for Lady Sarah's sake. So why would I try to bribe you?'

Thomas said nothing. Tired of the man's company, he was about to walk away. But Mead caught him by the arm. 'You despise me,' he said.

Unhurriedly, Thomas pulled his arm free.

'You think I care for your opinions?' Mead went on, his agitation rising. 'A servant, who runs at the beck and call of a mere country knight?' He was breathing fast. 'There was a time I rode at the side of men greater than your master, and anyone like you would have bent your knee to me!'

Thomas stared, seeing a strangeness in the man's eyes that he had first noticed when they met on the Downs. He saw now that beneath his veneer of arrogance, the mapmaker bore a self-loathing deeper than any he had known.

'If you seek absolution, find a priest,' he said. 'What is it you want from me?'

'What? Do you dare to judge me?' Mead cried. 'You know naught of me, or the burdens I bear—!'

'I do not wish to,' Thomas answered. 'You know as well as anyone, the harm you have done. You were a part of Mountford's conspiracy, to escape paying his fines. He drew others into the web, which became the Devil's Jury. It bought them little but misery – and lately, a terrible death. You're as much to blame as he was—'

'No!' Mead was staring, shaking his head vigorously. 'I am not! I am a man of science – I merely draw maps!' He spoke quickly, as if trying to make himself believe his own words. 'You think we all have such simple choices as you?' he demanded. 'That a mapmaker can do as he pleases?' He gave a bitter laugh. 'Do you know what the spies of France or Spain would pay for a copy, even a glimpse, of the work I do? Do you not think I have spurned their proffered gold, as you have spurned mine?' A grim smile appeared. 'Now, tell me that altering a few lines of ink, to wipe a few hundred acres off the land-holdings of a man like Mountford, is such a dreadful crime!'

Thomas said nothing. 'You see?' Mead cried. 'You have no

answer!' He drew breath, then turned towards the horse which stood patiently at his side. Gripping the rein, he spoke in a quieter tone.

'Some nights back, I drank more than was good for me, at the inn in Chaddleworth. The landlord's wife said she knew you, when I told how you and I had met on the Downs. I heard you're a widower, like me...' He frowned at the look which came over Thomas's face. 'But unlike me, you have a child.' He paused. 'My wife died before we were so blessed, hence the only legacy I leave behind me are my maps. Marks on paper to you, but to me they are like children – beyond price. The embodiment of everything we have, to be handed down for eternity! You think I would debase them lightly?'

He placed his boot in the stirrup, heaved himself into the saddle and looked down at Thomas. 'I pawned my soul, falconer. My mistake was I thought I could redeem it later – and I left it too late.' His voice rose, and there was a quavering in it. 'Now nothing lies before me, save the pits of hell.'

With a violent movement he yanked the reins, dug his bootheels into the horse's scrawny sides and drove it mercilessly forward, away into the night.

Thomas stood for a while on the path, hearing the hoof-beats recede into the distance. A nightjar flew above his head. From the woods about the ruined priory, a little to the south, barn owls hooted.

He did not wish to walk home to an empty cottage. Nell would be in the kitchens until late, and would sleep as she often did beside the wenches, all of them so tired they cared not where they lay. He drew a gulp of night air. The moon was high, and Chaddleworth lay but a quarter mile westwards. In a moment he was striding through the trees, to emerge on the green a short time later. The lighted windows of the Black Bear drew him.

The inn was still crowded, its reassuring odours enveloping him like a warm shroud. Beery voices assailed him on every side. As he shouldered his way towards the barrels, picking up snatches of conversation, he heard there was but one topic on folk's minds: Paulo's tent show in Great Shefford the previous night, and the uncovering of Ambrose Fuller as the murderer of Richard Walden. He realised that Grace's troubles had driven much else from his thoughts; he should seek out Frogg, and ask about the search.

'See who's here – the artificer of it all!' Dillamore was emerging from the throng, a brace of empty mugs in each hand. 'Half the village talks of you,' he said excitedly. 'They say you chased Fuller out of Great Shefford, and lost him when you stopped to help fight the fire...' He shook his head. 'By the Lord, who'd have thought that bow-legged soak of a thatcher, who's drunk in here most of his life, was a bloody-handed murderer?'

He stopped, peering closer. 'You look in need of a mug,' he said.

Thomas sighed. 'I'd best find Giles Frogg first.'

'You'll find him over at widow Gee's,' Dillamore informed him. 'Old hen barricaded herself in again, shouting everyone's after her gold.' He tapped the side of his head meaningfully.

Thomas frowned. 'I'll come back for that mug,' he said.

He crossed the green to Agnes Gee's tiny cottage. Giles Frogg and two or three other men were standing about outside, looking somewhat helpless. Thomas saw the exhaustion on Frogg's face, and knew the man had not slept since yesterday.

He nodded. 'I hear you've got more trouble on your hands, Giles.'

Frogg let out a sigh. 'I've told these men if she don't open her door within the hour, I mean to resign as constable. Then I'll walk over to the Bear and drink myself horizontal. Like to join me?'

Thomas gave a wry smile. 'Mayhap I will.'

One of the men who stood near grunted his displeasure. 'See, Thomas, I've told him we ought to break the door in and have done with it. Agnes bain't sound in her mind – she's a danger to herself, and her neighbours.'

As if in answer, there came a screech from beyond the door. 'I know ye spy on me!' Agnes Gee shouted. 'Ye want my husband's gold, and ye shan't have it!'

Frogg looked exasperated. 'I fear what she'll do if we try to force it,' he muttered.

The men exchanged looks, glancing at the cottage. Thomas met Frogg's eye, whereupon the constable gave a brief shake of his head, which told him all he needed to know: that the search had proved useless. Fuller, and presumably John Flowers too, were still at large.

He was on the point of making an excuse and walking back to the inn, when there came another cry from within the cottage. 'Jesu save me – it's gone!'

The men stirred, for there followed a series of fearful shrieks, of such a pitch that it was clear the business had gone on long enough. Action must be taken.

'Well, Giles?' one of the other men demanded.

'The devil with it,' Frogg said at last. 'Break the whoreson thing down, and hang the consequences!'

With relief the others sprang to the door and began shoving at it. From within, Agnes Gee's cries merely increased, especially when the old timbers gave way and the door flew inwards. Frogg shouldered his way inside. Stooping under the low lintel, Thomas followed with the other men.

The single, poorly furnished room was lit by a feeble rush

light, but the figure of Agnes Gee was visible, cowering by the chimney wall. As the men piled into her house, filling it with their bulk, she raised a shaking hand. In it was an old knife, fit for little more than cutting bread.

'Keep back!' she yelled. 'There's naught for you here. It's gone!'

Her gaze went to the ancient, blackened fireplace. To Thomas's surprise there was a gaping hole, seven or eight inches square, dug in the earth beside the hearth. Beside it lay a slab of thick slate which he assumed had been used to conceal it.

Frogg came forward and peered into the hole. He shoved his hand in, down to the elbow, then brought it out empty. The others exchanged looks.

'Mayhap he did have a sum squirreled away, after all,' one muttered.

But Thomas was watching the old woman, as she stared from one man to another, then at the hole, still holding the knife out before her.

'Who do you think took it, Agnes?' he asked gently.

'The ghost – it must have been!' Agnes Gee cried. 'Jane Kirke saw it, and I saw it! Creeping through the trees beyond the green, in and out of gardens – none would listen when I told of it! Now it's been in my house, and taken Nick's gold!'

The men stared. Giles Frogg straightened up, looking sceptical. 'You mean Walden's ghost?'

She shook her head fiercely. ''Ee don't look like Walden – 'ee's foul and naked, covered with hair, like the devils on the walls of the church!' Suddenly she dropped the knife and fell to her knees. 'Lord Jesu, rend me not for my sins... for I've borne all a poor widow can, and I can do no more!'

As the men watched, she burst into tears. Oblivious to their presence, she buried her head in her hands and sobbed as though she would never stop.

Frogg looked at the other men, who filed out, but signalled Thomas to stay. Soon they were alone with the distraught old woman, who remained on her knees weeping for her sins, whatever they might be. Within the hour, comforted by the two of them as best they could, she had quieted. Neighbours had gathered outside, but Frogg sent them away. Agnes sat at her old, rickety table on the only stool, while Thomas and the constable stood nearby.

Thomas's senses were reeling, for now another matter – one to which he had given little thought – was laid bare. The explanation had been before him, time after time, and he had failed to see it. There was no ghost, and the clever-handed young man who had drawn the likeness of one on glass, in order to scare a murderer into confessing, knew it better than anyone. Had the hour not been too late, he would have gone to the show field at once – now it must wait until the morrow. He could only hope that Paulo and his assistant had not already packed and gone.

Agnes Gee sipped the cup of warm milk a neighbour had sent in, and gazed at the two men. Finally she said, 'It was our secret... To keep us in our last years, Nick said. Only, he grew afeared to touch it.'

Frogg spoke up, in a tone of some awe. 'It's been troubling me, ever since the truth come out,' he said. 'I asked myself a dozen times: if they all took bribes – the jurymen, that is – then what did they do with the money?'

Thomas nodded. 'It crossed my mind too,' he said. 'I'll wager Simon Haylock drank most of his.'

'And the brewer, Rawlings,' Frogg added. 'From what I've heard in West Shefford, he spent all he had on a blowsy whore. Bought her jewels and kickshaws and such... They say his wife suspected it all along.' He turned to Agnes Gee. 'But your husband buried his.'

The old woman merely stared down at the table.

'You can tell us now,' Frogg said to her in a kindlier tone. 'Naught will happen to you; it was your husband's crime, not yours—'

'Crime?' The old woman fixed a watery eye upon him. 'Twas the Devil's wages... He knew it as well as I. That was why he feared to spend it. Will Kirke too!' She turned a haggard face from one to the other.

'Have ye not caught hold of the truth yet? 'Twas Kirke's gold too, and Haylock's! Nick kept it for all of them: twenty-seven gold crowns, wrapped in a bit of leather – our fortune. Now Jane will have naught for her old age, same as me... 'Tis the Lord's punishment on us both!'

Thomas watched her, and a chill fell upon his heart. It was Paulo Schweiz who had cast doubt about the widow's being as crazed as folk thought. But another doubt remained, and more of the showman's words sprang to his mind: *You are still unsure whether to trust me...*

'Who else knew of it?' he asked Agnes, somewhat sharply.

But the old woman seemed not to hear. 'Our fortune,' she repeated softly, gazing down at her hands. 'It should 'a been silver – and thirty pieces of it too.'

She began to weep again, quietly now, her eyes closed.

But Thomas persisted. 'Agnes, think on it,' he urged. 'When did you open the hiding-place? When did you last see the money?'

But she did not hear. Frogg rose from the table with a shake of his head. At last Thomas followed him outside.

* * *

In the morning, after a few hours' troubled sleep, he was up and waiting for Ned Hawes when the boy arrived at his work.

'I must leave all the birds in your care,' Thomas told him, 'and go to Great Shefford.'

Ned showed his disappointment; the village was seething with excitement, and the boy was eager to hear the news from Thomas's own mouth.

'We'll talk later,' he went on. 'For now I need you to hold off Sir Robert, or anyone else who asks where I am gone.'

Ned stared. 'You've heard something?' he began, but Thomas was already moving off. 'Before the day is ended,' he called, 'we will all have heard something.'

Ned watched him hurry down the slope and disappear round the wall of the stable yard. Had Thomas known it, there was more on Ned's mind than the far-off hunt for a murderer. For two nights ago, before he had set out for Paulo's show in Great Shefford, he had talked with Eleanor, and knew now that she would never be his wife. Feeling empty, he walked out on to the Downs to feed the eyasses.

* * *

On the same borrowed gelding he had last ridden, Thomas galloped down the Hungerford Road. The sky was overcast, with the threat of a storm later, but he barely noticed. His one thought was to get to Paulo's encampment before he pulled out, and confront him with what he knew. But as he approached the village, with the show field to his left, he saw that the tent was gone.

Cursing under his breath, he slowed the horse, but as he turned in at the gateway his spirits rose. The tent and all Paulo's accoutrements were packed, but the cart was still there. Nearby, the showman's old sway-backed nag was tethered. He reined in, quickly looking around.

There was a shout. Paulo was crossing the field towards him with hand raised, wearing his old scholar's gown.

'You are come to say good-bye!' The conjuror's smile was warm, and Thomas felt sick at heart. How he would play this, he did not yet know.

'Master Paulo.' He dismounted, and took Paulo's outstretched hand. 'I'm glad I was in time; no doubt you are eager to be gone.'

Paulo said nothing, but disarmed Thomas with one of his stares. Finally he said, 'You have much trouble, still.'

'I'll not deny it,' Thomas answered. 'Yet I believe I have solved one mystery, and without your help.'

Paulo frowned. 'You are angry with me... Why should that be?'

Thomas hesitated. 'Where's your helper?' he asked. 'Or should I ask, where is the ape?'

But Paulo merely gazed at him. Nor did he turn when there came a sound from the laden cart. Thomas looked round sharply to see Kit Page emerging from behind the covers. He climbed down from the cart and waited. Soon the ape appeared and dropped onto Kit's shoulders, whereupon the young man straightened up, looking without expression at Thomas.

'I would speak with him,' Thomas said quietly.

Paulo was silent.

'I know now, why things have disappeared from some of the houses around my village, including my master's,' Thomas persisted. 'Or I should say, I know how they were taken.' Still Paulo remained silent, until Thomas said, 'You wished for my trust. Was I right to place it in you?'

But Paulo's eyes narrowed. 'Did you ever truly do so?' he asked.

'I thought you my friend,' Thomas began, but the other threw out a hand.

'That is not an answer.'

Thomas drew breath. 'In truth, I no longer know what I should think,' he said. He indicated Kit Page, who was still watching them. 'Call him over, and let us put an end to the wrangling.'

Suddenly Paulo's expression changed. His heavy eyebrows sprang together, and anger showed in his eyes. Turning on his heel, he strode at once to where Kit still stood beside the cart. Thomas followed.

They drew close, and Kit flinched. His hands went up to grasp the long arms of the ape, which hung about his shoulders like a fur collar. 'Why is he come again?' he asked, with a jerk of his head towards Thomas.

But without hesitation, Paulo raised his hand sharply and cracked him across the face. The boy gasped and staggered, while the ape let out a screech, leaped off his back and flew behind a cartwheel, from where it watched the events wide-eyed.

'*Dieb! Verbrecher!*' the showman cried. 'You swore it was over! You are a serpent yet!' And to Thomas's dismay, he proceeded to beat Kit about the head with his hands, until the boy fell to his knees, then finally curled up into a ball on the grass, crying for mercy. Only then, his breath coming in rasps, did the showman cease, turn his back and walk a few paces. Then he stopped, bowed his head and gave into a sudden and overwhelming grief.

24

Thomas stared from Kit to his master, and back again. Finally he left the gasping boy, who had sat up and leaned back against the cartwheel, his head in his hands. With a mixture of feelings, he walked over to Paulo.

The showman had mastered himself. As Thomas drew near, he turned. 'You were right not to trust me,' he muttered, wiping his face with the wide sleeve of his gown. 'For I am a fool!'

'You?' Thomas shook his head. 'You're the cleverest man I have ever known—'

'*Nein!*' Paulo's eyes flashed. 'Only a fool deceives himself, as I did...' His gaze dropped. '*You* are clever, my friend. For you saw what I chose not to see, even though in my heart I knew it...' He took a breath, trying to summon some dignity. 'Come!'

He pointed to the cart. As the two of them walked towards it, Kit Page scrambled to his feet. The ape still cowered behind the wheel.

Paulo glared at him. 'Show me where it is!'

Kit hesitated. 'This is between us...' he began in a low voice, but stopped himself as Paulo raised his hand.

'Show me!' he snapped.

The boy made no move. Then as Paulo stiffened, he made a sudden lunge to one side, but Thomas was quicker. As Kit turned, he stuck his boot out and tripped him easily. Then when the boy fell, Thomas reached down and caught his arm.

'You're not leaving yet – at least, not in that manner,' he said, yanking him to his feet. 'Now do as your master says.'

Kit squirmed, but he was caught fast. Refusing to meet Thomas's eye, he gazed sullenly at Paulo.

But the showman had moved to the cart, and was banging on the side with his fists. He walked along it, cursing under his breath. Finally Kit tore himself from Thomas's grasp, and cried, 'Soft! I will show you!'

Watched by the other two, he went to the front of the cart and reached beneath the driver's seat. Angrily he smacked the narrow wooden panel, which fell in at once. Then he stood back, staring at the ground.

Thomas walked to the opening which was revealed and peered inside. Then he reached in and drew out a small hempen sack, which clinked as he lifted it. He turned to Paulo, raising an eyebrow. Breathing heavily, Paulo came forward, took the sack and tore at the cord which bound it. When he tipped the contents out a shower of coins, many of them gold crowns, fell onto the grass. There followed a necklace and several rings, a gold plate, a pair of gold cups and a silver dish.

In the silence that fell Thomas glanced about the field, but fortunately there was no one to observe the proceedings. Reaching into the recess again, he pulled out a sheet of fine linen. He unfolded it until an embroidered crest appeared, picked out in scarlet thread.

'My master's,' he said.

Paulo was gazing at Kit, but the boy merely stared morosely at the grass.

'It is how he was, when I first found him,' Paulo murmured, turning to Thomas. 'This was all he knew. I taught him new skills, and he called me father, and swore he had put away his old life. Until I caught him out, in another country – and yet again, he swore he would cease...'

He faced Kit. 'You wanted for nothing,' he said. 'What then, would you do with all this money?' When Kit kept silent, the showman turned away. But Thomas had seen the deep hurt in his eyes, and knew what he must do. Deliberately he bent down and began gathering up the valuables, stowing them into the sack.

Paulo raised his eyes. 'You will tell Sir Robert...' he began, but Thomas stayed him.

'I'll tell him you and I recovered what was stolen,' he said. 'And though I begged you to come with me to the high sheriff to receive his thanks, you had a show to prepare, and had to take your leave. They will hardly wish to pursue you.'

Paulo frowned. 'I would not have you lie for me.'

Thomas finished collecting up the coins and dropping them into the sack. Then he pulled what remained out of the recess under the cart's seat: several fine linen sheets and bolster-cases, and a velvet cloak.

He eyed Kit. 'You must have spent many hours, training the ape to do your will,' he said. And when the young man made no reply, he continued, 'It would climb up walls, and through windows while you waited. Am I correct?'

Kit still stared at the ground. Then he crouched, peered under the cart and gave a low whistle. After a moment the ape came out, loped towards him and leaped into his arms. The boy hugged it like a baby.

Paulo gazed at them both, and turned away.

* * *

Thomas led the gelding out on to the road. The bag of stolen goods was tied across his saddle with the rolled-up linen. He waited until the showman's heavily laden cart had lumbered out of the field. Kit Page was in the driver's seat, while Paulo walked behind.

The cart passed him and turned southwards, whereupon Kit drew it to a halt. He had not met Thomas's eyes since their earlier encounter.

Paulo drew close, looking as if he wished to speak, but Thomas shook his head. 'I know what I do,' he said. 'More, I know what you – and the boy, too – have done here. The Downlands may yet be in your debt.'

Paulo looked subdued. 'All the while he stole – and I who am deemed so gifted, could not see what lay under my own feet.'

Thomas favoured him with a smile. 'I've often found myself in that case,' he said. 'Besides, it was the ape who stole, was it not? And how might such a creature be brought to trial?'

Paulo gave a short laugh, though it had not the ring of earlier times. Then he grew sombre. 'There is yet much for the high sheriff to do, is there not? Our little plan succeeded, yet your murderer is fled, and his fellow too.' He nodded, as if to himself. 'Only later did I understand how it was they were known to each other, yet not known.'

'I fear the avenger – the young man we all thought we knew – will find his victim first,' Thomas said gravely. 'Then there will be but one murderer to hunt: the one who worked with poison, as you revealed.'

Paulo sighed. 'I've learned much, these past weeks. Foremost is, I do not wish to entangle myself again in the law's business. Let others play discoverer.'

He held out his hand, and Thomas gripped it. 'We will not meet again,' Paulo said. 'I may sell my tent and my cart, and take ship for France. Mayhap I will work alone thereafter, as I used to.'

'That would be a loss,' Thomas told him. 'Your *Mundus Peregrinus* shows us worlds that folk have barely heard of.'

Paulo smiled, with something of his old mischievous self. 'So I am told,' he answered. 'I have yet to see them for myself – an intriguing ambition.'

Thomas looked surprised. 'I thought you had seen them.'

'I am a Switzer,' the other replied, 'who has ventured into Naples and France, and a few smaller countries of Europe. The other lands I have but heard of – from greater travellers than me.'

He touched Thomas on the arm, turned to go, then paused.

'The letter you seek...' he began.

'I know, you said it will be found,' Thomas broke in.

But the conjuror's smile had faded. 'Do not judge her too harshly,' he said, then walked briskly to his cart and climbed onto the driver's seat. There was a crack of the whip, and the travelling show of Paulo Schweiz drew away along the lane and passed out of sight. As he mounted his horse, Thomas heard its wheels rumble over the Lambourn bridge, then fade into the distance.

* * *

No sooner had he reached Petbury than he found his absence had not gone unnoticed. Sir Robert was displeased, and had left word that Thomas should attend him the moment he returned.

Ned was nowhere to be found, and Thomas guessed he was

exercising a bird on the Downs. After quickly tidying his appearance he made his way to the house, carrying the bag of recovered valuables with him like an offering. At least, he had something to show for his pains. But on entering the Great Hall, he encountered an atmosphere of some hostility.

There were several people at the high table: Sir Robert and Richard Ward the high sheriff, together with Lady Margaret and another very elegant lady: pale and auburn-haired, in a richly embroidered gown, and wearing a small ransom in jewellery. He guessed, correctly as it transpired, that this was Ward's wife.

Sir Robert, sombre-faced, gestured him forward. The remains of a more sumptuous dinner than the Vicarys were in the habit of taking, were still spread on the table. Serving-men stood by attentively, as did Martin the steward, at his most officious.

Thomas approached and made his bow, whereupon Sir Robert's words fell like a blow. 'The high sheriff has a mind to arrest you,' he said.

Thomas blinked and turned to Ward, who was looking at him with unconcealed anger. 'I hope you have a goodly tale to spin by way of explanation, falconer,' he said. 'Else you may find yourself bound for Reading gaol, in place of your friend Saltmarsh.'

Thomas's heart sank. It seemed that what he had achieved since Saltmarsh's escape was of no account: the sheriff held him responsible, and that was enough. 'Sir...' he began, but Ward held up a hand.

'I knew you were a sly one from the moment I first saw you,' he said in a cold voice. 'Had I known how resourceful—nay, how slippery you could be, I might have acted differently.' He glanced at Sir Robert, who did not respond, and back to Thomas. 'There has been a deal of toing and froing between here and Great Shefford, wouldn't you say? More, you appear to have talked my men into doing your bidding not once but twice – and the result is an escaped felon, one of my servants poisoned, another man dead in a fire – and two suspected murderers fled into the night, with half the village tripping over their feet in pursuit!'

Thomas said nothing. He sensed that hard words had passed between the sheriff and his master before his arrival. And there was no escaping the fact that Sir Robert's own hopes of bringing matters to a speedy conclusion had come to naught. He had but one card to play: he held up the small sack, which nobody seemed to have noticed.

'May I beg leave to speak, sir?' he asked, fixing his eyes upon Sir Robert. His master met his gaze and nodded.

'These are the valuables that were taken from here, as well as Poughley manor and elsewhere,' Thomas said. 'Master Schweiz, the conjuror, used all his skills to help me locate where they were hidden.'

He came forward and placed the bag on the table before his master, making sure that the metallic clink from within was heard by all. He turned to Ward. 'If I might make so bold, master sheriff: Will Saltmarsh was not the thief. And since we know now he was not the killer of Sir John Mountford either—'

'You dare to harangue me?' Ward's eyes were blazing. He pointed at the sack. 'I think it more likely you struck some bargain with the rogue Saltmarsh, and in return for telling you where those goods were, you helped him escape!'

Thomas met his gaze. 'How might I have done such, sir? Your men were on watch the night he disappeared, and I was here, attending upon my master and mistress.'

Ward's gaze shifted to Sir Robert, who raised an eyebrow. 'That's true enough, Master Ward. More, it was Thomas who then drove the four men who were under my protection to Great

Shefford, to what we believed was safety – where they would be guarded by your servants.' He paused. 'Is it his fault one of them chose to accept ale from a stranger, and got himself poisoned? Moreover—'

'Yes, indeed!' Ward was controlling his anger with difficulty. 'We have trod that ground already, sir, have we not?'

He eyed Thomas again. 'I know in my vitals, that there is more to this than you have told.' And when he turned back to Sir Robert, his tone was scathing. 'I am disappointed, sir, to find that much of what I had heard about you has proved true. You seem barely capable of controlling your own servants.'

There was a stifled gasp from several throats. Martin the steward stared frostily at Ward. The other servants stood like wooden posts.

But Sir Robert kept his eyes upon the table, picked up his favourite cup and drank from it. Whereupon it was Lady Margaret who spoke.

'How perceptive you are, master sheriff,' she said, wearing one of her faint smiles. 'I have berated my husband a hundred times for his *laissez-faire* ways... We are but simple country folk, as you know. We laughed about it at Easter, when my Lord Godwin dined here. As did the Fettiplaces, and the Plowdens... They all think Sir Robert too kind for his own good.'

Ward bristled. 'I must ask the lord lieutenant for his opinion when I next see him, my lady,' he murmured, forcing a smile.

But Lady Margaret was not done. 'Why not speak with him here, when he dines with us next month?' she asked. 'He comes for the sport, as always... We count ourselves blessed to live in the heart of some of the best hawking country in England, as you know.' She paused. 'And we have the best falconer, too.'

Ward inclined his head, biting back some reply. Sir Robert

remained silent, but there was a glint in his eye that was not lost on his more perceptive servants.

Then, unexpectedly, there came a voice Thomas had not heard before, and it was from Ward's own wife.

'Indeed, madam,' she said in a languid tone. 'Now I observe Master Finbow for myself, I have small difficulty in imagining what an asset he must be to you.' She threw what was intended to appear a casual glance at Thomas, but as the receiver of it he felt a stir; Mistress Ward, he saw, was a woman of some mettle.

At the high table, there was a tension between the two men and their ladies, until mercifully Sir Robert took the initiative. 'You've done well to recover what was stolen,' he said to Thomas. 'The details of how it came to pass, we might leave until later.' He turned to Ward, who sat rigid with a glassy look on his face.

'Master sheriff, Thomas has done little without my leave,' he said. 'And he is but a falconer, not a man-at-arms. The failing lies surely with your own servants?'

Ward hesitated. 'I would still like to question him,' he said acidly.

'And more,' Sir Robert continued, raising his voice slightly, 'the cunning device he hatched with that mountebank exposed the wretch who murdered Richard Walden. At least we know whom we seek – as we know at last who was poisoning the members of that ill-starred jury.'

'Again, sir, we have already touched upon that,' Ward retorted. 'Even now a search is being mounted across the county, and beyond.' He glanced at Thomas, but before he could continue, his wife spoke again in a bored voice.

'Heavens, sir, have you not beaten the matter to a pulp? I thought we came here for the hawking first, and for matters of office second?'

Ward's sickly smile reappeared. 'Madam, Sir Robert and I have duties...'

'Then should we not leave you to them?' his wife asked, with a smile at Lady Margaret.

Lady Margaret smiled in turn. 'Wise words from your spouse, master sheriff,' she said to Ward, and turned to Sir Robert. 'With your leave, sir?'

Sir Robert inclined his head, and several relieved servants sprang forward to attend Lady Margaret. But before she rose, the knight faced Ward.

'Since we speak of duties, sir, might my falconer be permitted to go now, and return to his?'

There was a brief silence before Ward gave a short nod, but it was enough. Thomas acknowledged Sir Robert's dismissal, made his bow and headed for the entrance. As he passed through the doorway he caught the baleful look that was directed at him by the high sheriff, then got himself outside.

25

He found Ned at the mews, unhooding Tamora after her exercise. The leather pouch he carried bulged with small game. With a nod of approval, Thomas took Caesar on his gauntlet and carried him outside. Ned followed with Brutus.

Thomas told him briefly what had occurred at Great Shefford. But though he listened attentively, it was clear the boy had other matters on his mind. 'There's odd things going on at the eyas mews,' he said. 'I think someone's been hiding out there.'

Thomas frowned. 'Are you certain?'

'I found some rinds of bread this morning, and a chicken bone or two. More, looked like a sack's been used as a pillow.'

Thomas was looking down towards the house. 'Have you told anyone else?' he asked. When Ned shook his head, he said, 'We'll walk there now, take a look.' He glanced at the pouch. 'You can go down to the kitchens later and give the catch to Nell.'

'You'll want to speak with her yourself,' Ned said. 'And I've no business at the house, now.'

'So you've talked with Eleanor,' Thomas said, understanding at last. When Ned made no reply he added, 'Remember, she's still young – younger than you. Mayhap she's not yet sure what she wants.'

Ned raised his eyes. 'You've no need to try and soften the blow, Thomas.'

'Then my hope is, it will not spoil our friendship,' Thomas murmured. Caesar twitched on his wrist, so he drew the plumed leather hood from his pocket and slipped it over the old tercel's head to quiet him.

'No,' Ned answered. 'Naught I know of would ever do that.'

Thomas led the way up the path towards the Downs.

But as soon as they reached the nursery mews, he saw that Ned was right. For one thing, the eyasses were nervous as though they had been disturbed, their quiet routine broken. Leaving the adult falcons tethered outside, he and Ned did their best to settle the birds, while making a search of the hut. There were indeed food remains in a corner, and signs that someone had slept there, at least once.

They stood outside in the late afternoon, watching the clouds thickening to a slate grey. The storm which had threatened for hours was close now.

Thomas was thoughtful. The eyas mews was remote enough for a temporary hideaway. From here, there was little but empty Downlands in two directions. A fugitive could cross the border into Oxfordshire within hours, or he could go west into Wiltshire... He frowned. If he were on the run, which way would he go?

Ned had been looking at the grass. 'I'm no woodsman,' he said to Thomas, 'but I'd say somebody was here last night, and moved off south this morning.'

Thomas walked over to him. Gazing down, he saw several broken stems as clearly as did Ned, but they proved little.

'And it's not just that,' Ned added. He peered across the wide plain of long grass, rippling in the rising breeze. He walked off a few paces, then stopped and bent down. 'It's more this!' he called, holding something up.

Together the falconers they examined the object: it was a man's leather heel, badly worn at the rear, and torn where it had worked loose from its nails.

'Well,' Thomas mused. 'Whoever he is, he won't get far with those boots.'

Ned squinted at the sky. 'Storm's upon us.'

Thomas gazed southwards. 'There isn't time to get back to Petbury before the birds get a soaking,' he said. 'I think we should make for Boxwell Farm.'

'Why there?' Ned asked. Then seeing Thomas's expression, his face cleared. 'By the Christ,' he muttered, and hurried back to pick up the falcon.

* * *

They had barely gone a half-mile before the heavens burst.

The falcons were hooded, but they hated a heavy downpour, and shifted restlessly on the gauntlets. Thomas and Ned were obliged to open their jerkins and cover up their charges as best they could. Uneasy at being exposed on the open Downs, they broke into a trot through the sodden grass, while thunder growled in the distance. There was not a tree within a mile's radius, and they would not be the first men of West Berkshire to die from a lightning strike. The thought spurred them on as there came a blinding flash, quickly followed by a thunderclap.

Ned drew alongside Thomas, shouting as they ran. 'Why would he go south?'

Thomas shook his head. 'I don't know... just a notion.'

They travelled for half an hour, sometimes slowing to

recover their breath, then hurrying on. But at last they were running through pasture, the ground dipped and the roof-tops of Boxwell Farm showed dimly through the driving rain. The thunder had passed by them, rolling north-east towards Wantage. On the Downs, knots of sheep were huddled together. As they hurried downhill they saw more, sheltering under trees by the lane. The farmyard was ahead. Thomas was first through the gateway, the rebuilt barn to his right with its new roof of firm yellow thatch.

He halted, feeling Caesar's body pressed against him under his jerkin. Thankfully the bird was quiet. Ned came up behind, his wet hair plastered to his skull. Both of them were soaked to the bone.

There was a sound. Peering ahead, they saw the farmhouse door open and a figure appear. A hand was raised, beckoning them inside. At once they hurried forward, to pass over the threshold into the warm kitchen. But as they stood dripping inside the doorway, Beatrice Ames's taut manner struck them both.

'John's out with the boys,' she said quickly. 'They got to get the new lambs under cover.'

Thomas nodded, acknowledging the woman's smile, which to his mind seemed forced. As he watched, she lowered her eyes.

'So you're all alone, mistress,' he murmured.

She nodded quickly.

'Powerful storm,' Thomas added. 'Caught us out like a couple of townsfolk.'

Beatrice gestured to the chimney, where a fire burned. 'You'd best get your wet clothes a-drying,' she said. 'I'll find something you can wrap yourselves in.'

Still she avoided Thomas's eyes. After a moment he said, 'If we might place the birds somewhere quiet...?' He opened his jerkin to show Caesar still perched on his wrist. Startled, Beatrice stepped back.

'Lord, I didn't see...' She glanced at Ned, who also revealed the bird he carried, then glanced about the kitchen. 'I'm not sure where...'

'The barn would do,' Thomas said.

There was a silence. Deliberately he turned and looked through the doorway to the barn. Its doors were shut.

Beatrice's hand flew nervously to her throat. 'Yon corner would be fine,' she said. 'I'll fetch stools. You won't want to go outside again.'

Thomas met her eye. 'Can't get any wetter than we are already,' he answered. 'Unless, that is, you don't want us to go in the barn?'

She had paled visibly. Holding Caesar close to his side, Thomas took a step towards her. 'Let me help you,' he said in a low voice.

Beatrice flinched. 'Nay, Thomas...' she began, but there was a catch in her throat. Then, with the eyes of both falconers upon her, she took a sudden breath.

'He's been in there since this morning,' she blurted. 'He's got Gilly with him. Matty's out with his father...' She threw a fearful look towards the barn. 'He said if I told anyone, he'd kill him!'

Ned's jaw dropped, but Thomas remained calm. 'You mean John Flowers?'

Beatrice shook her head violently. 'Nay, I mean Ambrose Fuller!' And when the falconers took in the news, she seemed to throw caution aside.

'He swore he'd be away come nightfall,' she said, and moved away from the door, indicating the other two should follow. 'He was hiding, waiting for John and Matty to be gone. Then he caught Gilly, put the fear of God into him – into me too! He's got a poniard. He's half-wild and in terror for his life. I fed him, and found him a pair of John's boots, though they're way too big...' All at once she was near to tears. 'What more could I do?'

'You did right,' Thomas said. 'Now let us try—'

'Nay! Think of Gilly!' she cried. 'He's barely thirteen...'

But Thomas drew closer to her, and somehow she took heart from his presence. 'Let us place the birds safely,' he said. 'Then Ned and I will decide how to act.'

* * *

A short time later, her head covered against the rain, Beatrice Ames stepped out of the farmhouse and hurried across to the barn carrying a covered basket. Nervously she banged on the door.

There was a muffled sound from within, then a voice. 'What d'ye want?'

'I've food and a costrel,' Beatrice called. 'John and Matty will return soon...'

Nothing happened for some time. Then the voice again. 'Leave it outside, and get ye gone!'

'I will,' Beatrice replied, but as she turned to go, there was a growl.

'I know someone's over the house! I heard 'em running in!'

'They're but taking shelter,' she called back. 'Sitting by the fire 'til their clothes dry, then they'll be gone. They know naught of you!'

'You better be telling truth,' Ambrose Fuller answered. 'Or this boy loses an eye! I've a dagger close to 'ee...'

Beatrice's hand went to her mouth, but her nerve held. 'I'm going,' she called. 'Take the food before it gets wet.' She hurried back to the house. Even from within the barn, the slam of the door would have been audible.

Or so Thomas reasoned, crouching in the rain beside the barn wall.

A minute later the door creaked open. There was a moment while someone looked about for the basket, which was at one side. Then a hand appeared, and Thomas leaned forward and grabbed it.

There was a cry of pain and rage, and Ambrose Fuller shot out of the barn, drawn by the unexpected momentum of Thomas's strength. He lurched across the muddy yard, slipped and fell on his side. Immediately Thomas was upon him, twisting his arm behind his back. Fuller bellowed, struggling to aim a kick at his assailant, which went wide. But even as he struck out with his free hand, craning his head to peer upwards, Ned Hawes, dripping like a sodden rat, appeared from the other side of the barn. Bending quickly, he put Thomas's poniard against Fuller's throat.

'Best be still, Ambrose,' he said, 'or it's you as might get spiked.'

Fuller grunted, his eyes darting about, rapidly becoming as soaked as his two captors. Now they had occasion to look at him, he appeared a deal less threatening. His face was dirty, his clothes too. There were scratches on his cheek as if he had run or crawled through undergrowth, which was likely the case. His breeches were torn. On his feet, far too big for him, were John Ames's boots.

There came a shout from inside the barn, and Thomas turned quickly, thinking of the boy. But Beatrice Ames was quicker, running full tilt from the house, her skirts slopping through the mud, and she flew through the open door. A moment later, to the relief of both Thomas and Ned, she appeared, weeping tears of relief, arms about her younger son. Thankfully the boy looked unhurt, though his hands were tied behind him. Pale-faced, he stared at the man lying prone in the yard with Thomas and Ned Hawes bent over him.

Thomas turned back to Fuller, whose arm he still held in a tight grip. 'What possessed you to come back here?' he asked. 'Was it the last place you thought he'd look for you?'

Fuller made no answer, but his eyes slid towards the poniard Ned still held to his neck. 'You wouldn't use that thing, boy,' he breathed.

Ned stiffened, but Thomas leaned down and shoved his face close to Fuller's. 'I might,' he said. Then, as an afterthought, he added, 'But the one I spoke of would do it slower, and make it hurt more, would he not?' He paused. 'Mayhap you should be glad it's we caught you, and not him.'

Fuller's rage broke. 'You whoreson rogue, Finbow!' he cried. 'I should 'a broke your head in this very yard—!'

But Thomas jerked his arm, making him cry out. 'Your days of breaking heads are done,' he said. 'You'll hang for what you did to Walden, and not a soul will weep.'

Fuller's breath came in rasps, but his head had sunk onto his chest. Thomas's gaze wandered to the roof of the great barn, which loomed above them. 'You did a good job here,' he observed. 'Neither of us knew it would be your last, did we?'

He signalled to Ned, and between them they pulled the prisoner to his feet. Fuller's eyes darted about, and for a moment it looked as if he would try to break away. Then he looked down at the boots, whose ends had bent upwards beyond his toes. How far would he get?

He sagged, and stared at the muddy ground.

* * *

It was dusk by the time John Ames and his older son returned home, to a scene neither would forget: Ambrose Fuller, muddy and trussed like a fowl beside their door, with Thomas the falconer and his helper sitting inside clad in blankets, while their clothes steamed before the fire.

Word was sent to Sir Robert, and within the hour a small party arrived on horseback. It consisted of Will Ashman, the high sheriff's servant, together with James the groom and a couple of his fellows. Ashman had orders to bring the prisoner to Petbury at once.

The sheriff had urged speed, and his servant had little time to speak with Thomas; nor, it appeared, did he wish to. It was but a short time before the two falconers watched them leave, with Ambrose Fuller bound and led on a rope between them. He looked like a beast on its way to slaughter.

Mercifully the rain had ceased. Thomas and Ned had retrieved their birds, and stood in the yard to take farewell of John Ames and his wife, both of whom were profuse in their gratitude.

'What a May-time this has been, falconer,' the farmer muttered, shaking his head. 'Seems like the world's been over-turned since the night our barn was set afire. Who'd have thought there was such wickedness to be uncovered?'

Thomas made no reply; he had no wish to voice his fears that the matter was not yet ended. But if he was startled when Beat-rice Ames hugged him, it was nothing to the surprise Ned showed at receiving a hug in his turn. To Thomas's mind, the boy seemed to grow an inch taller. With a wave, the two of them set off up the path, the shortest way back to Petbury.

* * *

After the storm came a clear night, bright with stars. Ned had gone home bursting with excitement and not a little pride, after Thomas had praised his quickness and bravery. There was little doubt that he would be the toast of the Black Bear when the momentous events of the day were known, which would be soon enough. Thomas could already hear the tongues wagging.

For his part, he was subdued. Having settled the falcons he walked down to the stable to speak with James the groom. But no sooner had he rounded the wall than he saw torches, and several men standing in the yard – most prominent among them, Sir Robert and the high sheriff himself.

'Finbow!' Ward seemed in a better humour than he had earlier that day. 'It seems you are to be commended for your action, though it was a somewhat fortuitous encounter, from what I hear.' He smiled slightly. 'Mayhap there's some affinity with barns that draws you to them.'

Thomas made his bow stiffly. Will Ashman stood by, refusing to meet his eye. But Sir Robert spoke up briskly. 'The prisoner is under guard, and has been placed in the hayloft, which seems to have become a repository for undesirables of late,' he said. 'The sheriff will convey him hence to Reading...' He eyed Ward. 'I trust that will be soon, sir?'

Ward's faint smile now looked like one of unconcern, and it seemed to Thomas that he had the manner of a man with all the time in the world.

'Of course, Sir Robert,' he murmured. 'Though naturally there are matters to be put in hand first. The arrival of a proper guard to escort the prisoner for one, and my issuing of letters and warrants...' He raised an eyebrow. 'Is it an inconvenience to you?'

'None at all,' Sir Robert answered coolly. 'I would merely like to have my stables returned to their proper function.'

'Understandable.' The sheriff indulged himself in an elabo-rate yawn. 'Shall we retire now? The night grows chill.'

Without waiting for a reply he strode off towards the house. In the absence of any orders, Will Ashman looked abashed then hurried after him. Sir Robert stood with Thomas and the grooms who, now that the other men had gone, drew closer to their master.

'I want a good watch kept,' Sir Robert told them. 'I mean not on the prisoner – that is for the sheriff's man. In any case, Fuller is bound and without shoes – he is in no condition to go far. I mean on the surrounds, in all directions.' He looked keenly at Thomas and at James, who nodded. Then he walked off to the house.

Thomas and James exchanged looks, for their master's meaning was clear: whatever the sheriff had said, there was a strong suspicion that their prisoner was being held, like the former jurymen in the barn at Great Shefford, as bait.

26

A day passed, on the surface as ordinary as any that passed at Petbury, save that there was a murderer lodged in the hayloft and a bad-tempered sheriff's man in the yard asking folk their business. An air of suppressed excitement hung over the manor as details of what had occurred were raked over, again and again. But the heroes of the hour, Thomas and Ned, remained out of sight. Thinking the boy would like nothing better than to stop by the kitchens and bask in the attention of the wenches, Thomas made sure they were both occupied.

'The eyasses,' he asked, as they swept out the mews. 'Have they settled?'

Ned nodded. 'They're all well, far as I could see.'

The boy seemed unusually distant. 'All a bit much for you, was it? Yesterday's coil?' Thomas enquired.

'It's not that.' Ned straightened up. 'It's...' He shrugged. 'Folk I've known all my life – or thought I knew. Now it's all come bubbling up, like some foul sludge that was hidden. I stood in the Bear, looking at them – it's like Chaddleworth seems a different place to me now.' He shook his head. 'Old Agnes with a fortune in gold hidden under her hearth... Now she don't talk to a soul, only sits all day staring at naught. And Jane Kirke won't live in the village, but is gone to her daughter's. Seems only Giles Frogg's content, now matters are passed out of his domain and he can take a mug at the Bear in peace.'

'He's earned it,' Thomas said.

'True enough.' Ned brightened. 'Tomorrow's Saturday. Will you walk over in the evening and take a mug with me?'

'I will,' Thomas answered, and clapped him on the shoulder. 'After I have attended to some matters of my own. That is, if I am permitted to.'

* * *

Night fell, and no guard had arrived from Reading to remove the prisoner. After bidding Ned farewell, Thomas walked down to the kitchens to take supper. Though he spoke with several of the servants, he heard little that was new. The high sheriff, it seemed, had been out riding all afternoon as if at leisure. Sir Robert had accompanied him, merely for hospitality's sake. Meanwhile, Lady Margaret entertained Ward's wife in the gardens and in her own chambers.

He had almost finished his pottage and read, when Nell found a moment to come and sit with him.

'They dine late again tonight,' she said. 'I will sleep here. Tomorrow...' She trailed off. Tonight she was not tender; rather, she looked worried.

'I said a while back, there was something I should tell you,' she said. 'It has been on my conscience too long.'

He waited.

'Eleanor has fretted enough,' she continued. 'And I...' She stopped, and Thomas grew concerned.

'What is it? Tell me.'

She hesitated, then: 'It's I who took the letter that came for you. I hid it.'

He froze. 'Why?'

'Because I knew who sent it,' she answered. Hurriedly now, she went on, 'I gave the carrier a drink and a bit of dinner before he went back, and he told me where it came from.' She paused. 'I have not opened it.'

He stared. 'All this time...'

'Nay, do not judge me yet.' There was sadness and regret in her eyes. 'I'll bring it to the cottage tomorrow, and you will read it, and then we will see.'

'See what?' His anger was rising. 'How could you let me accuse Eleanor...'

'Eleanor knows!' she said, striving to keep her voice low. About them, the business of the kitchens proceeded, though with less bustle than usual. Abruptly she rose. 'Eleanor knows now,' she repeated, 'and she has forgiven me. My hope is, that you will too.'

He rose in his turn. 'That may be somewhat hard to do,' he said.

Before she could say more, he moved to the door and went out.

* * *

He awoke in the owl-hoot time, after but a short sleep, and sat up. His dreams had been fleeting, but what troubled him most was Nell's confession of that evening. It would seem a long wait until the next, when, she had given him to understand, matters would become clearer. He sighed, got up and dressed. He would not lie abed all night fretting; a walk in the cool air might help him sleep.

He left the cottage, glancing down towards the great house. The only lights that showed were from the upper chambers, whose high-born occupants habitually kept later hours than their servants. With barely a thought, he walked down to the stables. Whoever was on watch would at least be better company than none at all.

The yard was unlit and the main door open, which surprised him. Then, if Will Ashman were guarding the prisoner, he would likely not think to close it. He looked in through the doors; all seemed quiet, with Sir Robert's horses snorting softly in their stalls. He squinted up the ladder to the hayloft. There was no sound from above; presumably Fuller was asleep. After his recent spell of living as a fugitive, no doubt it was a welcome enough respite.

He turned away, thinking he would walk on the Downs for an hour, then realised what had unsettled him: there was no one on guard at all.

Where were Ashman, and James, and the others whom Sir Robert had charged with keeping watch? On impulse, Thomas found himself climbing the ladder, as quietly as was possible in his heavy boots. He reached the hayloft and peered round in the dark, looking for the pallets against the wall where once the terrified jurymen had lain. Sure enough, he thought he could make out a figure, sitting upright...

A whiff of disturbed air behind him came in an instant, followed by a sickening crack on his head. His last thought, as he swayed on the ladder, was that he would fall to the floor below. Then he was sinking into unconsciousness, as a pair of strong arms lifted him up and laid him on the loft floor.

He woke in considerable discomfort. The reason, he soon discovered, was that his wrists were trussed behind his back with baling twine. Pain shot through his head, making him nauseous. He breathed deeply, then without moving looked about – and almost gasped.

There was a lantern on the floor, throwing its feeble light about the loft. To one side, on the pallet where John Palmer had expired the previous Sunday, and which no one had seen fit to remove, sat Ambrose Fuller, his legs bound in front of him. But if his hands had been tied too, Thomas saw, they were now free.

They were free because John Flowers, who sat before him on a sack of oats, had freed them.

And uncannily it was the same Flowers, the young fair-faced man Thomas had felt such respect for, whom he had watched drinking in the Black Bear, his arm about Ned Hawes's shoulders. Flowers, sitting easily opposite Fuller, looking for all the world like a friend who had come by for a consoling talk with a condemned man. His clothing was neat, his blond locks too. He even wore his easy smile that, as Will Ashman had said, would have charmed any maid into his bed...

Then it occurred to Thomas, uncomfortable as he was on the dusty floor, that for reasons perhaps best known to the high sheriff, Ashman and the rest of the watch had been removed. And it could be no accident. Did the sheriff intend that Fuller should be found? Did he even intend his escape?

Thomas knew then that he was alone. But while he remained still and quiet, he hoped Flowers would think him unconscious. For the present he could do nothing but listen. For they were talking, or at least one of them was – Flowers.

'You'll drink it, Ambrose,' the young man said. 'As I see it, you've little choice.'

Thomas started, and his eyes flew towards the fateful barrel of poisoned ale, which still stood against the wall: no one had thought to remove that either. Then he saw the mug, on the floor beside Fuller, and he saw Fuller's face. The man was petrified. His eyes flickered from the other man to the mug, and back again.

'By the Christ, John,' he whispered, 'I won't.'

Flowers looked disappointed, like a host whose guest refuses another cup of wine. 'You must. You can't imagine what a deal of trouble I had to make up such a brew, let alone get it in here.'

Fuller shook his head slowly. 'You can't make me...'

'Oh, now...' A warning note sounded in the young man's voice 'You're sorely mistaken there, Ambrose. I *will* make you.'

There was a flash of bright steel as Flowers drew a long blade of some kind from his belt. Fuller's body jerked in fear. Then, as Thomas watched helplessly, the young man raised the blade and brought it down with a thwack onto the bare boards where it stood, quivering. It was no knife, but a sharpened billhook.

'I was prenticed in a carpenter's shop, not in the fields,' Flowers said softly. His eyes gleamed in the lantern-light. 'Yet if I chose to take your fingers off one at a time, I could do it clean enough with this.'

Fuller let out a gasp. 'Then why not cut my throat, and have done with it?' he cried. 'I'm for the gallows anyway! For the love of God, John—'

'No!' For the first time Flowers raised his voice. Thomas, striving to keep still, sensed at last the rage contained within the fair form of this handsome young man, one who, he knew now, burned with the lust for revenge. How else could it be, in one who had killed so many?

'Talk not of God, Ambrose,' Flowers said icily. 'For you will not meet Him in the hereafter – you'll broil in hell for what you did to my father.'

A sob came from Fuller's throat. 'Lord above...' He swung his head from side to side, clenching his hands. 'I know it, and I rue that day as I rue no other... I swear I've lain in torment every night since, for what I done. You don't know what I suffered! It was dark, I was afeared – I didn't know twas him came upon me—'

'Enough!' Flowers reached out quickly, prised the billhook from the floor and levelled it at Fuller. 'I've heard your paltry excuses already, in that tent in Shefford,' he said. 'I waited ten years...' His voice shook. 'Ten years... Three since I watched my mother eat herself up with grief, after she took me away from Chaddleworth. You remember Rebecca Walden, Ambrose? A woman without a cruel bone in her body – even when she married Flowers, and he gave me his name and I thought we'd have a fine new life, the pain was working inside her – like a worm, gnawing at her! I watched her waste away, 'til she couldn't even leave her bed, but lay wrinkled like an old costard, while my step-father prayed night and day at her side. Even when she was gone he prayed. Wouldn't listen when they told him it was over. What he didn't know...'

The blade shook; Flowers was trembling, working himself up to some terrible act, and Thomas could do nothing. He strained at his bonds, with a fervent hope he would not be heard. But soon he realised that neither of the other men had any thought but for themselves.

'What he didn't know, Ambrose,' Flowers went on, 'was that I'd sworn to her before she died, I would avenge our loss. That if it took the rest of my days, I would find a way to come back from London, where I'd been sent, and track down whoever beat my father to a carcass. And if it took the killing of every last one of Mountford's cursed jury, so be it! But what I never thought on...' He broke off, breathing steadily. Tugging desperately at his bonds, Thomas saw the young man struggling to contain himself.

'What I never thought on,' he continued in a voice of disbelief, 'was that the bullying oaf I hired as a thatcher, who worked beside me day after day, whose wages I paid from my own pocket, was the one – and he hadn't even sat on the jury! He wasn't called! No one wanted to give you a share of the spoils, Ambrose – because none of 'em could abide the sight of you!'

Flowers broke into a harsh laugh. 'What a fool I was! I could have done for you at my pleasure, any time I chose...' He looked away. 'Now think how many men had to die, before I got to my father's killer. Though they deserved it, thieves and varlets all, taking the bribes only he refused – Richard Walden, a fool but an honest one, isn't that what folk like you dubbed him? A simple gravedigger, who never harmed a soul in all his life!'

Flowers seemed to have forgotten where he was. Thomas heaved at his bonds, fearful of losing circulation; still neither man heard him.

Then Flowers raised the billhook and brought the blade down hard upon Fuller's thigh. The man let out a howl of pain.

'Now drink the brew, Ambrose,' Flowers said. 'Every last drop.'

He waited, and to Thomas's surprise Fuller picked up the mug. His hand shook.

Flowers showed his approval. 'Friar's cap is the best for putting down vermin,' he said. 'That's what the Genoan pedlar I bought it from told me. *Aconitum,* the alchemists call it. Cost me a pretty penny, too.'

Fuller's hand still trembled. But to Thomas's eye, the man seemed to be calculating in his desperation, as if he might yet stall his captor. Slowly he lifted the mug to his nose and sniffed. 'I'll drink it,' he muttered at last, and winced with pain. Blood showed on his breeches where the blade had pierced him. 'I've no life left... and there's none will mourn me—'

Flowers raised the billhook again angrily. 'Stop whining. You think I care for the dredgings of your wicked heart? I'm here to watch you die, Ambrose – and I'll not leave 'til I hear the rattle in your miserable throat!'

Then he started and whirled round: he had heard the snap of the frayed twine as Thomas broke free.

'Stay, falconer!' he shouted, raising his billhook aloft. 'I've no fight with you!'

'But I'm afraid you have, John,' Thomas said, and got stiffly to his feet.

Flowers rose too, then came a thud. Both he and Thomas looked, and saw Fuller had dashed the poisoned mug to the floor. Its contents ebbed away between the boards.

There came a shriek of rage. And before Thomas could gain the few yards that separated him from Flowers, the young man had leaped to stand over Fuller, who was fumbling at the binding on his legs. He gave a cry of his own, one of terror, as the billhook rose, glittering in the lantern-light, and fell. Thomas watched as, seemingly taking an age, the bright blade arced downwards. But because he had dodged aside, it sliced into Fuller's shoulder.

He cried out, but in his desperation there was a kind of courage. Moving swiftly for a heavy man, he grabbed Flowers about the legs and wrenched them from under him. As he lost his balance, Flowers lashed out again with the billhook, catching Fuller's arm. The man yelled again, but in this last-ditch struggle knew he had some sliver of advantage. For as Flowers fell, the blade dropped from his hand, and Fuller was upon him. The next moment he had grabbed the young man's head in both hands and banged it hard on the floor.

Flowers went limp, a sigh escaping from his mouth, whereupon Fuller saw that he was still the loser. Thomas had come forward and picked up the billhook.

'Be still, Ambrose,' he ordered.

Fuller glared up at him. Blood ran everywhere from the deep wounds he had received. His breath came in bursts.

'Well, now...' The thatcher fixed Thomas with a look of mingled malice and resignation. 'You and I had a brabble of our own coming, right enough,' he growled. 'Like I said to 'ee – you'd best slit my throat and put an end to it.'

But Thomas shook his head. 'Such work's for the hangman.' He gestured to Fuller's hands. 'Hold them out while I tie you.'

'Nay, I'll die for loss of blood first,' Fuller said, with a grim smile. 'You can't make me do your will now, falconer – nor can any man.'

Thomas glanced at his injuries. 'I've seen men in worse shape than you pull through,' he said.

'Do I care what you've seen?' Fuller threw back. 'In God's name, leave me to die. I couldn't walk in any case.'

A moment passed, while Fuller's gaze shifted to the still form of Flowers. 'Always knew there was a devil in 'ee somewhere,' he said. 'Working away behind that smile of his... I couldn't ever get a handle to him.'

He looked up at Thomas. 'That witchcraft in the tent,' he muttered. 'You had a hand in it, didn't ye?' When Thomas said nothing, he hissed with pain. Blood ran from his arm onto the floor, Thomas saw; an artery...

'A clever one, aren't you, falconer?' His voice was weak. 'A whoreson clever cove, a mite too high and mighty for a hawks-man...' He coughed. 'You and that rat-faced German wizard. The way I see it, he conjured up spirits who told you all, save what truly mattered: who it was poisoned half the village, and who it was killed Sir John Mountford!'

He gave a harsh laugh, coughed again and inspected his blood-soaked sleeve – but in Thomas's mind, something fell into place. He drew a sharp breath.

'You...?'

'Aye!' Fuller grinned wickedly at him, enjoying his moment of triumph. 'You think that boy had it in 'ee?' He raised his other hand to indicate Flowers, and let it fall weakly. 'I went to Mountford to get money off him, to get myself away. I saw it was all coming loose... like my boot-heel come loose, only none could mend 'ee. I said I'd spill all, about the jury, only the whoreson cove wouldn't help me. Turned to his faith, in the end – they all do. When he said he'd call the constable, brand me a house-breaker, I told him twas I killed Walden! None else!'

He threw a look of hatred at Thomas. 'Don't 'ee see? Twas I got rid of the juryman no one wanted... Mountford owed me – and I told him that! 'He should have showed gratitude, and paid me off! Instead he called me murderer, said he cursed me for doing it, for laying another weight on his conscience... Whoreson papist...' He broke off, banging his hand on the floor in rage.

Thomas stared, thinking bizarrely of Ned's words earlier that day: *Folk you've known all your life – or think you've known...* He peered down at Fuller.

'So you stabbed him,' he said. 'Hacked him to death, in his own chapel...'

Fuller returned his gaze, then his eyes darted past Thomas. Thomas turned, hearing a scuffling, and found himself shoved aside. Caught off balance, he fell over the sack Flowers had sat on, landing heavily. The billhook flew from his hand, and even as he started to rise, he knew it was too late. John Flowers was on his feet, had caught up the weapon, and turned to stand once again over Ambrose Fuller. And this time, Thomas knew, he would not miss his target.

The blade fell, sinking into the side of Fuller's neck like a butcher's cleaver, severing the great artery. Now blood gushed anew, in fearful quantity, but the victim never saw it. He merely fell back, his body racked with convulsions.

Then he closed his eyes and died.

27

Thomas and John Flowers eyed each other for what seemed an age. Finally the young man lifted the billhook, which dripped with blood. Thomas stepped back.

'I said before, I've no quarrel with you, falconer,' Flowers breathed. 'I've done what I came to do and now I'll climb down, and you will let me leave.'

Thomas shook his head. 'Where will you flee, John? You think the high sheriff will brook your fleeing Petbury, where he is my master's guest, after you've done murder under his very nose? He'll hunt you down, and kill you like a buck.'

Flowers made no response, but beneath his calm Thomas saw his agitation.

'I'm a dead man if I stay,' he muttered, and took a step towards the ladder-head. 'Let me leave, and I'll not harm you.'

Thomas eyed him. How many could have wreaked the mayhem this young man had done, he wondered, and escaped capture all the while? He was about to make a last attempt at remonstration, when he heard the shouts. Flowers heard them too. His head snapped round towards the ladder.

'Think, John,' Thomas said. 'Someone's bound to have heard the noise... There's a sheriff's man out there would stick you, and claim his reward for doing it.'

But Flowers had made his decision. Holding the blade towards Thomas with a warning look, he moved quickly to the ladder and placed his foot upon it.

'If you come after me,' he whispered, 'I'll stick you.' Then he descended rapidly, his head disappearing below the floor.

Thomas looked at the body of Ambrose Fuller, lying on the blood-soaked pallet. Then he took up the lantern and walked to the ladder well. From the yard, he heard footsteps on the cobbles. But the shouting, he realised, was farther off, beyond the paddock. Horses snickered nervously in the stalls below.

Feeling almost exhausted, he climbed down and went outside. Sir Robert's hunting dogs were barking in their kennels. Raising the lantern he peered about, but saw no one. The truth was plain enough: Flowers had escaped, and Thomas had let him walk free.

The shouts drew closer. Putting the lantern down, he rounded the wall of the stable yard and began to hurry towards the paddock. Thirty yards away, another lantern was swinging wildly about. He called out, was answered, and moved towards the light. Out of the dark two figures appeared: James the groom and Will Ashman the sheriff's man, both out of breath.

'Did you see him?' Ashman cried. It was he who held the lantern.

Thomas shook his head. 'I was about to ask you the same... He's killed Fuller.'

Ashman swore a loud oath. 'When?'

'Only minutes hence,' Thomas answered, then realised there was confusion. 'Did you not hear the cries?'

'Nay, it's not possible...' James was recovering his breath.

'Will's been chasing him all the while, from the kitchen yard down to the paddock—'

'You mean John Flowers?' Thomas broke in.

Ashman drew a breath and pushed his face closer to Thomas's. 'Flowers? He means that whoreson thief Saltmarsh – my escaped prisoner!'

Thomas thought quickly. 'Saltmarsh doesn't matter,' he said. 'Flowers got into the hayloft, hacked Fuller to death... He's got a billhook, sharpened like a sword.' He eyed Ashman. 'Where were you all the night?'

Ashman's face was haggard in the lantern-light. 'He killed Fuller?' There was an odd look in his eye. 'Then there's one less to fret about...' He glared. 'Don't tell me Saltmarsh doesn't matter!' he snarled. 'He got my friend killed, and near lost me my place—'

'Listen!' Thomas snapped. 'It was Fuller killed Sir John Mountford. You catch the man who killed him – and who poisoned all the others, including your friend – and you'll have a place for life. And a reward too.'

James drew closer. 'Thomas is right,' he said urgently. 'Let's spread out quick, before he gets onto the Downs. I'll call everyone out...'

At last Ashman nodded, though the last part of James's suggestion was superfluous. There were shouts, and figures appeared from the stable yard.

'Which way, then?' the sheriff's man asked, but Thomas was already moving off. 'I know not,' he called. 'We'll have to cover every direction!'

He disappeared into the dark. But while James hurried off to gather more helpers, Ashman walked towards the great house.

* * *

Thomas ran uphill, past the falcons' mews and onwards to the Ridgeway. Later, he could not explain what it was that drove him. As he cleaved the long grass, startling birds into flight, he almost laughed to himself, guessing what Paulo Schweiz might have made of it. *My friend, you were drawn... What else?*

He gained the path, a sliver of chalk showing faintly in the moonlight. The wind was getting up. He stood and breathed deeply, looking from west to east, and tried to reason. Flowers would not run south; the chance of capture was greater. Then, Thomas had reasoned so the day before, as he stood with Ned at the mews: north into Oxfordshire, or West into Wiltshire – and Ambrose Fuller had chosen neither.

He peered into the dark. Perhaps a hundred yards to his right was the spot where he had met with Saltmarsh; it seemed an age ago now. Again, not knowing why, he turned in that direction, breaking into a trot along the path. After a few minutes he halted, dropped to one knee and listened. A silence had fallen which unsettled him. The nights were never silent on the Downs. Unless every living thing were watchful, and afraid...

He turned, and his gaze fell upon something lying in the grass. He straightened, walked forward and looked down, to see Saltmarsh's boots lying where he had discarded them, beside the path.

Then he heard the footsteps, running.

He dropped to the ground again. The footfalls were closer, but from his right, where the Wantage road crossed the Ridgeway. Had Flowers run eastwards, then changed his mind and retraced his steps? He waited.

The runner drew nearer, then stopped. The silence was so intense Thomas could hear his own heart. He squinted into the gloom, but whoever it was remained lost to sight, whereupon the last thing he expected happened: he heard another set of footfalls, lighter than the other, hurrying along the path towards him. But these came from the other direction, and could only belong to one man...

He got quickly to his feet, and stepped onto the path in plain view.

'I told you flight was foolish, John,' he called out, at which a figure stopped ten yards away, visible now by the moon's glow.

It was Saltmarsh.

'Finbow?' He was panting for breath. 'What the devil...?'

But Thomas groaned inwardly even as he whirled about, realising too late his mistake. Sure enough, as he started to move he glimpsed ahead of him a familiar figure, blond locks flying as he turned and ran.

Thomas ran too, as fast as he was able. *You're no longer young*, he told himself. *You think you can outmatch a boy of Flowers's age...?*

But Flowers knew not the paths as the falconer did; he knew not the hillocks and dips, the hare's forms, the rabbit-holes, the patches of gravel and loose chalk. He had all but drawn out of sight, when with a muffled cry he tripped and fell headlong beside the path. By the time he had scrambled to his feet, grazed and panting, Thomas was upon him.

The billhook flashed once again, silver in the moonlight. Thomas leaped back, the blade missing him by a hair. He grabbed for the outstretched arm, but Flowers had rolled aside and was quickly on his feet. There he crouched, bent double, so short of breath he was almost faint. Sweat glistened on his handsome face, about which his hair hung in ragged locks. How far he had run in the short time since his flight from the stable, Thomas could only guess.

'Let me go, or I'll kill you!' he cried, then gave a start. But Thomas did not turn; he had heard the footfalls too, coming up behind him. Unlike Flowers, however, he knew to whom they belonged.

'There are two of us,' he said. 'Give up the blade, else my friend will likely hack your arm off.'

Flowers gasped, rooted where he stood, as Saltmarsh materialised from the gloom and drew to a halt. The silence that fell was charged with possibilities.

'Jesu, pikeman...' the newcomer's voice was hoarse. 'What made you go off full tilt?' He looked at Flowers, then at the bill-hook. 'Who're you?'

Flowers made no reply, merely struggled for breath.

'When I ask a question,' Saltmarsh said, 'I like to get an answer.'

Flowers eyed him. 'I've no quarrel with you,' he breathed. 'Nor with this man...'

'Odd, that.' Saltmarsh took a step closer to the young man. 'Seeing as you just tried to slice him with that whoreson sword – what is it, a Switzer's *Hauswehr*?'

Flowers backed away, looking from one man to the other. 'Leave me be!' he warned.

Saltmarsh shrugged, made as if to turn away, then with a lunge that caught Flowers utterly off guard, kicked his right leg out from under him. The young man sprawled on his back, but held on to his blade.

'Away!' he cried, jabbing upwards. 'I'll slice you!'

Saltmarsh stiffened, as Thomas's blood froze; the murderer had just sealed his own fate. 'Will...' he began, taking a step forward while knowing it was futile. 'Let me deal with him—'

'I'm sergeant, to you,' Saltmarsh said. For a moment, he looked as though he had decided to leave Flowers where he lay. His gaze wandered idly towards Thomas. Then with the speed of a striking snake his right arm shot out, gripped Flowers's wrist, and twisted it. Flowers cried out and dropped the billhook.

Saltmarsh picked it up. For a second he stood motionless, etched against the moonlight, as Thomas had seen him once, on a rain-soaked battlefield in the low countries... And on that day, too...

He opened his mouth, but knew that the deed was already done, and all words useless. Like one of Paulo's tent show pictures, but stark in its clarity, the image stood before him: Saltmarsh thrusting downwards with the billhook, into John Flowers's heart. There was no scream; only a child-like whimper, then silence.

* * *

The two of them stood some way off, beside the path. Thomas had no words to speak. He had never felt so tired in his life.

'A man draws his own fate, pikeman,' Saltmarsh said. 'One way or another, we all pay.' He looked at Thomas, then away. ''Twas for you that I came back here.'

'That was rash,' Thomas said.

Saltmarsh snorted. 'I can evade those sheriff's dolts any time,' he snapped.

'Can you?' Thomas realised that whatever camaraderie he might once have felt for this man had evaporated. 'Last time I saw you they had you in chains in a barn, ready for carting off to gaol.'

'And you helped spring me,' Saltmarsh admitted. 'Which is why I came to give you thanks, before I leave for good.'

'I don't need your thanks,' Thomas said. 'And it wasn't me who sprang you.'

'Nay...' Saltmarsh's eyes narrowed. 'I know that. Yet I also know twas because of you he did it, not for my sake.'

He peered up at the moon. 'I'll be gone, and won't trouble you again,' he said. 'I'm for Deptford, where there's a ship for the Golden Horn... Ever heard of the seraglio, Finbow?'

Thomas said nothing.

'Anyways...' Saltmarsh took a step, but did not offer his hand. 'You saved my neck; now I believe we're even.'

But Thomas frowned suddenly, surprised at his own turn of thought. 'Answer me just one thing,' he said. 'How in heaven did Paulo Schweiz get you out of that barn, when there was neither window nor opening, nor burrow, and the doors were barred from without?'

Saltmarsh hesitated, then a thin smile appeared. 'That,' he replied, 'is a secret known but to me and our friend, that I promised never to reveal as long as I live.'

With a last look at Thomas he turned and walked swiftly away. Thomas watched until a cloud shadowed the moon, and he was lost to sight.

28

The day following was Saturday, and in the afternoon, having attended upon his master in the morning, Thomas was given leave to order his time as he would. The first thing he did was instruct Ned to go home early, having grown weary of telling and retelling the events of the past night. But only when Thomas had promised to come into Chaddleworth and let Ned buy him a mug, did the boy take his leave. As Thomas stood by the mews and watched him walk away, he saw the spring was back in his step, and was content. Then he went to his cottage, and cast himself down on his pallet.

He had not slept, since for him the night had merely merged into dawn, when he helped bring the body of John Flowers, born John Walden, down off the Ridgeway. That of Ambrose Fuller had already been taken away. So it was that when the sheriff's guard finally arrived in late morning there was no prisoner for removal – or at least, none that lived. As to who it was that killed John Walden, the gravedigger's son who left Chaddleworth a boy, and whom none had recognised when he returned as a man, rumours flew thick and fast. There were some in the village, it was true, who might have wanted him dead, but since there were no witnesses, this was one murderer who would never be found. Some wondered if the fugitive Saltmarsh had been responsible. Thomas, for his part, could add little; he had merely reported finding the body.

With some relief he had stood beside Martin the steward and others from the household late that morning, watching the high sheriff and his party take their leave. Sir Robert and Lady Margaret were there to bid formal farewell to their guests, the ladies kissing like old friends; and indeed it was said they had become friends of a kind, though there was small love lost between Richard Ward and Sir Robert. The knight rode his own horse to the gates to wave the high sheriff off, as if to make sure that this guest who had long outstayed his welcome, was finally gone from Petbury. Thomas had exchanged glances with Martin, both of them noting Ward's sober demeanour. His manner was altered considerably since the news of Fuller's and Walden's deaths reached him. He would not, after all, be able to claim credit for capturing the murderer of Sir John Mountford, nor even for discovering his identity. And it was Lady Margaret who mentioned in passing, that the full story would be told to the lord lieutenant of Berkshire when he dined at Petbury soon. No doubt thereafter, it would become common currency...

Alone now, Thomas felt as empty as was his cottage. Indeed, he thought, it had seemed empty ever since Grace left. He could picture her still, sitting by the chimney with her needlework... But as he reasoned, he knew the hollow feeling in his own heart had less to do with the violent events of yesterday, than with what Nell had told him. He sat by his fireside, frowning to himself; no – the cottage had been empty long before, ever since Eleanor went to live in the great house. He had not seen her today, though like everyone else she would know what had happened. Surely she guessed how much he wished to see her?

The evening drew in, and Eleanor did not come. At last, growing restless, he rose to go out and tend the falcons, when the latch lifted. It was Nell.

She came in, closed the door and moved towards him, but he stepped away, gesturing her to the fireside. Kindling was laid, though he had not yet lit a blaze. She hesitated, then sat down while he knelt, struck a light and held it to the dry grass and twigs, pushing them together as the flames sprang up. He placed larger sticks, and finally small branches, then sat back. Together they watched the flames grow, sitting in silence. Outside, the sun dipped behind Lambourn Down.

Finally Nell spoke up. 'First, read,' she said, and drew the letter from her sleeve.

He stared, afraid now of what it might contain. Then he took it somewhat quickly, unfolded the stiff paper and read.

To Master Thomas Finbow, Falconer to Sir Robert Vicary, the manor of Petbury in the County of Berkshire.

From Moll Kynwardine, formerly called Moll Perrott of Tadworth in Surrey.

Thomas: these are my wordes but sett down by Cousin Will in my parlour, him having a better hande for letter writing than do I.

I am married but not to Niccolo who died last spring, he was verie weak by the end and I did playe nurse and physician both to him in the best chamber until the last. He was brave and did speke of you at tymes and made me swear his blessing and frendship.

I was an empty vessel after he was gone, I did naught but

worke and sleep and folk did not supp at the Red Bull so heartily as before since I did not sing for them now.

I have thought of thee my faire hawksman and your smile and was minded to send worde yet knew not what I might say. Last Palm Sunday when William Kynwardine who farms forty acres beyond Chipstead did ask for my hande I consented. For I will not keep an inn any more. He is a good man a widower and needs a mother to his two sons and he will treate me well, though he is stern at times.

Cousin Will commends himself to you. He is married to Doreth and they have a daughter. I ask pardon Thomas, for when I told ye I would be there if you came backe I shall not, now the Red Bull is sold. Judge me not harshly, for I was once, and remain in a corner of my heart,

Your Moll.

Her name writ here, first day of May, year fifteen ninety-two.

He lowered the letter and stared into the fire, but did not see the flames. He was back in Armada Year, seeing a dark-haired, smiling woman in a good russet gown, singing to a spellbound crowd in an inn in a Surrey village, an ageless tale of lost love.

Judge her not harshly... Paulo's words came back.

Nell was still. When at last he looked at her she would not meet his eye, but continued to gaze into the fire.

He told her. When he had finished he half-expected her to weep, though Nell never wept. She merely nodded, and waited.

'You knew who it was from,' he said. 'Hence you thought...'

'I thought she was calling you,' she finished. 'Why would I not? I thought you would go to her, and I would lose you. I asked you, a fortnight since, remember? You would not give an answer!'

He lowered his gaze. 'Because I could not.'

She took a breath. 'Well, now we both know what's in it...' She broke off, her green eyes blazing fiercely.

'I would have stayed,' he said, 'and I say it not only because she's beyond my reach – I had already chosen my path.'

She frowned slightly, watching him closely.

'You've not heard all that happened last night,' he went on. 'I believed I came near to death. And I swore to myself if I lived, I would waste no more time, but ask you to marry me.' He sighed. 'If I weren't such a fool, I'd have listened to what was said to me from every side, and knew it chimed with what was in my own heart.'

Then as Nell watched, he balled the letter up and threw it into the fire. Together they saw it curl and blacken, then burst into flames.

And gradually, she relaxed, and her face grew soft in the firelight.

'You haven't answered me,' he said, and put out his hand.

She arched her brows. 'You have yet to ask.'

But she took his hand and placed it against her cheek. Without speaking they rose, and she leaned against him. 'You'd best choose a good time to tell Sir Robert,' she muttered. 'Else I could lose my place.'

Then she looked up and kissed him, so hard his lip smarted the moment she drew away. 'How can I ever be certain you have told the truth?' she demanded. 'Suppose what she wrote, had been as I feared?'

'That's a matter of trust,' he said.

Whereupon she sighed, and rested her head on his chest.

* * *

On Sunday after dinner he rode beside Sir Robert on the Downs, while Tamora and Caesar flew high overhead. The knight and his falconer were alone, and judging the time to be as good as any, Thomas made his request. Though he felt confident enough that his master would give his blessing to a union with Nell, he was surprised by the other's air of amusement.

'What held you back?' Sir Robert asked for the third time, as they reined in an hour later, watching Tamora gliding above. And for the third time Thomas's reply was evasive, so that at last his master snorted and gave up. Touching heels to his mount, he rode uphill a few paces, then halted. As Thomas drew his own horse alongside, Sir Robert turned to him.

'I meant to ask you,' he said. 'What happened to that mapmaker? The fellow with the fair daughter.'

Thomas looked blank. 'I believe they've gone away, sir,' he answered.

Sir Robert grunted. 'His work is finished, then.' He frowned. 'Something odd about them... I suppose I'll never know what it was. Then, that's a Cambridge man for you. Yet I loathe leaving a puzzle unsolved, don't you?'

Thomas nodded, shaded his eyes and peered into the sky, where Tamora had dropped and was hovering, her mighty wings beating. His master followed his gaze, then tugged at the rein again and urged his big hawking horse uphill, towards the towering falcon.

* * *

MORE FROM JOHN PILKINGTON

The next book in the Thomas the Falconer Mysteries series from John Pilkington, *The Maiden Bell*, is available to order now here:

https://mybook.to/TheMaidenBellBackAd

ABOUT THE AUTHOR

John Pilkington has been a writer for over forty years, having written plays for radio and theatre, television scripts, children's series and numerous works of historical fiction, concentrating now on the Tudor and Stuart eras. He also ventured into speculative fiction with his biography of Shakespeare's famous jester, Yorick. John lives in Devon with his partner.

Download your exclusive bonus content from John Pilkington here:

Visit John's website: www.johnpilkington.co.uk

Follow John on social media here:

 bsky.app/profile/johnpilkington.bsky.social

ALSO BY JOHN PILKINGTON

Boldwood

Boldwood Books is an award-winning fiction publishing company seeking out the best stories from around the world.

Find out more at www.boldwoodbooks.com

Join our reader community for brilliant books, competitions and offers!

Follow us
@BoldwoodBooks
@TheBoldBookClub

Sign up to our weekly
deals newsletter

https://bit.ly/BoldwoodBNewsletter